Cause for Concern

Margaret Yorke

Cause for Concern

LITTLE, BROWN AND COMPANY

A *Little, Brown* Book

First published in Great Britain in 2001
by Little, Brown and Company

Copyright © Margaret Yorke 2001

The moral right of the author has been asserted.

A CIP catalogue record for this book
is available from the British Library.

ISBN 0 316 85744 0

Typ   ted,

Cause for Concern

1

The train took him from the airport back to London. At Victoria, he rang her, telling her when to meet him at Rotherston Halt, then burrowed into the Underground. He was tired after his trip and he didn't like waiting around, so she'd better be there.

His call had been from a public telephone at the station, so Susan realised that he must have lost his mobile phone again, or failed to charge it, but, as always finding an excuse, she thought that might be difficult overseas, though he often needed it to contact the office; at least, so he'd told her. Some of the through trains now had telephones installed, but it wouldn't occur to him to use one, or even to ask to borrow a fellow passenger's mobile. If he missed the train, he'd enjoy thinking of her waiting at the station in the cold, damp night.

He'd sounded curt, and her heart sank as she backed the Citroën out of the garage and into the road. After these trips, occasionally he was briefly in a good humour, ready to appreciate being home and comfortable, but if he'd been drinking his mood would already be aggressive. One of these days he'd drink too much while leading a tour and then what would happen? There had already been complaints about his aloof manner and he had been angry enough to let her know about them. If he were violent to a client, there'd be no more chances.

She didn't think he was ever intimate with a guest. There were often lone women on the tours he conducted, and she sometimes wished he would find one to whom he could get close; it would offer her an escape. But he was too comfortable in their well-run house, with her dancing to his tune. And he saved his rage for her.

Linda was already sitting in the window seat when the man in the ginger tweed suit got into the train just before it left and sat opposite her. He opened a plastic bag and took out a can of beer, which he opened and proceeded to drink. After it had gone, he produced a second and began on that.

Linda frowned. She had avoided looking at him as he heaved a large briefcase into the overhead rack and edged behind the table between them, dumping the bag beside him when he sat down. To get up and move away would be obviously hostile; while she hesitated, more people entered the carriage and another man took the seat next to her, effectively pinning her in. From the tail of her eye she noticed that he wore a dark suit. He carried a laptop which he put on the table and opened. She could not move now, but he was a sort of protection. Linda determined to ignore the beer drinker and opened her book – the latest Maeve Binchy – knowing it would soon carry her mentally away from the train and her immediate surroundings. When the man opposite stretched his legs so that his feet bumped hers, she drew her own back, tucking them under her, reading on.

As the train moved off, the man facing Linda pulled a pack of onion rings and another of crisps from his plastic bag, opened both, and began thrusting the contents into his mouth, munching away. Crumbs fluttered on to the table and a strong smell of onion mingled with vinegar was wafted towards her. Her suited neighbour also noticed it, and leaned against the back of his seat, pulling his computer closer to him. He's afraid of crumbs, Linda thought, shrinking back too, resting her book on the table's edge to protect Maeve Binchy from contamination.

It was dark outside now. In the warm lighted cocoon of the train, hundreds of people, mostly strangers to one another, many of them commuters returning late after a long working day, were borne through the night towards varied destinations, isolated, solitary individuals sharing only the experience of the journey. The man facing her finished his feast and abandoned the empty packs on the table in front of him. Then he began drumming his fingers on it and humming a tuneless dirge.

Linda bent lower over her book, while the man in the dark suit carried on with what he was doing on his computer, apparently undeterred. Linda could still smell the mixture of onion and vinegar. The man moved his legs again, stretching them, knocking her feet, not apologising. Everyone else in the carriage was reading their paper, or sleeping, in temporary limbo. Linda tried to pretend a wall had arisen between her and her opposite neighbour. She breathed lightly to avoid the fumes, and reminded herself that they might have been garlic. In less than an hour she would reach her station and the nuisance would be past. It could happen sooner, if the man left at an earlier stop.

He didn't. He continued to fidget and hum until he lapsed into a brief slumber, when he snored, waking as the train stopped. They got off together, but Linda was before him at the door. She had started negotiating her release in good time, before the train slowed down, with a muttered request to the man with the laptop, who clicked it shut and stood aside to let her out. He walked to the further end of the coach before he, too, left the train.

A few other passengers disembarked at Rotherston Halt. Linda went ahead of them, hurrying to collect her small Fiat from the car park. She had caught an early train up that morning and had found a slot near the entrance so she was soon on her way; as she drove past the station forecourt, a car pulled out in front of her and Linda had to brake to avoid it. She followed it down the road. It was raining now, a light, depressing drizzle, but Linda, though ruffled by the careless driver at the station, was glad to be free of the crisps and the obtrusive feet of the man in the train. She knew his movements had not been an attempt to engage with her; he was totally obliv ious of anyone but himself.

Lights of oncoming cars dazzled Susan as she drove steadily through the rain towards Bishop St Leon.

'Go faster, can't you?' said Martin.

'It's not safe. I can't see well enough,' said Susan.

'I'll drive then,' he snapped. 'I can see. I'm not blind.'

Susan was not blind either, but the rain and the lights refracting from the glasses she wore for driving limited her distance vision.

'No – it's all right.' Susan accelerated for a short spurt, then gently slowed, hoping he wouldn't notice. He mustn't drive; his licence had been suspended for a year.

He was quiet for a while until, as they approached the Crown, one of Bishop St Leon's three pubs, he called out, 'Stop!'

Susan jammed on the brakes, thinking he must have seen some obstacle ahead which she had not noticed, but already he was opening the car door and getting out. He left the door swinging and went into the pub. A car behind them was forced to stop suddenly when they did; it pulled out and passed them, with a flash of headlights. Susan was trembling. She sat for a moment crouched over the steering wheel, and then she undid her seat-belt so that she could lean across to close the door. The passing driver had every reason to be annoyed; one of these days she'd have an accident because of Martin's sudden instructions or changes of mind. She switched off the ignition and turned her lights down. How long would he be?

After several minutes it occurred to her that she need not wait. He could walk the rest of the way, several hundred yards. The rain was not heavy; he would not get very wet. She waited another few minutes, to give him one more chance, and then she drove on down the road and round the bend to Cedar Cottage. She was still trembling as she heaved his heavy bag and his satchel out of the boot and took them indoors before putting the car away. She locked the garage, hiding the car keys in case he thought of going for a spin to a more distant pub when he finally returned; it had happened before and the car bore dents to prove it. She struggled upstairs with his bag, hefting it up, step by step, and dragging it across the landing to his room. Then she made another trip with the satchel. She had drawn the curtains before she left the house. Now she turned on the bedside lamp, which she would leave on so that when he reached his room he could see his way around, if he was capable. Slowly she unpacked his bag, taking out bundles of dirty washing, putting his other clothes away – his good trousers for evening wear when he had to eat with the clients, which was as seldom as he could manage, and his maroon sweater, which seemed clean. She put his books and papers on the chest. A sour smell came from the soiled clothing as she bundled it up and took it downstairs to put in the washing machine.

He had not returned by the time she decided to go to bed. She had left a casserole in the oven. Now she put a serving on to a plate, covered it, and wrote in big letters on a plastic message board, 'Dinner. Heat in the microwave. 3 minutes', and went upstairs again. Her bedroom was at the other end of the house, but that wouldn't stop him from blundering along and dragging her out of bed. Locking her door was no protection; once, he'd broken it down. That was after he had lost his job at the university and the publishers had turned down his outline for a book about the Celts. He'd implied that it had been commissioned and that they'd changed their mind about it, but she no longer knew what to believe. It might be true. He had had a good brain before he started drinking, though he hadn't got a First, telling her that the examiners had set unfair questions and the work he had done was not covered. However, he'd secured a post as a lecturer and that had lasted for a long time. He'd been sacked for no reason, he had said. Susan wasn't sure whether he had been accused of harassing a student, or whether it was because his pupils' results had been poor. It hadn't been fair, he had complained. Nothing ever was. His whole life had gone wrong because he was the child of a single mother; why did his father desert them when he was only three years old? It all sprang from that, he said.

Susan had a bath, which warmed her up, then lay in bed unable to read, thinking about the past. Why did Martin blame everyone except himself for his own weak character? He and his sister had been raised in modest comfort; grandparents had helped care for them, often having them to stay for their holidays; plenty of working single mothers brought up their children effectively and with far less support than they had had. Perhaps it was genetic.

Martin, when a young man, had tried to trace his father, but without success. There had been a postcard from New Zealand some months after he left, but nothing since. Years later Patricia, Martin's elder sister, said it was good riddance; their father was an alcoholic.

'And who made him one?' Martin, aged fifteen at the time, had demanded. 'Our mother.'

Patricia thought it was a wonder their mother hadn't hit the bottle too.

Before he got the travel courier's job, he had secured some relief teaching, interspersed with routine clerical jobs, but there were several spells of unemployment between assignments. For weeks, after an earlier prosecution for drink driving when he lost his licence for three months, Susan, on the way to her own job, had taken him to work at the office where he was putting routine information on to a computer. He had no natural affinity with computers and made heavy weather of the task, hence, Susan explained to herself, the urge to drink. But then the travel job had come along. He'd thought of it after hearing from his sister about the ineffective courier she had had on a holiday in France. Patricia, a management consultant, annually went on guided tours, sometimes to European cities, sometimes further afield, and had become a connoisseur of their efficiency. Good guides could make or mar them, she declared, and in a throwaway remark had suggested he might try it. Martin took up the idea with an enthusiasm he had not shown for years. He wrote to various companies, starting with the most expensive and gradually working his way downwards until he was engaged by a middle-market group which had been let down by the sudden illness of a regular courier. At that late date, it was difficult to find a replacement. Martin's degree, his university and teaching experience, but not particularly his professed expertise in Celtic lore, qualified him intellectually, and his good manners, infrequent since he became so dependent on alcohol but brushed up and improved for his interview, ensured success. He had worked for them intermittently ever since.

Soon after he started his new career, his sister married an American she met on a holiday in China, and went to live in California, where she became stepmother to several teenage children and seemed to be living happily ever after. She kept in touch, but spasmodically. She thought Susan should move away from Bishop St Leon and make a fresh start somewhere new, shedding Martin, but he said all their friends were here.

What friends, Susan had wondered; no one came to the house except, very rarely, in his absences, for she had lost the habit of inviting people in.

Her problems were returning now. She heard Martin opening the front door and there was a crash as he entered the house. Susan pulled the duvet round her ears and prayed for a peaceful night. He might pass out downstairs, and sleep it off. It had happened before.

In another part of Bishop St Leon, Linda parked her car on the wide gravel sweep in front of Field House, where she was employed as nanny to Georgina, aged three, and Henry, seven months. Her employers, with their children, were on holiday at the moment, but they were due back from Florida early the next morning. She had arranged to sleep in the house that night in order to be on the spot when they arrived. Normally, she lived in Rotherston, where she shared a flat with another girl, but she occasionally slept at Field House when her employers' timetables made it necessary, compensating with time off later. She'd been with the family since Henry's birth.

She had spent the day in London with a friend. They'd been shopping, then to a film, and they'd had an early meal before she caught the train. She'd very nearly run into that car when it stopped so suddenly outside the Crown. This was the same car that had pulled out in front of her at the station; she'd followed it all the way to Bishop St Leon, and now the driver had nearly caused an accident. Whoever it was, wasn't safe on the road.

Everything was in order in the house. A voice-mail message told her that the plane was expected on time. She went to bed: best get some sleep – transatlantic planes sometimes arrived early. Georgie and Henry might be fractious when they reached home, and their parents, Edward and Hannah, would probably be tired.

Under the primrose duvet in the small bedroom which was hers when she stayed, Linda spent a moment in con-demnation of the errant driver and the man eating crisps on the train. Then she banished them from her thoughts; it would be good to see Georgie and Henry, both lovely children, in the morning. She liked their parents, too; this was a happier family than the last one she had worked for.

Martin had stayed drinking in the Crown until it closed. Though licensing hours were now elastic, the landlord found little need to stay open much after eleven in mid-week. Martin had leaned an elbow on the counter, telling the company that he had just been in Venice with a group of tourists with whom he had shared his deep knowledge of history and art.

'Some were keen students,' he told his uninterested audience. 'Others weren't.'

There had been the woman who had shunned all his arranged visits and gone off walking on her own, and another who had known far more Venetian history than he did. Most of the group were interested in art and had spent hours in the Accademia gazing at the works of Bellini and Giorgione, while one woman had wanted only to visit the Rialto, intending to imagine Shylock and Antonio in dialogue upon the bridge. Martin had sent her off with a map, on her own. She had missed the trip to Torcello included in their package, and had not returned to the hotel when the rest of the group did. Some of them – all strangers to her for she was travelling alone – had shown concern before going off to various recommended restaurants for dinner, which was to be taken independently, as the tour brochure prescribed. After the first night, when they all ate together and he described the delights ahead, informing, not conversing, Martin seldom joined clients for these meals; he ate and drank unwitnessed and uncensored. He had to get away from them; their inane chatter and demands tested him sorely and he needed a few drinks to strengthen him for the following day.

The Rialto woman was there at breakfast in the morning.

Martin wasn't. He breakfasted late, if he ate at all, appearing just before the planned time of departure for that day's sightseeing. By lunchtime his parched system was crying out for a restorative and several beers slid down, helped by a salad or a sandwich. On the last day, once they had reached the airport and checked in, his responsibilities were, in his opinion, at an end; they were adults; they could find their own way home.

If anyone, on a trip he led, had an accident or fell ill, it was exasperating, for then he had to make an extra effort. Fortunately these incidents were rare.

'Where are you off to next, Martin?' the landlord asked, hoping it would be somewhere far away, and the departure soon. Martin was sometimes quite a problem when he overdid it.

'I've got nothing until March,' said Martin glumly. 'These trips ease off in winter. But I might get an emergency call, if another leader drops out.'

'What'll you do till then?' asked Nicholas Waters, captain of the village cricket team and, though a financial consultant, a lost soul between seasons.

'Get on with my book, of course,' said Martin.

Everyone knew he was writing a book about the Celts; he had not revealed the rejection he had suffered.

Tonight, no one was interested in the Celts. Martin became sentimental and began talking about the changes in the village, where he had lived for a long time, longer than most of the pub regulars and the landlord. Now, he alleged, it had become a nest of money-mad commuters who cared nothing for the past, simply sleeping there.

This was one of his pet themes.

Refusing to be drawn into a discussion about the transformation of old, dilapidated cottages into comfortable houses, Nicholas, who lived in one of them, challenged him.

'Why don't you sell that place of yours?' he asked. 'It must be worth a fortune. You could live anywhere.'

'Good idea,' said someone else. 'I've got a friend who wants to move here. I could put you in touch.'

But Martin didn't want to move. It was true that the house was worth a lot, and it would be worth more with every year. Why should he share that sum, when one day it could all be his? He said nothing, and the company, already about to break up for the night, began to leave. Martin, ignored, switched moods and as he set off down the road, the damp night air accelerated his descent into anger.

'We'll have him in here most nights now,' the landlord said, closing up. 'More's the pity. Drives people out.'

But sometimes other drinkers indulged the sport of taunting Martin, getting him to tell tales of how the village used to be and of the people who had lived there. He could be quite amusing, once launched, until it went too far.

*　　*　　*

Martin was the last to leave the Crown. Four of the other seven who had been there until closing time lived within walking distance of the pub but the rest had cars, all parked in the yard at the rear. Martin expected to see the Citroën still outside the front entrance, but the road was empty.

'Bloody bitch,' he said aloud, and fumbled for his mobile telephone, forgetting that it was dead. In any case, he could not see to hit the right buttons for his home number.

He blundered off down the road. The rain had stopped, but the sky was overcast; no moon shone. It wasn't far to Cedar Cottage and his feet could carry him almost automatically to its door, but there was time enough for his resentment to build up so that his head was spinning with anger when he reached the gates. She'd even closed those. He rattled and clattered the latch, pushing one open, leaving it swinging as he scrunched his way on the soft gravel to the front door. He banged on it, thumping the heavy old iron knocker against the wood; when nothing happened, he began to shout. She'd have to come and let him in.

Upstairs, Susan heard the banging. She pulled the bedclothes over her head and cowered there. He'd got his key; he had only to put it in the lock and turn it.

Outside, Martin continued to crash the knocker and call out, cursing, and across the road, Bill and Mary Church stirred awake.

'Ruddy Martin,' said Bill. 'He's back again.'

'Mm.'

'I'll go and sort him out,' said Bill.

'Don't,' said Mary. 'You'll be arrested if you bash him.'

'He's the one who ought to be arrested,' Bill replied. 'He broke her arm once, didn't he?'

'She said she fell down the stairs,' Mary said. 'Go back to sleep. She'll let him in. She always does.'

'More fool her,' said Bill, who was now wide awake. 'Why doesn't she chuck him out?'

'Where would he go?'

'Where do people go? He'd have to rent a room somewhere.'

'He'd drink himself to death or end up on the street, sleeping rough,' said Mary. 'She can't let that happen.'

He'll kill her one day, Mary thought.

'Let's call the police,' she said. They'd thought of it before, but never done it.

'If he doesn't stop soon, we will,' said Bill. He got out of bed and went across to the window overlooking the road. The porch light was on at Cedar Cottage, and, as he watched the figure standing there, the front door opened. Martin almost fell across the threshold and the door closed.

Bill went back to bed. He listened for a while, then lapsed back into sleep. Now it was Mary who lay awake, wondering what was happening inside the house opposite.

2

Bill, once a morning jogger, had taken up power walking instead, after spraining an ankle rather badly. He pounded round a circuit of the village every morning at six-thirty before driving to Rotherston station. He was a city trader and longed for the day when he might work from home.

Remembering the night's events, he glanced across at Cedar Cottage as he left his own house and again when he returned, glowing, from the exercise. It beat the gym any time, especially when the weather was fine, as it was today after the rain. The air smelled fresh and clean, until a car passed – Nicholas Waters, off to the station already. Often they caught the same train; perhaps Nick had an early meeting today.

Cedar Cottage looked tranquil in the pale light of autumn. Susan was often up at this time, and then the curtains would be drawn back from the windows but this morning they were still pulled across. He felt mildly anxious as he entered his own house, ran lightly up the stairs and took his shower, while downstairs Mary was making breakfast. They ate fruit and muesli, believing in a healthy diet. Mary was a teacher, head of English at Rotherston Comprehensive, a sought-after school whose excellence was a reason for the area's popularity with ambitious middle-class parents.

While they ate, both of them wondered if they should go over to make sure that Susan was all right, but, as often before, they decided not to; she wouldn't thank them for prying, Mary thought, but Bill said it wasn't prying, it was watching out for one's neighbour.

Once, they used to visit to and fro occasionally, but that had stopped years ago, when Martin lost his job and started to hit the bottle. Or had he begun hitting it before losing his job? Cause and effect, probably, thought Bill.

Bill left first, and Mary hurried to get her papers together before she followed. With no off-street parking at their house, they kept their cars in the road. North Street, in Bishop St Leon, was partly composed of blocks of terraced cottages, once occupied by agricultural workers but now renovated and combined so that two or three together made attractive houses which fetched increasingly large sums when they changed hands. Bill and Mary had bought theirs soon after the motorway made the village easily accessible to commuters. Gradually the population had changed as the retired people who had formerly lived there died or moved away and there was a thriving younger element with small children and new babies. Several of these families, where the wives had well-paid jobs with salaries essential in meeting heavy mortgages, employed nannies. Mary felt rather sorry for the mothers, handing their infants over at a few months old; she had stayed at home, resuming her career only when their children, now adult, were ten and twelve.

The nannies had a busy social life. Mary knew some of them; Jo, at The Old Chapel, had been a pupil at Rotherston Comprehensive before she did her training; after that, she had been an air stewardess for a while as a way to see the world, but had eventually gone back to working with children. Three or four nannies often took their charges to one another's houses; instead of the mothers socialising, it was the nannies. Mary, witnessing this activity during school holidays, decided that it stopped them from being lonely, and the children learned to interact. Probably it was good preparation for the world they would inhabit as they grew older, with, in some cases, long journeys by bus to school. Not all the children went to local schools.

The curtains were still drawn at Cedar Cottage when it was time for Mary to leave. Martin always slept in; perhaps, unusually, Susan was doing the same after the racket in the night. Though this was not the first time Mary and Bill had been woken by his noise, always before, there had been signs of life opposite before Mary left.

Signs of life: Mary felt uneasy, driving off without seeing some across the way.

*　　*　　*

During Martin's absence in Venice, a new couple had moved into the house next to Cedar Cottage. Dan and Fiona had left London because his company had moved to Banbury, an easy commuting distance from Bishop St Leon, while she could travel the other way to her office in Chiswick. They had taken a week off work to settle and begin painting, moving in hard on the departing heels of the previous householders, but so far had seen little of Susan, though the people on the other side had called round with a bottle of wine, and Bill and Mary, opposite, had given them flowers.

Last night they had heard Martin banging on the door and shouting. Dan had looked out of the window but at that moment the noise had stopped, apart from some muffled sounds which could have been raised voices. Up to now, their new life had been peaceful; they had been aware that Susan drove off just before nine and returned about six o'clock, but otherwise they had scarcely seen her, and since they would soon be out all day themselves, had not attached importance to the question of their neighbours. Their own house, built nearly thirty years ago on land Susan had sold during a building boom, would be perfect when they had refurbished it and had a new kitchen fitted. In two or three years' time, with luck, they'd start a family; meanwhile, there was plenty to be done before tackling their long garden, which was well stocked but somewhat overgrown.

They'd noticed Susan mowing. Their own lawn needed cutting, but they hadn't got around to it yet; it was more important to get the house straight first. Dan, an urban man, had said that the grass could wait, but Fiona, who had grown up in the country, remembered her father's annual anxiety lest he be foiled by the weather and fail to achieve a final cut before the winter; she feared that, if left, their lawn would become a wilderness. There was a pergola beyond it, covered in climbing roses which needed tying in and pruning; the vendors had been enthusiastic gardeners, and Fiona meant to improve upon their efforts.

Now there was only the coming weekend before they returned to work. Intent upon their programme, both forgot the noise last night and concentrated on their tasks, while along the road, at Field House, Linda set off to take Georgie to her playgroup, wheeling Henry in his small, cosy pram. The children had slept for most of the flight back, but not their parents, who had now succumbed and were in bed. Today, Friday, was a playgroup day and it was agreed that Georgie might as well return to her routine; besides, she was eager to see her friend Tamsin again. While she was occupied, and Henry slept, Linda would tackle the large pile of washing which the family had brought back with them.

She walked past Cedar Cottage but, intent on chat with Georgie, did not glance at it. Returning, though, with Henry in his pram and Jo, Tamsin's nanny, pushing baby Clare, both young women halted as a man on foot emerged from the gate. He walked briskly past them, prams and all, head down, in a hurry.

'Rotten so-and-so,' said Jo.

'Who is he?' Linda asked.

'That's Martin Trent,' said Jo. 'Thinks he's God's gift. Drinks enough to float a galleon, my dad says. Gets nasty with it, too.' Jo's father farmed land on the fringe of Bishop St Leon, and had switched from cattle to vegetables and fruit. Her mother had started doing bed and breakfast and now had several regular guests who stayed when doing audits or other recurring work in the area. 'But the Crown's not open yet. He's probably going to Rotherston to a pub that is. He'll come back in a taxi – he lost his licence a while ago. He gets nasty when he's drunk.'

'Oh,' said Linda. Because she returned to Rotherston most nights, she had not taken heed of many village residents except for various toddlers and some of their parents whom she met at playgroup. 'Doesn't he have a job?'

'He's a travel rep, I think,' said Jo vaguely. 'Lives with his mother.'

'Mummy's boy?'

'No. He's been married but it didn't work out so he came home to Mum. Or maybe he moved in when he lost his job. I'm not sure. His mum's brought him and his sister up on her own since they were little kids,' said Jo. 'Their dad walked out. Dad says there's a jinx on that house. It's got a history. Everyone who lives there has bad luck, going back to mediaeval times.'

'Do you believe that?'

'I don't know. If it's an old house, people must have died there – people used to die at home but they don't very often now, do they? Maybe there were murders,' Jo said. 'There was some mystery about Martin's father. He just disappeared. Went to New Zealand, it was said.'

'Well, in that case, he didn't die here,' said Linda robustly. 'That's superstition.'

'I expect so,' Jo agreed. 'Anyway, Martin's bad news.'

The girls parted at the fork in the road, Jo turning up North Street on her way back to Chapel Row, and Linda walking on to Field House. Later, after they'd collected Tamsin and Georgie at midday, and given them lunch, they were due at another nanny's house to spend the afternoon. It was all go for them in the nursery world.

Susan heard Martin leave.

He had hit her again last night after she had come downstairs to let him in. First, punctuating every sentence with four-letter words, he'd asked her what she thought she was doing, going off and leaving him to walk home, and when she'd summoned up the courage to tell him he had a useful pair of legs and could walk a few hundred yards, he'd said it was little enough to expect her to wait when he'd returned from arduous work overseas in a job which was demeaning to one of his skill and ability.

'You don't contribute to your keep. Why should I consider you?' Susan had demanded, surprising herself.

'It's your duty. I'm your son. I have no father. You owe me. He abandoned me because of you.'

'That isn't true,' said Susan, as her frail flame of courage faltered.

'It is. If you'd been a decent wife he'd not have gone off and left his defenceless little children,' Martin had snapped.

But Martin's father had beaten her and abused her. Martin had witnessed some of the scenes and had been chastised himself, but he had been too young at the time to remember them. He had convinced himself that his father's rage was justified and, since the failure of his own marriage and his return home after losing his job, he had adopted the same pattern of conduct. In her lowest moments, Susan thought he might be right. For one thing, if she hadn't been pregnant she and Norman would never have married, but in those days, more than forty years ago, to be an unmarried mother was to become an economic and social outcast. Besides, at the time, she had thought herself in love with Norman, and he with her. Her infatuation had lasted far longer than his, if his had ever existed. It had certainly vanished by the time the children were born.

The years after Norman left had been happy, though the family was short of money. They had continued to live in Cedar Cottage, which Susan had painted throughout to expunge all trace of him and, when she could afford to, she had gradually replaced items of furniture that had bad associations. Her parents – never keen on the match – had helped her financially while she trained as a teacher; she had taught at a primary school in another village for twenty years, and when she took early retirement after the school merged with another, she had been offered a job by Brian Marsh, a former pupil who had started an estate agency in Rotherston. She was his only employee at first; later, when the business grew and he engaged a bright young negotiator, soon followed by other staff, she stayed on as his personal assistant. When she sold the building plot, she was able to pay off the mortgage, and later, with money she inherited after her parents died, she had some improvements made to the cottage, including the addition of a modern kitchen at the rear of the building.

When Martin came home after he lost his job, her own was her salvation, for it got her out of the house and provided a steady income.

Where did I go wrong, Susan had asked herself, as so often before, when Martin had at last gone to his room and she managed to drag herself upstairs. Then she must have fainted, she thought in the morning, waking to find herself still in her dressing-gown lying on the top of the bed. Her head hurt, and in the mirror she saw that she had a large bruise on her cheek. Now she remembered hitting her head as she fell down after he punched her. Well, he hadn't killed her this time; one day he would, and what would happen to him then?

Surveying her face, she realised that with this evidence she might be able to get an injunction to keep him away. But she couldn't prove he had hit her. He would deny it, saying she must have tripped over after he had gone to bed. Anyway, she probably deserved it, for being a useless mother.

It was difficult, now, to remember the bright little boy with the brown curls who had cuddled up to her, wanting a story, and had held her hand as they walked across the fields to the mill stream to fish for tiddlers. In those days he used to hug her and tell her he would take care of her when he grew up. What had happened to him?

At the onset of adolescence, he had vanished, to be replaced by a moody, brooding, though clever boy, who did well at school but was idle and sulky at home. Those were difficult years, inevitably, she told herself, because the boy lacked a father. Another woman who lived in the village, who was divorced, also had problems with her son who had become rebellious and difficult. She said that she thought some boys, when they were on the cusp of maturity, and who had been brought up by their mothers, resented what they saw as their dependence. Without this mere woman, their subconscious told them, what would have become of them? Her son had settled down and grown out of this phase; he was now a decent family man. Martin, facing adversity, had turned to drink like his father, and when drunk, his basic nature erupted. Not every man, when drunk, became aggressive, but too much alcohol would make anyone's true disposition emerge.

Susan was afraid of her son. She admitted to herself that she did not like the man he had become in middle age, but her instincts made her protective; she could not cause him harm; a sort of primitive love somehow endured.

With the house to herself, she was able to relax. He had probably gone off to Rotherston on the bus to see the girlfriend he had somehow acquired, a woman she thought he had met through a lonely-hearts advertisement in the local paper. Susan had found the discarded newspaper with various advertisements highlighted in bright green, his favoured colour. All the romance seekers sought also a g.s.o.h. It took Susan some time to work out that this meant Good Sense of Humour. Her son had none, and she feared that she had lost any she might once have had. A woman he met in this or any other way would need to be tough enough to look after herself.

Martin couldn't. Not altogether. That was why he lived at home, and why, very rarely, he would shed maudlin tears and beg her forgiveness for his conduct. She always forgave him, and he always bullied her again.

This morning, she was already late for work, and was tempted not to go in at all, but Martin might return, and if his lady friend was not at home, he would be angry and frustrated. Susan did not know which of the advertisers had been successful and so knew nothing about her. Occasionally he stayed away all night, and would return jaunty the next day; more often, a taxi brought him back in the early hours.

Martin caught the bus at the end of the road. He still had a car, an old Honda Civic, now in the large double garage, and he would be out on the road as soon as his licence was restored. In an isolated village like Bishop St Leon, five miles from the nearest town and with few buses, without one life became impossible.

Accustomed to waking early, and angry rather than very drunk the night before, he had not slept late. His head was, for him, reasonably clear, and he remembered lashing out at his mother's pale, frightened, accusing face. He could not bear to see that terrified expression and felt compelled to wipe it out. Though he had long ago ceased to feel shame, he did not want to see her till he had made himself feel good again. A visit to Debbie would soon put him right and she'd be glad to see him. He had not realised that his mother was still in the house when he left.

Martin got off the bus outside Rotherston library and walked along several streets until he came to where Debbie lived with her two daughters. It was a pity about the children; he wished she didn't have them, snotty little creatures; he'd never liked children and never saw the one he had sired himself, a boy who must now be adult, he realised if he thought about him, which he preferred not to do.

Debbie ought to be at home this morning; she knew he was due back from his trip and would be waiting for him. He'd met Debbie, not as the result of a newspaper advertisement but in the Grapes in Rotherston. Martin had been feeling very sorry for himself, the night they met; drink made him maudlin at first. He'd soon told her that his wife had left him and he never saw his son and that he'd been made redundant due to cuts in the education budget, tailoring the tale to elicit sympathy; he'd done it before, with other women, with success, but these relationships were fleeting. He chose not to remember that each time it was the women who had ended them; he'd picked wrongly, was his view. Luck was never on his side.

He'd never been tempted to get close to any client on a tour he was conducting; most of the single women clients were too confident and experienced, some travelling with a female friend. Martin's targets were the vulnerable.

Debbie was out.

Of course, she had a part-time job now, at the supermarket. He'd forgotten that; she'd started it just before he

left, as Rose had got a nursery school place; Lily already
went there.

Rage soared in him again. He fumbled in his pocket
for his keys. He'd got one to her house; he'd persuaded
her to have one cut for him, to show her trust, he'd said.

He let himself in and went to wait for her in her sitting room. He'd got nothing to read and she had very few
books. Sinking low by his erstwhile standards, Martin
turned on her television.

3

Susan had put cover-up fluid over the bruise on her cheek but it did not hide the mark.

Brian Marsh, her boss, was talking to a client when she entered the office over an hour late. Before leaving home, safe in the knowledge that Martin had already gone out, she had telephoned to apologise, saying she had over-slept, which was the truth. Now, she merely waggled her fingers at Brian before disappearing into the back part of their premises to leave her coat; then she went to her own desk in time to answer a telephone call asking for an appointment to view two houses in the town. Soon, she was absorbed in her work, able to forget for several hours the problem that she could not solve.

Brian, busy, did not notice her injury; Nigel, one of the younger negotiators, was already out measuring up and taking photographs of a house they had been asked to sell; the other, Amy, handing details of some properties to an elderly couple seeking a retirement bungalow, very quickly did. Since Amy had been with the firm, Susan had never before been late, but Amy had met Martin because he was a frequent customer in the bars in Rotherston; she and various friends went to some of them, especially the Grapes on Fridays, and he had tried to chat them up. Amy had thought he was rather nice at first, though much too old for her, but one evening she had seen him transformed in minutes from someone pleasant and well mannered into an argumentative boor. She had not learned who he was until he came into the office one day shortly before they closed and, quite civilly, said he had just arrived back from Greece and had come to cadge a lift back to Bishop St Leon with his mother. He sat quietly enough, glancing through some papers taken from a satchel he carried; he was tanned and had lost weight; he was quite presentable. Amy's own life was too full to let her spend time wondering about the two sides to his nature. Now, seeing the mark on the older woman's face, she did not make the connection.

Apart from selling houses, the firm functioned as a letting agency, and after dealing with the clients wanting a bungalow, Amy was consulted by a man in his thirties who was looking for a house share. With a man his age, Amy knew what this probably meant; he was one half of a divorce, and dispossessed. She gave him details of some possibilities, two in Rotherston and others in surrounding villages. There was a room in Bishop St Leon that was not officially on their books but the lease for the whole house had been arranged by them and she knew the vacancy, a sudden one, would be advertised in the local paper. She gave him details.

Later, in the staff room, while they ate sandwiches for lunch, bought by Amy at a nearby sandwich bar, she mentioned it to Susan.

'He seemed quite interested,' she said. 'I'd put him down as more likely to favour Rotherston.'

'Depends where he works, I suppose,' said Susan, indifferently. She knew the house in question, an Edwardian one in Chapel Row. Her head ached and so did her side; she thought she might have cracked a rib when she fell last night. Though normally she enjoyed the imaginative fillings for their crusty rolls which The Lunch Box produced, today she had no appetite. She would like to be in bed with a hot-water bottle and something soothing on the radio, but it wasn't safe at home, not when Martin might return.

'You're not feeling too great, are you, Susan?' Amy asked at last. 'What have you done to yourself?'

She was alarmed to see sudden tears, quickly blinked away, spring to Susan's eyes.

'I slipped and fell last night,' said Susan, speaking the truth. 'Silly, wasn't it? I banged my head against the bookcase.'

'Oh – bad luck,' said Amy, adding, 'Arnica is good for bruises.'

'So it is,' said Susan brightly. 'I must get some.'

Amy went back into the office while Susan spent time in the cloakroom putting on more masking fluid.

'Susan isn't feeling too good,' Amy told Brian. 'Says she fell and banged her face last night.'

'Hmph,' said Brian. 'That probably means Martin's back. Venice, wasn't it, this time?'

Susan usually told them when he had gone off somewhere, and her colleagues had noticed how she seemed to relax during these periods.

Amy stared at him.

'Oh no!' she said. 'You can't mean what I think you do.'

Brian shrugged.

'I haven't said anything,' he answered, and before Amy could reply, Susan came back into the office. At the same time, two of their telephones started ringing. Brian stood up. 'I'm off now,' he said. 'Back about three.' He had an appointment to show a client round a former rectory, a beautiful house which would command a sizeable sum; this was the client's second visit.

'You wish,' said Amy, but she smiled. Brian would do his best to wrap up the sale today.

Susan seemed to be functioning normally during the afternoon. Amy kept an eye on her, between drawing up particulars of new properties on the computer, and preparing to mail them to potential buyers. The office stayed open over the weekend, for that was when people had time for inspection and Susan was always willing to work then. What must her life be like, Amy wondered, in spare moments, and solicitously made her a cup of tea earlier than their usual break.

'Wouldn't you like to go home?' she asked. 'I can manage. Nigel will be back soon.' Nigel was taking a couple recently returned from working overseas to see a number of houses, which could be a lengthy business, if, as today, they were scattered round a wide area. The clients needed to be near the station and the schools, but wanted to be in a village. At present they were renting a house on an estate in Rotherston.

'I'm fine,' said Susan. She felt safe here, in the bright office which was on the ground floor of a Georgian building in the main street. Rotherston was an attractive town whose council had tried, with varying degrees of success, to limit ugly renovations. There were a number of offices – building societies, travel agencies, two other estate agents and several solicitors – and three restaurants where once there had been shops, some still with flats above them; the town was not dead at night, but on Saturdays it could become rowdy when the pubs closed.

'It must have been quite a tumble,' said Amy.

'Yes,' agreed Susan, eyes on her computer screen.

'Is Martin back?' Amy asked, lightly.

'Yes.' Susan did not enlarge.

'Venice, wasn't it?'

'Yes.'

'Oh – had a good time, did he?'

'You'd have to ask him,' Susan said. 'I've scarcely seen him.'

'Have you ever been there?'

'Long ago,' said Susan. 'It was lovely,' she added. 'Beautiful.' It had been more than forty years ago, before she was married, with a school friend; they had toured around in the friend's car which they had left at Mestre while they went over the water to the city. The friend now lived in South Africa; they corresponded from time to time and she urged Susan to visit, but it hadn't happened. Susan's holidays were rare; she was reluctant to leave home; her respite came when Martin was away. 'I'd better get on,' she added. 'I must have these letters ready for Brian when he comes back.' If he didn't return before the office closed, she would sign for him.

Occasionally she wondered if Brian would soon force her to retire. She was almost sixty-five; she couldn't expect him to keep her on for ever, especially if she started coming in late and finding it difficult to concentrate.

If Martin's current girlfriend had given him a warm welcome, he might stay out all night, and be in a better humour when next they met. His moods varied with the success or failure of his so-called love life. Susan had got past the stage of imagining that Ms Right – she was unlikely to be Miss – would bring about his reclamation, but no doubt this latest woman was shown a side of him seldom revealed to her. What would happen to him, if he went on drinking and becoming violent whenever things failed to go his way? He might kill her – it could happen, accidentally, if he knocked her over again; his father had almost managed it.

She could escape herself, save him by doing it for him: killing herself. She had thought of it before. There were pills; a dose of paracetamol and some whisky, perhaps a plastic bag: then peace. It was an appealing idea. If he stayed at home long, and went on in this way, she would be tempted, but it would upset Patricia who might feel she should have kept an eye on things. Susan had hidden the true situation from her daughter.

But if this romance worked out he might move in with the woman, perhaps; it had happened before, more than once, but the arrangement had not lasted long.

That evening Susan drove home full of fear. Would he be there, waiting for her, angry?

When Amy returned to her flat after work that day, Linda, who shared it with her, was already there.

'Hi – how did it go?' Amy asked. 'Did they get back all right? Did they have a great time?'

'Yes, they did. Glad to be back, of course.'

Linda, looking for a flat or house share when she came to Rotherston before taking up her job at Field House, had answered an advertisement in the local paper; this had led her to Brian Marsh's estate agency where Amy was in the office when she called. Amy had just bought the flat, which was above a florist, and wanted a lodger to help with the mortgage; the two young women eyed each other cautiously, then decided on a month's trial to see if it would work. It did; they were friends now, independent, but sometimes going out together. Amy had a boyfriend who was in the army and was often away; Linda, wanting to get out of London where she had worked before, and unattached after a relationship had ended in tears, was glad to be accepted by Amy's established circle who met casually in the pubs in the town or went out for meals in groups. Some of them went to the gym a few nights a week and others played tennis or badminton, or swam. The more relaxed pace of life, in and out of work, suited Linda, whose London employers had both been high fliers – as were Edward and Hannah, in Bishop St Leon – but they had been very demanding, inconsistent in their behaviour towards their children, and had quarrelled a great deal with one another. Whilst she was sorry for their children, fond of them, and wanted to help them, the atmosphere had become so strained that Linda had decided to leave even before her personal life came to a crossroads. A clean break from everything was what she wanted and had achieved, though she kept in touch with a few London friends.

'Did Georgie and Henry remember you?' Amy teased.

Linda had thought Henry might forget her, but he had greeted her with chortles and happy cries.

'Seemed to,' she said.

She had started to make her and Amy's supper. Most

evenings, they ate together, and well, for Amy's lunch was almost always a snatched sandwich, and Linda's often was, too, though she prepared the children's meal and shared whatever Georgie was having. Henry's diet was still a pulverised mix.

'Do you see much of Susan Trent?' Amy asked. 'She lives in Bishop St Leon, but I'm not sure where, in relation to your place.'

'I've barely met her,' Linda answered. 'Apart from knowing she works with you, that is.'

'She's got this violent son,' said Amy. 'At least, he seems to be,' she amended. 'Came into the office once and looked as if butter wouldn't melt while he waited for her to give him a lift home, but Susan's got a big bruise on her face today and she looks awful. Brian seemed to imply that it might be Martin bashing her up. It can't be true, though,' she added.

Linda remembered Jo's remarks that morning.

'I saw him today,' she said. 'He came out of his house and nearly walked right into Jo and me when we were taking the children to their playgroup. Jo told me who he was – she said he's bad news. Drinks a lot, she said. So he's Susan's son?' Linda had met Susan in the office, before she moved into the flat. 'He's a travel rep, Jo said.'

'That's right. He's just got back from Venice,' Amy said.

'And he beat up his mother?'

'She says she fell,' said Amy. 'That's what battered wives say, isn't it? Or they walked into a door.'

'But that's dreadful!' Linda exclaimed. 'Poor Susan! And he lives with her?' She remembered that Jo had said he did.

'Yes. I don't know too much about it. She doesn't talk about him and Brian didn't say much.'

'Oh dear! That's dreadful. Poor woman. Can't she turf him out?'

'You'd think she would, wouldn't you? But I suppose, seeing he's her son—' Amy did not finish her sentence.

'I'll ask Jo about it,' said Linda. 'Her family's lived in the village for ever. Her dad thinks the Trents' house is spooked in some way.'

'Haunted, you mean?'

'Not exactly. She says bad things have happened to people who lived there.'

'Bad things can happen anywhere,' said Amy, who had helped Brian sell a house where a man had recently murdered his wife. She shuddered, remembering. 'I don't see what we can do about it,' she added.

Nor did Linda. It wasn't really their business but in a way it was; you couldn't just let someone go on beating up their mother and take no notice.

'We sent someone out to look at a house share in Bishop St Leon today,' Amy said. 'He came in this morning. Nice bloke. Quiet. Thirty-five-ish, at a guess. He's probably splitting up from his wife.'

'Is he?'

'Well, he's marrying age, or relationship age,' said Amy.

'He may not have met anyone,' Linda said. 'People don't, do they, once they get past clubbing and pubbing, and are into chasing money in their careers. What does he do?'

'He didn't say. No need,' said Amy. 'He was going to see some other places too.'

'Where's he staying meanwhile?'

'Who knows? On some pal's floor, I expect,' said Amy.

'Which house is it?' Linda asked. 'In Bishop St Leon, I mean.'

'It's in Chapel Row.'

It must be near The Old Chapel, where Jo worked. Linda said so, adding that she didn't know the village well.

'Yet you've been there for seven months,' said Amy, laughing at her.

'Yes, but I don't walk all that far with Henry or Georgie,' said Linda. 'Only to the playgroup and Jo's, really. The other nannies we meet live in other villages.'

'You do have a social time,' said Amy.

'Well, we need it,' Linda replied. 'And it's all girls. So far we haven't met any male nannies.'

'What a shame,' said Amy.

Debbie didn't return until nearly three.

Martin, frustrated that she hadn't come back by one o'clock, when he reasoned her shift would have ended and she would have collected her children, went up to the Grapes, intending to have something to eat; perhaps he'd go back to her place later, or on the other hand he might leave her to lament at his absence. Once in the pub, he began on the beer and soon his appetite disappeared. He returned to her house when the bar closed.

Debbie was there, but so were the children. Martin persuaded her to shut them in the sitting room with their toys and the television while they went up to her bedroom.

She didn't like to protest; Martin was funny that way. Besides, she was glad to see him and pleased that he seemed to have missed her. When he was in a good mood he was nice, and mostly, with her, so far, he had rarely been anything else.

4

The house in Chapel Row, Bishop St Leon, was a red brick villa with a gabled front and bow windows. Beside it was a garage, the black-painted doors now closed. Adam Wilson had made an appointment to see the room at seven o'clock that evening, when there would be someone at home to let him in, but he drove over to the village on Friday afternoon to have a look at it. Unless there were any obvious and serious disadvantages, he meant to take it, for Bishop St Leon was where he would find answers to his questions, and if he lived there, on the spot, his task would be simplified. For the present, he was staying at the Grapes in Rotherston. The previous day he had been in London, checking registers of births and deaths, but he had gleaned no new information.

Marsh's, the estate agent which dealt with the letting of the room, would be open the following day, Saturday. Adam wanted to move in immediately if the room was suitable and the paperwork could be dealt with promptly enough; it might be possible. He would have to pay a month's rent in advance; the young woman in the agent's office had made that clear, handing him the details. Adam had a wad of cash in the inner pocket of his dark suit; after his father's death, when he realised what he had to do, he had arranged to take three months' unpaid leave. There had been no problem about that; his job would be there for him when he returned.

The agent had provided him with a map of the village. In the centre, the main road from Rotherston became the High Street, off which branched North Street with, leading from it, Chapel Row, a cul-de-sac. Opposite number seventeen, with its vacant room, there was a building which had clearly once been a church or chapel but which had been converted into a dwelling. Roses and other climbers grew up its brick walls and the front garden was elaborately laid out with shrubs and small ornamental beds edged with box. At the side, there was a lawn; he could see a child's swing and a climbing frame beyond the house. The front door, made of mahogany, had shining brass fitments – letter-box, knocker, and there was a brass-trimmed green box for newspapers in the front porch. Adam turned the car and drove out of the short road into North Street and back to the High Street, where there was a small square with several houses fronting it, all modernised, well maintained and one for sale, but the agent was not Brian Marsh. There were also a newsagent's shop which sold groceries, and a post office. In pale, fading sunlight, Adam found it charming, yet what went on in all these houses? Secret lives, different from what was perceived by outsiders.

He took a right turn which would lead him, eventually, round to the further end of North Street. Here there was very little traffic and, at this time of day, few pedestrians. He saw a woman pushing a toddler in a pushchair, and another with two children and a dog, which was on a lead. He knew where Cedar Cottage was; that, at least, he had been able to discover.

It was detached, but very little land separated it from its neighbour on one side, though on the other there was a driveway leading to a large garage. Three first-floor windows overlooked the road under a tiled roof; below, there was a window on either side of the front door, which was oak, like those further up the village but less handsome, with black fittings – cast-iron, Adam surmised. His urge to get out of the car and look round was almost overwhelming but he must not give in to it: not now, and maybe never. Susan might not live here any more.

He did not know that he had already seen her, though he had not spoken to her, in Brian Marsh's office earlier that day.

Debbie was not finding her reunion with Martin easy. He had had a lot to drink, she realised, smelling it on his breath, as she had before, but she knew he drank; she'd met him in the Grapes. All men drank; they started young, for a laugh; often enough, she'd heard them say so, but her husband, Jim, a freelance television sound operator, hadn't, or not to excess. He'd just never been at home, except between shoots, but then he'd got a contract with a team making a documentary and had been overseas for weeks. When he returned, they had nothing much to say to one another; he had seen unspeakable scenes of deprivation and moved on, while she had simply been busy with Lily. Rose had been conceived during that difficult time, and soon Jim had gone away again, returning for the birth, but after that, though he reappeared from time to time and was a loving father to the girls, the gulf between them widened and eventually he admitted that he had met someone else.

He had moved out and was living with his new partner, who also worked in television. He paid Debbie as much as he could for herself and the children, and she had stayed in their house, which they'd both been so thrilled with in the beginning. When he was not working, he came to see the children and Debbie did not put any obstacles in his way; he was a good father and he had been a good husband. She wished things had worked out differently; she'd been so lonely, and then Martin had come along, but he was often away, too. She had no luck, picking absentees, but she must make the best of things now, for a woman with two small children was not one many men wanted.

'It's all right,' she told Martin, when, in bed that afternoon, he couldn't manage it. In fact she was quite relieved,
for she was worrying about the children on their own
downstairs. Lily was able to open the door; they might
get into the kitchen and start climbing on to cupboards
or opening drawers. 'It'll be better later,' she reassured
him. 'After you've had some supper. I've got mince. I'll
do spaghetti Bolognese – the girls like that. You stay here,
if you like.' She swung her legs out of bed, hoping he'd
sleep off the effects of too much alcohol. 'You must be
tired after your journey,' she told him, willing to believe
that was part of the problem.

He was tired: of course he was tired. But it was his
mother, causing a scene the night before, not the journey
which had tired him. Not answering Debbie, Martin
pulled the duvet round his ears and burrowed under it.
Curled up, warm, as in the womb, he need take no action
for the moment. Later, he'd go down and read to the little
girls. They liked that; Martin read with feeling, putting
on different voices for the characters. It kept them quiet
while their mother got through her chores with which,
occasionally, he helped her in a way he never did at home.
He'd dug her garden, too, and trimmed the privet hedge
along one fence. Debbie needed help; she couldn't manage
on her own.

He didn't want to go home. He might stay the night;
he often did. Debbie would be more relaxed later, when
the kids were in bed. To think that less than forty-eight

hours ago he'd been in Venice: what a life of contrasts his had become. It wasn't his fault that he'd been made redundant from his teaching post; if his wife had been more supportive it wouldn't have happened, but she was intent on her own career, which had overtaken his. In Debbie's bed, Martin easily wallowed in self-pity, casting himself first in the role of a fatherless child, then as a gifted but wronged teacher, and finally that of a father deprived of his only child, whom his cruel former wife had taken with her when she went to Edinburgh, embarking on what became a successful academic career.

Martin had lost touch with them, to his own mother's great distress.

He had paid nothing towards the upkeep of either the child or his former wife, but she'd got the house, which she sold when she went to Scotland. She'd had all she was going to get from him. She'd wrecked his life. Women were bad news. The only ones worth tangling with were those like Debbie, helpless, pliant creatures who needed a man around the place to tell them what to do.

After a period spent brooding on the misfortunes he had been forced to endure because of other people's actions, Martin got up and dressed. Debbie had been punished long enough by his remaining upstairs; he'd go down now and help her with the children. Having convinced himself that Debbie was to blame for his recent attack of impotence – it had happened before – Martin, smiling benevolently, went to join the little family.

*   *   *

Debbie wanted her children to like Martin. When he read to them, they were responsive, but he would suddenly get bored and switch his attention away. Once, worryingly, when a fair came to Rotherston, in an expansive mood of ostentation which she was beginning to recognise as one he occasionally indulged, he had taken them all to it, paid for their rides and insisted that Lily go with him on the Big Wheel.

Lily hadn't liked it; she hadn't wanted a turn on it and she'd been in tears when they got off; Debbie had said that maybe she wasn't old enough, but Martin had brushed aside such protests; he said it would be fun and he wanted company, eventually persuading her. He'd been laughing all the time they were in the air. Afterwards, Lily had been coaxed out of her tears by being given a goldfish Martin had won in a hoop-la, but that night she'd had bad dreams.

Debbie was grateful that he took an interest in her daughters but she knew she should have insisted that Lily went only on the rides for little children. Both of them had enjoyed trundling round on the small carousel, but Martin had said that Lily was a big girl now and deserved promotion. Still, that was in the past; there was nearly another year to go before the fair came again; by then they would all be more used to one another, and Lily would be that much older.

Martin, spasmodically, liked playing father to Lily and
Rose. They were pretty little girls, fair haired like their
mother, doll-like, very different from his own son, who
was dark and sturdily built with a determined jaw. Paul
did not resemble either parent; Martin had questioned if
he was, in fact, the father, but Susan knew Paul took after
her own father. Now, Martin suggested that the girls
should do a jigsaw; they had some easy ones, suitable to
their years. He watched them trying to fit the pieces
together and praised them when they succeeded. Debbie
went out to the kitchen to prepare the meal, leaving them
to it, and peace reigned.

Susan couldn't postpone the moment of her return home
by shopping, for she had already stocked up with food
ahead of Martin's return the day before.

She tried to convince herself that he would have
received a rapturous welcome from his new girlfriend and
was staying overnight. When past relationships had pros-
pered, Martin had not spent much time in Bishop St
Leon; she had seen him only when he came to collect
mail and his washing, but he had never moved in properly with any of the women. Most of them were divorced
or separated and would lose maintenance or benefit –
whichever applied – if they had a resident partner. The
only one she had met was young, small, thin and pretty,
and Martin was nearly old enough to be her father. He

hadn't found her as the result of a lonely-hearts advertisement or club meeting; she was too young to have felt
the need for such a service.

They had had tea in the garden, which the girl had
admired. Susan had shown her round it while Martin, in
exemplary fashion, carried the tray indoors, though he
didn't wash the crockery nor put the remainder of the jam
sponge Susan had made in a tin; wasps were walking on
it when she went into the kitchen later.

'How did you meet Martin?' Susan had to ask it, as
they strolled over the lawn which sloped towards the
boundary fence. A weeping willow was in full leaf, casting
shade in that part of the garden.

'Didn't he tell you?' The girl, whose name was Jenny,
blushed a little. 'We met in Oxford. I was on my bike
and I nearly ran into him when he was pulling out of a
parking place. He was lovely about it. It was all my fault.'

It had happened while Martin was doing a relief spell
at a language school in the town, and Jenny was a pupil,
learning how to teach English as a foreign language before
she went to South America. Jenny wasn't in his class; he
was teaching English to a group of Chinese students.

She fitted the pattern Martin needed: vulnerable and
naive, but as she had enough courage to go overseas in
such an enterprising manner, both these attributes would
diminish, making her less attractive to him by the time
of her return. And by then she would have found other
fish to fry, nearer her age. Susan could not wish such a

nice girl to be seriously involved with a man who had so much anger in him, even if he was her son.

And so it was: a few letters came at first; then silence, and Martin went on a drinking bout of great magnitude when he realised that he'd been rejected yet again.

Susan, since those days, had learned to make the most of the peaceful spells during which Martin found sexual, if not emotional satisfaction, and in the intervals while he was away on a courier assignment. She could cope in between, however difficult it was.

He didn't really mean his rages. It was the drink, just as it had been with his father, who at first had been penitent when he realised what he had done to her, the bruising and the fractures; his solicitous behaviour after such bouts almost made the suffering bearable.

She left the office when Brian came back from a successful afternoon and told her to go home. She'd done the letters, left messages for him, cleared both their desks.

'Will you be all right?' he asked her.

'Yes – I'm fine now,' Susan said.

'Sure?' Brian, who had shaggy eyebrows which would overhang his eyes as he grew older, peered at her intently.

'Yes,' she repeated.

'You can always ring me if you need me, Susan,' he told her earnestly.

She knew that he suspected what had happened, and she knew, also, that he meant his offer.

'Yes,' she said, for the third time. 'Thank you, Brian.'

There was nothing anyone could do. If there were to be a solution, only she could find it.

When she reached home, the house was blessedly quiet. Martin was still out. What a relief! She went into the garden, moist-smelling after the rain. She enjoyed working in it; she had planted more bulbs in the grass beside the fence separating her garden from Dan and Fiona's. They had to be renewed from time to time, for mice uprooted them and ate them, and they rotted if left in clumps instead of being dug up and divided every few years, as was recommended. She put in snowdrops, too; the small white spears, appearing at the end of January and at their best in bleak February, were a heartening sight on dreary winter days. There were so many different sorts; Susan did not differentiate, but enthusiasts collected various varieties. Perhaps she ought to learn about them; it could be interesting. It was almost dark when she returned to the house. Martin never let her know whether he would be back for supper or not; for a long time she had prepared a meal for him if he came in wanting to eat, and she always did so when he returned, as last night, from a tour, but after she had bought a microwave oven, often all she did now when he demanded food was to heat something through. If she didn't, or told him to get something for himself – the fridge was always well stocked – he'd cook nothing, settling down with a four-pack of beer instead, or, if there was no alcohol in the house, he'd go up to the Crown.

Last night's casserole had been large enough for several meals. Susan, cheered by the calm of her solitude, felt quite hungry; she heated a modest helping for herself, and parcelled the rest into plastic tubs which she put in the freezer. Martin, meanwhile, had eaten spaghetti at Debbie's, and had opened a bottle of red wine which, anticipating his return, Debbie had brought back from the supermarket. They were steadily drinking it, nestling together on her small, squashy sofa, both very content. He was a dear, really, Debbie thought, feeling a rush of affection; what did it matter if sometimes he drank a little too much? No one was perfect.

5

In the Crown, Adam made half a pint last some time.

He was alone in the bar. It was still early; only a few people had come in on their way home from their offices or other places of work. After driving round the village on his trip of exploration, he had parked his car and walked back along North Street to look at Cedar Cottage again, and had continued on past Field House, where the road went round a bend. A stone wall ran along the boundary, but at one point he could see across it to where Susan Trent's garden marched beside the larger one at Field House. He wondered if her house had once been its lodge, or a gardener's cottage. He could see several tall trees – willows, and some poplars, but there was no sign of a cedar. As he retraced his steps towards the centre of the village, a small Fiat turned in between the gateposts and pulled up outside the house. Adam walked slowly on, curious enough to stare in as a young woman got out of the driver's seat and began extracting two small children from the rear. He was too far away to recognise her as the woman he had sat next to on the train the previous evening when an obnoxious man seated opposite had eaten some strong-smelling crisps and cast crumbs about.

He walked on up the road and then turned back. By the time he passed Field House again, the young woman and the children had gone. He'd like to see inside that house.

Beyond it lay the church. He walked towards it, going up the path and trying the door, but it was locked. Turning away, he wandered through the churchyard, which was tidy, the grass recently cut and no dead flowers visible on the graves. In the fading light, he peered at the tombstones, deciphering the names and the dates of those interred. Some went back a very long way and were difficult to read; he saw no Trent among them, but a shiver ran through him as he circled the ancient building, coming round its east end and reaching the front again. Ghosts, he thought, and shook his head to rid it of morbid thoughts. It was time to find some company.

It was warm in the pub and the landlord, Des, glad to have a customer so soon after opening for the evening, was genial.

'You haven't been in before,' he remarked.

'No. I'm hoping to move into the village,' said Adam. 'I've an appointment to see a room in a house in Chapel Row.'

'Oh yes?' said Des. 'Is that while you look for something to buy?'

Adam laughed.

'I'm afraid not,' he said. 'I'm just here while I do some research.'

'I see. Linked to Oxford, I suppose.' There were a number of people in Bishop St Leon who worked in Oxford in various capacities, ranging from the academic to commerce.

'You could say that,' Adam acknowledged. 'There are plenty of sources there.'

'Good libraries,' said Des, encouragingly.

'And laboratories,' Adam added.

'So what do you think of the village, then? Seen much of it yet? Have you been here before?'

'No. It's very attractive,' said Adam. 'I've driven around. I've been as far as the church. Couldn't go in. It was locked.'

'It's locked most of the time,' said Des. 'Some of our older residents remember when it wasn't, but there are bad types around. If it's not stealing the charity box, it's vandalising the building. You can't leave anywhere unlocked now.'

'Are there many vandals in Bishop St Leon?'

'They come and go,' said Des. 'A few youngsters get a bit wild at times, and then others have been known to come in from Rotherston, looking to make trouble, but it's no worse here than anywhere else. Better than most.'

'No village policeman?'

'Not now. They all cruise around in cars. It'd be better if they walked around the streets, made their presence felt. Too many of them are out catching motorists going two miles faster than the limit while old ladies get robbed,' said Des.

'Do old ladies get robbed in Bishop St Leon?'

'It's been known. When they let confidence tricksters into their houses,' said Des. 'Fake council callers or knockers.'

'Knockers?'

'They call themselves antique dealers – they go round knocking on doors wanting to buy furniture or china or silver – this and that,' said Des. 'They spot bargains – things the householder doesn't realise are valuable, and offer, say, fifteen pounds for something they know to be worth a hundred. They come in waves. We've had none here recently, I'm glad to say.'

'Sharp practice,' said Adam.

'Very.'

'I suppose you know everyone in the village,' Adam said. 'If you've been here long.' He estimated that the man was in his early forties.

'Not really. You get to know the regulars,' said Des. 'I've run the Crown for five years. Even in that time the place has changed. Folk used to live here all their lives but now they move around. Older people move into smaller houses and younger ones come in from London, wanting a country life. We do fairly well because we serve good food but some country pubs are having a struggle because people can't risk having more than a drink or two if they're driving. A few have turned into smart restaurants and they're OK – one member of the party is the driver and doesn't drink, or they have a taxi.' He laughed. 'Running a cab might be profitable for a second career,' he said. 'I worked in a bank. Got made redundant.'

'Tough,' said Adam.

'Too many machines,' said Des. 'Taking the place of humans. It was either run a pub or join the police.'

'The police?' Adam was astonished.

'I'd have liked that, but I was too old to make it worthwhile,' said Des. 'Even if they'd have taken me.'

He'd have been a good policeman, Adam thought, looking at his plain, pleasant face: reassuring.

'Do you know the tenants in the house in Chapel Row?' he asked. 'Number seventeen?'

'Yes. They come in here sometimes. Not together,' he emphasised.

Adam waited. Would the chatty publican give him a rundown on the two men?

'They're both out at the moment. At work, I suppose,' he tried.

'Yes. One of them's a carpenter – well, a craftsman. Makes wonderful furniture – bespoke stuff, to order. He's got a workshop over the other side of Rotherston,' said Des. 'That's Christopher. The other one,' he paused, for dramatic effect, and began to polish an already gleaming glass. 'Roger. He's a copper.'

'Really?' Adam was intrigued. 'So you should have plenty to chat about, as you're interested in police work,' he remarked.

'Not really,' Des replied, and would say no more, beyond stating that Roger had been living there for only a few weeks. Soon after his arrival Jeremy, a musician, presumably the tenant whose room Adam planned to rent, had decided to move out.

'Is that significant?' asked Adam, and when Des did not answer, he added, 'But you're in favour of having a policeman in the village.'

'He doesn't work here. He's in the CID,' said Des. 'Based in Reading, I believe.'

'A detective, eh?' That was interesting.

'You'll be meeting him soon enough,' said Des.

'I'll look forward to it,' said Adam.

'I shouldn't be in too much of a hurry,' Des said.

At this point, some customers entered the bar, two women in business suits, one in a skirt and the other in neat tailored trousers, and a man. They greeted Des with cries about their exhaustion after leaving their offices, but thank goodness it was Saturday tomorrow.

'This is——?' Des indicated Adam. 'He's thinking of living in the village for a bit.'

Adam supplied his name.

'I'm going to see a room in Chapel Row,' he told them.

'That'll be Jeremy's,' said one of the women.

'Good luck,' said the other, adding, 'It's a nice house and Christopher's great.'

Nobody mentioned Roger.

Adam looked at his watch.

'I've got to go, or I'll be late,' he said.

'There are other places to rent,' said the man. 'Or Des would put you up. Wouldn't you, Des? He lets rooms now and then.'

'I'll remember that,' said Adam, getting up to go. Roger, though a police officer, did not seem to be flavour of the month. Nevertheless, he might be a useful person to know.

It was Christopher who opened the door to him. It had to be; Adam knew it before the man spoke. He smiled, shook his hand – his own was hard and dry, rough to the touch – looked him in the eye and said, 'Hi, I'm Christopher Castle.'

'Adam Wilson,' said Adam.

'I'll show you the room,' said Christopher. 'Come this way.'

He led Adam round the house. The vacant room overlooked the garden; it was large, with fitted cupboards along one wall and a wash-basin in a corner. There was dark blue and silver striped wallpaper along one wall, and moss green on another.

'It's not everyone's choice of décor,' said Christopher.

'But Jeremy, who used to live here, is a musician and has esoteric tastes. You can always redecorate. The bed's OK. His girlfriend used to stay here with him sometimes, and there were no complaints.'

'I see.'

'He's moved in with her for now. Maybe they'll make it permanent,' Christopher said. 'You attached?'

'Not at the moment,' said Adam. 'What about you?' He might as well ask, since cards were being marked in this way.

'Off and on,' said Christopher. 'Rather more off than on, you could say. Same girl, I mean, but she's a free spirit.'

'Oh – tricky,' said Adam, not sure how best to respond. 'The room seems fine,' he added.

''The bathroom's along here.' Christopher showed him. 'We provide our own sheets and towels. And we cater independently. We each have a cupboard in the kitchen and a shelf in the fridge. It mostly works out all right.' He would let Adam discover for himself that Roger was likely to raid someone else's store if he'd forgotten to shop. 'Roger's out quite a bit at night. He puts in long hours when he's on a case – he's in the police.'

'Useful,' said Adam. He wasn't going to reveal the fact that he'd already received potted biographies of the two men. 'What about you?'

'I'm a journeyman joiner,' said Christopher. 'I make furniture. Tables, chairs, boxes – whatever you want. In my spare time, if any, I carve things.' He opened the door of the room facing the one Adam knew he was going to take, and somewhat bashfully waved a hand round.

The room had the same modern fitments as Adam's, but a shelf ran along under the window and on it were displayed, carved from various types of wood, an eagle in flight, a leaping horse, a mare with a suckling foal, several swans in different positions, and the head of an old man, chiselled from a solid block of what Adam thought was elm.

'May I?' He moved towards them. 'They're splendid,' he said, at a loss for praise that would not be gushing. 'That head, in particular. Who is it?'

'My grandfather,' said Christopher. 'He was a merchant seaman. Dead now. Killed in an accident – a road accident. Hit-and-run. At night, two hundred yards from where he lived. He was harmlessly coming home from the pub.'

'Oh – I'm sorry.'

'Yes. Me too.'

'Did they get the driver?'

Christopher shook his head.

'A kid, probably. A TOK.'

'TOK?'

'Technical term. Taking without owner's knowledge,' said Christopher. 'A stolen car.'

He turned away to show Adam the bathroom, then led the way downstairs. 'Roger has the top floor,' he said. 'He's got his own shower. En suite, as they say. Pays more than us. Come and see the rest of the place.'

There was a large living room which all could share, and the pine-fitted kitchen was spacious. Outside, there was a garden which it was now too dark to inspect.

'It's not bad,' Christopher said. 'I'm not a gardener but Roger's turned out to have green fingers. He's tidied it up and planted vegetables.'

'Sounds good,' Adam said.

'You'll take it, then?'

'Sure,' said Adam.

'Let's go down to the pub and seal it,' said Christopher with enthusiasm. 'How about trying their steak and chips?'

'Right,' said Adam.

Christopher hurried him out, and they got into Adam's car to drive the short distance back to the Crown. Adam had the strong impression that Christopher wanted him out of the house before Roger returned.

Why? In case he changed his mind about moving in after he met the third tenant?

It was Friday night and the pub was now much busier than when Adam had left it, less than an hour earlier.

Christopher seemed to know most of those who were gathered in the bar and he introduced Adam around. People wanting food had come from further afield and Des was now busy filling glasses. A young woman was helping him and taking orders for dishes which unseen hands were preparing.

'Do you play cricket?' Nicholas asked Adam.

'Yes,' said Adam. 'But not well – and surely you don't play in November?'

'I'm planning ahead,' said Nicholas. 'We've got to win the Brinton trophy back.'

'Brinton trophy?'

'It's an inter-village tournament,' said Nicholas. 'Bishop St Leon lost it this year.'

'After holding it for three years,' said Des.

'I see.' This was serious stuff. 'I might not be up to your standards,' said Adam.

'We'll try you out as soon as the season starts,' said Nicholas.

But Adam might not be here then.

'Pity about Martin Trent,' someone said. 'As a young lad he was a useful batsman.'

'Martin Trent?' Adam was alert, hearing the name.

'Chap who lives here. Played as a youngster. Not now.'

'Why's that?' The speaker had used the present tense; so Martin Trent still lived in Bishop St Leon.

The man who had mentioned him raised his arm in the gesture of one drinking, but without a glass in his hand.

'When he's home, he comes in here most nights,' said someone else. 'Might be in yet.'

'He's probably in Rotherston,' said someone else. 'Got a woman there, hasn't he?'

'Poor cow,' said someone else.

'He was in last night,' said Nicholas. 'Back from Venice, as he told us.'

'Venice?' Adam did not need to form a proper question.

'He's a travel rep. Courier. What you will,' said another man. 'Used to be an academic, or so he'd have us believe.'

'It's true,' said Nicholas, who had lived in the village for a long time. 'He taught at a poly – it's become a university since then. Not in this area. That was while he was married.'

'He lost his job and his wife at much the same time,' said someone else.

'She died?'

'No – she dumped him, sensible woman. Took the boy and left,' said the other man. 'And Martin came home to Mummy.'

'Where he's been ever since,' said Nicholas. 'Poor Mummy.'

'Has anyone seen her today?' asked another man. Adam thought he'd been introduced as Bill. 'Only it was a bit rowdy over there last night.'

No one had seen Martin's mother.

'Where's Mary tonight?' someone asked Bill.

'She had to see some parents after school, and then she was going to do the big shop. She'll be in later.' Bill turned to Adam. 'My wife's a teacher. On Fridays we often have supper here. Mary likes to get the shopping done so that we have the weekend clear ahead of us.'

'Are you a cricketer?' asked Adam, though what he

really wanted to know about was the Trents, mother and son.

'Used to be,' said Bill. 'I still turn out when needed.'

'Demon bowler, that's Bill,' said Nicholas.

At this point, Christopher and Adam's steaks were ready; the girl carried the plates over to a table in a corner and the pair separated from the group at the bar.

'Friendly crowd,' remarked Adam.

'Yes,' agreed Christopher. 'I've been here two years and they've never made me feel a stranger.'

'Aren't villagers supposed not to accept you until you've lived there for two generations?' said Adam.

'There are some original families still here,' said Christopher. 'They may still feel like that. But things have changed such a lot in recent years in these places. Young people can't afford to live in the country because property is so expensive. Most of the old cottages have been tarted up and modernised and have been bought by commuters, and the new houses are well out of young people's price range.'

'Hence renting,' Adam remarked.

'All my assets are in my business,' said Christopher. 'Eventually, I'd like to live where I could have my workshop on the premises, or hard by.'

'You'll do that, won't you?' Adam said.

'I hope so. Maybe not in this area, but this is where the customers are,' said Christopher. 'This is a prosperous part of the country.'

'What was all that about the former batsman – Martin, was it? Do you know him?' Adam's tone was casual. He did not want to seem too curious, but he wanted to follow up the information that fortuitously had come his way. He was keeping a lookout, too, for Mary, the wife of Bill, due soon.

'I've been here when he's been in,' said Christopher. 'Fond of a drink, as you gathered. I don't know much about him. He lives with his mother, who's a widow, and he gets argumentative when he's past the sentimental stage. One or two people have hinted that she has a hard time of it with him.'

'Do you know her? The mother?'

'No. I'm not even sure I'd recognise her,' said Christopher. 'I know a lot of people by sight, but I don't spend much time here. I work late, usually.'

'Did you cut your day short to show me the room?'

Christopher shrugged.

'You shouldn't have done that,' said Adam. 'The agent would have done it.'

'I thought it would be good to meet. For both of us,' said Christopher. 'Not that we need see much of one another in the house, unless it works out like that. I don't have much time for evening activities. Squash, swimming, the things people do.'

'Cricket, for instance.'

'Yes.'

'There's always Roger,' said Adam.

'True. There's always Roger.'

'Doesn't he have a say in whether you take me in or not?'

'Up to a point. We're doing this in an ad hoc sort of way because Jeremy left rather suddenly. He told the agency as he knows Brian Marsh.' And for the unlet period, Jeremy, or, at the end of the month, Christopher and Roger, would have to pay the extra rent. 'You want a room. Put the two together and there you go.'

There you went, indeed. Adam, cutting his last piece of steak, was wondering how to reply when a small commotion by the bar advertised Mary's arrival. She was greeted warmly, not only by her husband but by the assembled group; it seemed like a club, friends gathering, a welcoming place. Perhaps they were all cricketers. Adam glanced across, curious.

'Mary does a lot in the village,' Christopher told him. 'Helps with fêtes and so on. Sings in the choir.'

'Popular lady, then?'

'Very.'

'And you said you don't spend much time in the village,' Adam mocked gently.

'Come into the Crown enough and you hear the gossip,' Christopher told him.

It was true. Adam had learned a bit himself before he went to see the room. If he stayed there long enough, maybe he'd meet Martin Trent.

But not that night. Martin had not come in by the

time Adam and Christopher left. All being well, Adam would move in the next day.

Would Roger be there, when he did?

Adam drove back to the Grapes in Rotherston wondering about the missing member of the household. What had he done to make himself so unpopular? Surely a police officer would be welcome in the community?

6

As soon as he entered the house, Christopher knew that Roger was back, for a smell of frying fish greeted him in the hallway, accompanied by clouds of steam. The kitchen door was open; Christopher advanced towards it, prepared for the familiar sight of Roger standing over a pan on the stove, whence came the fumes. In another pan, chips were heating through. As Christopher entered, Roger tipped the chips on to a plate, followed by the fish.

Roger often bought fish and chips on his way home, then got delayed so that the food grew cold and needed heating up. Once again, Christopher resolved that they must get a microwave. Adam, when he'd been exposed to this experience, would be certain to concur and might split the cost with him, though Roger might be less willing to join in. He'd have to be persuaded to use it, though.

'Hi,' said Christopher. 'Not had supper yet?'

'As you see,' said Roger.

'Hard day, then?' Sometimes Christopher, making conciliatory remarks to Roger, felt he was like an anxious wife, trying to ease the atmosphere in a stressful relationship.

'Some of us have to work,' said Roger, who, having seen only Christopher's ornamental carvings, not his furniture, had made it clear that he considered Christopher's occupation to be dilettante stuff.

'I came back early to meet the new lodger,' said Christopher, wincing at his own ingratiating tone. Why did he let Roger do this to him?

Roger did not answer. He sat down at the table and proceeded to pour quantities of vinegar on to his chips before starting to stuff food into his mouth as if he had had nothing to eat for weeks.

'Nice guy,' Christopher continued bravely. 'Means to move in tomorrow. He's doing research of some sort.' He hadn't discovered exactly what, and hoped Roger would not ask, but he did, not looking up from his plate, speaking with his mouth full.

'Into what?' he growled.

'I didn't ask. Something scientific, I expect,' said Christopher.

'Hmph.' Roger's snort indicated that Christopher wouldn't stand much chance if he were on Roger's police team investigating crime.

'Quiet chap,' said Christopher. 'Thought you'd like to know. We had a bite at the Crown.'

'Mates already, then.' It wasn't a question. Roger, having uttered the remark, picked up one of the two cans of beer sitting on the table and drank noisily.

Christopher sighed. He'd got on well with Jeremy, and had been sorry to see him go. Jeremy wouldn't have left but for Roger. They should have toughed it out and forced Roger to mend his ways or depart. Maybe Adam would be on for that, once he understood the situation.

Cheered by this reflection, Christopher said, 'I'll let you enjoy your meal in peace,' and turned away, closing the kitchen door behind him. If Roger would remember to close it, and put the extractor fan on when he was cooking, life all round would improve. He went into the sitting room and turned on the television; there might be a programme worth watching before he went to bed. If he heard Roger go up first, he'd open the kitchen window and the back door to let out the steam and smell. Christopher wondered if Roger was a good detective; he fitted some of the more unattractive stereotypes portrayed in press and television, but that did not mean he was ineffective. On the whole, Christopher had found most police officers civil and agreeable; two who had come to his workshop after he had had a break-in, when expensive tools were stolen, couldn't have been more helpful. They even caught the thieves – opportunist lads – and were able to return his property.

There was nothing to interest him on television. He went up to his room, where he had his stereo, a comfortable chair, and Dick Francis's latest paperback to read. He hoped there would be plenty about horses in it; those were the ones he most enjoyed.

Left alone, Roger soon finished his fish and chips, washing the food down with beer. He scarcely tasted what he ate or drank; it was simply fuel to keep him going till the morning. Following enquiries he had made in London, he had spent much of his day with officers from the Fraud Squad who were pursuing a financial scam; they had infiltrated a woman officer into the building society where, after she had covertly investigated all the staff, suspicion had fallen on an employee who had a more lavish lifestyle than his salary would warrant. She had found evidence that he had been running several accounts with other societies and banks, transferring funds, and an arrest was imminent. Roger would be involved in that part of the operation, planned for early the next morning. Most of the credit was due to the woman officer, a computer expert, who had explored the files and gathered the information which would send the suspect to prison.

Roger swilled his plate and cutlery under the hot tap and put them to dry on the drainer. Poor bloke, he thought, sparing the culprit a moment's sympathy; there he was, happy as Larry, probably planning a flit to Spain with his loot, but he hadn't got out in time. He'd swindled honest folk; that's what he had done, and he didn't deserve any sympathy.

Nevertheless Roger, another sinner, felt a pang of pity.

*   *   *

He didn't want to go straight up to bed. Sleep wouldn't come quickly, and when it did, images from the past would haunt him in his dreams. He'd hear the squeal of brakes and see the child's body hurtling into the air. Drink might help; sometimes it did, dulling memory. He needn't talk to anyone; he'd made no friends in Bishop St Leon but making a new start, anonymous in these surroundings, had been his reason for transferring to the area and coming to the village. No one knew him here; no one had known Elaine. There was no need to be sociable; it certainly wasn't necessary at work.

He put on his leather jacket and left the house.

Christopher heard the door. Giving Roger time to get clear, he set his book aside and went downstairs, where he opened the kitchen window and back door. Then he walked down the garden in the dark and stood looking at the solid, serviceable house. Strange, wasn't it, he thought, to be thirty-five years old and sharing a rented house with two men whom he had never met before they were connected in this way. It was student life prolonged, though all were employed adults and sometimes they got drunk and suffered emotional rebuffs, yet none had any responsibility for the others, nor commitment to them. It should be satisfactory and undemanding, and so it was, until Roger's arrival. He sighed. Jeremy hadn't had the stomach for a confrontation, however artfully manoeuvred. Perhaps

Adam, who seemed a calm, controlled individual, when he discovered the problems, would find a solution. Cheered by this reflection, Christopher strolled back towards the house. He had rather hoped the new tenant would be female; a woman joining the household might have been a civilising influence. Still, if a woman had met Roger, she'd have been put off instantly.

The fumes in the kitchen had abated when he returned; he closed the back door and the window; then, leaving the room, shut the door leading into the hall.

Roger, who in Christopher's opinion was a compulsive eater, was capable of having another fry-up when he returned from wherever he had gone – probably the pub. With this thought, Christopher went up to bed, resolved to make an early start in the morning to compensate for time lost today; it wasn't often that he came home before eight at night, and sometimes it was later still.

Meanwhile, Roger had found the Crown full of cheerful people looking forward to the weekend. He'd been welcomed in a friendly manner, but when he had bought his beer, he took it to a corner of the bar and stared at it morosely between swallows.

After the initial greetings of those who recognised him, no one made an effort to include him in conversation. Their impression was of a sulky, brooding man, and they were not going to put themselves out for someone so unresponsive. Roger, however, was not deaf; he listened to what was going on around him and he was aware of who was speaking. He was a trained police officer, and it was habit. A young couple, whom he had not seen before, were at a table near the bar counter and were talking to a middle-aged pair at a neighbouring table. The older woman was leaning across to ask the younger ones if they had heard a rumpus in the night.

'From the Trents, you mean?'

'Yes.'

'We heard someone banging at the door. It was noisy, but then it stopped,' said the younger man.

'Have you seen Susan today?' asked the older woman, Mary Church.

'No – but then we don't see her much,' said the younger woman, Susan's new neighbour, Fiona. 'She was friendly the day we moved in – said hullo, but that was it.'

'Did you see her leave for work this morning?' asked Bill Church.

'No, but then we don't really know her. We wouldn't notice,' said Fiona. 'Why? Is something wrong?'

'Oh, I'm sure everything's all right,' said Mary quickly. 'It's just that Martin Trent – Susan's son – has been away and he came back last night. I expect he'd forgotten his key and Susan must have gone to bed.'

The older couple exchanged glances. Should they warn the newcomers that there might be trouble at the neighbours'? Bill shook his head very slightly; time enough, he was thinking. They'd soon find out, though as it was winter now, rows were likely to be indoors rather than outside.

Going home, the Churches discussed whether or not to knock on Susan's door and make sure that she was all right, but when they reached their own house they saw a sliver of light shining between the curtains at her sitting room window. They decided that she was probably watching television, and that Martin, if he were at home, had, by this time, calmed down and was being pleasant company. Even so, before they went to bed, they opened their bedroom window and leaned out, listening.

Opposite, all was silent.

After the Churches left the Crown, Roger had another beer, listening to the talk, but the Trents were not mentioned again. Breaking his silence, he asked Des, the landlord, about them.

'I heard someone mentioning Susan Trent,' he said.

'Oh yes?' Des picked up a glass to polish.

'Which is her house?' Roger asked. If the landlord would not tell him, he could soon find out, from the telephone directory, or, if she wasn't in it, from the voter's list.

'Cedar Cottage,' Des replied. Roger, though not his favourite customer, was a police officer; if there were to be real trouble with Martin, and he was in the bar, he could be useful. Besides, Des knew that the Churches were anxious about Susan Trent; no harm in Roger knowing about it. 'Heard Bill and Mary mention the disturbance, did you?'

'Something was said about the son,' said Roger. 'Forgot his key, they said.'

'Yes – well, you weren't in last night. Martin was here and had a drop too much,' said Des. 'As people do.' He looked at the other man's red face and amber eyes, a most unusual colour; they were not staring eyes, nor hostile; they had a haunted look, he thought later, startled, as he replayed in his mind their conversation. 'The Trents live opposite Bill and Mary Church, at Cedar Cottage. It's a stone house with a tiled roof, and a big willow tree in the garden, down the road before a bigger house and the bend,' he said.

Roger nodded.

'I'll be off,' he said, and added, most surprisingly, 'Good night.'

'Good night,' said Des, astonished at this cordiality.

Outside the pub, Roger hesitated. Then he turned left instead of right, and walked along North Street until he reached Cedar Cottage. The name was on the gate, and Roger had a torch. The house was quiet. A light burned at an upstairs window. He stood there for a while, then turned back and retraced his steps, passing the Crown and going back to Chapel Row. He let himself in noiselessly and went upstairs to his self-contained accommodation on the top floor. As he passed Christopher's door, he heard soft music, something melodious and pleasant.

Roger shuddered. Once, he had enjoyed listening to music; easy listening, it was called, the type he had liked. Now, hearing it upset him, made him emotional. He hurried on, out of earshot.

*   *   *

In the morning, Roger was up early. He had to be in Reading in time to go with the uniformed officers to make the arrest, and he left the house at half-past five.

Christopher woke because he heard the cistern refilling after Roger had flushed the lavatory. He looked at the time on his clock radio and sighed; waking at half-past six would have been soon enough for him.

Roger left the house without going into the kitchen. He went quietly down the stairs and closed the front door as silently as was possible; you had to bang it slightly. Christopher appreciated his efforts; he might not have heard him if he hadn't already been awake. Was Roger hung over after last night? He must have had several drinks down at the Crown, on top of what he'd drunk in the house. Ruminating on the enigma of his house-mate, Christopher rose himself, had a cup of coffee and some toast, then set off for his workshop; Saturday was one of his busiest days, when customers who were working during the week called in.

Soon immersed in his own work, he forgot about Roger and about Adam moving in, only remembering them on the way home that evening.

Adam arrived at the estate agent's soon after the office opened. A young man was there, gathering papers in the background, and an older man who greeted him, telling him that he was Brian Marsh.

Adam told him that he would like to take the room in Chapel Row, Bishop St Leon, and had come to do the paperwork.

'I expect there's something to sign,' he said. And money to pay up front, he knew, warned by the young woman who had given him details of the let the day before, and who had arranged for Christopher to be at the house to meet him. She would have shown him round, she said, but suggested that he might like to meet at least one of the other tenants.

He had brought enough money in cash to pay the deposit and two months' advance rent. Brian seemed surprised.

'I thought you might need to clear a cheque before you let me move in,' said Adam. 'And with the banks being closed today, I came prepared.'

'You liked it, then?' asked Brian.

'It's fine,' Adam assured him.

The formalities were soon concluded. Adam was given his key and he went back to the Grapes to pay his account there and collect his belongings.

Susan arrived at the office just after he had gone.

Martin Trent had spent the night with Debbie. While she put Lily and Rose to bed, he watched television, channel

hopping, to pass the time till she reappeared; the programmes on offer were, in his opinion, mind-numbingly
banal. He felt restless and impatient; coming home was
always a disorientating experience and he needed instant
diversion, but how much was there, either in Bishop St
Leon or here? At least, when he was leading a tour, he
had a role and was important to his clients, and some of
them listened to what he had to say with apparent interest.
Also, he could bustle busily in hotels and on tour buses,
establishing his authority, setting timetables, checking
names.

'You're Mum's boyfriend, aren't you?' Lily had asked
him this evening, during their meal.

He smiled genially at the little girl.

'You could call me that,' he acknowledged.

'You're quite old. Much older than Mum,' said Lily.

'Lily!' scolded Debbie.

'It's true,' said Martin, still smiling.

Debbie gave a small, relieved sigh. When he smiled,
he was transformed and then she knew why she loved
him – if she did; she often asked herself that question.
His slightly puffy face would lighten up; all the down-
ward curving lines would turn the other way and his
forbidding scowl would vanish. Then, she was not afraid
of him; then, she wanted to hold him and comfort him,
cling to the happy moment and forget the moody dis-
pleasure which he occasionally displayed and which was,
she knew, provoked by her own inadequacies. She swept

the children off to bed before Lily became still more tact-less, but Martin surpassed himself by going upstairs with them and helping with their baths, then patting Lily dry while Debbie towelled Rose. Afterwards, he read to both girls in their room, a book that he had bought them, *The Little Prince*. They loved it.

Debbie left them to it and went downstairs to do the washing-up. After a while, Martin followed. He told her the children had settled down and Rose was already asleep. He and Debbie made love then, successfully, but without joy, on the rug in front of the gas coal-effect fire.

Was that love, Debbie wondered sadly, afterwards, or was it simply sex?

Martin was still there in the morning, covered with a duvet Debbie had brought down after he had fallen so deeply asleep that it seemed a shame to wake him.

She was glad to go upstairs, explaining to herself that one of the children might wake; in any case, the floor was hard and not too comfortable, though Martin did not seem to notice.

Thank goodness it had been all right – sort of: he'd be happy in the morning. She wondered if he meant to stay all day; Jim, unless he were called away on an assignment, which often happened when he had arranged to collect the girls, was due at any time. It would be so much better if he and Martin didn't meet.

The children had woken early and had come into her room, as they did every morning. She felt awkward if

Martin was there with her but she couldn't stop them from coming in, nor could she dismiss Martin. Modern children got used to this sort of arrangement, she told herself; if Martin moved in permanently, it would happen all the time, but so far he had never stayed more than three nights. He soon became bored, tied to the house because of the children, and often he'd gone up to the pub, coming back late having drunk a lot. He was sometimes sentimental then, weeping into her neck and saying that no one understood him, nor was he appreciated properly. He would claim he had been neglected as a child and, in his various jobs, cheated of seniority that was his due. Debbie would comfort and console him, petting him as if he were another child.

Now and then he would snap and seem angry, but that had happened only if one of the girls had cried, needing her, or the telephone rang, or there was some other distraction to take her attention away from him.

Everyone had moods, Debbie reminded herself, and Martin had reason. His mother must be a heartless woman; instead of being grateful that he lived with her, she seemed to regard his presence as a nuisance. Debbie, however, made him feel needed and wanted.

She was glad of that.

This morning the girls didn't mention Martin; they were excited because their father was coming and he'd take them up to London. As he was living in her flat, that woman would be there, whatever she was called.

Debbie did not want to admit that she had a name; to do so made her into a real person. If Jim could have her, she could have Martin.

Buoyed up by this positive thinking, when it was time to get up, Debbie sent the girls to wash and dress – Rose could put on her clothes now, except for doing up any buttons – gathered up her courage, and went down to wake Martin. She couldn't let Jim come and find him sleeping in the sitting room.

7

Jim had planned to pick up his daughters at half-past nine, which was late enough for Debbie not to feel rushed and for him not to have to get up so early that Kate complained, but this morning they had fallen asleep after making love when they woke and Jim had then dashed off after a hasty shower and a snatched cup of coffee, leaving Kate fighting against the feeling that she had been pushed aside as of small account.

It was unfair to react like that, she told herself, as she finished her own coffee. Of course he loved his daughters, and they were dear little girls – Lily shy but composed, and very capable, responsibly looking after her little sister, who was liable to burst into tears and cling to Jim when it was time to go home. Kate hoped that they would learn to trust her. Liking might, if she was lucky, come later. She had offered to go out for the day and leave him alone with the children – it was what they wanted, she was sure – but Jim had said that they must get used to her. On the other hand, if there was something else she wanted to do – visit a friend – go to a museum – go shopping – she must.

Kate was tempted, after he had gone, to do just that – disappear, not returning until he had left to take the children back to their mother. She and Jim were not joined at the hip; each could pursue separate interests and keep up with friends not known to the other; she had to, when he was away on an assignment, which was often. The situation, after all, was reversed when she went on location, which had happened twice since they moved in together.

Kate admitted to herself that she would like a child of her own – his child – but they hadn't discussed it, or the possibility of eventually marrying. She had two little rivals in Lily and Rose, and she still feared that for their sakes he might go back to Debbie. If Debbie were more independent, they might not have parted for he would not have been so vulnerable, worn down by her clinging nature. Kate, who had not met her, understood that Debbie could not cope with their separations, yet now she had to do so. How was she managing, if she had been so unhappy when she had a sometimes absent husband, now that because of Kate's intrusion into his life, she had no husband at all? Kate thought Jim had been drawn to her because she was so different – self-reliant and not collapsing in tears when they had to be apart. There was also the chemistry between them; loyally, he hadn't talked much about the sexual side of his marriage, but she inferred that after Rose was born, Debbie was perpetually tired and had lost interest. Kate understood that; she knew from friends that it was often a consequence of mother-hood, needing time and patience to be overcome.

Instead, Jim was with Kate. What had begun as an illicit but understandable affair when they were working together had developed into what both knew was real love.

Because of an earlier sad experience at the Natural History Museum – Rose was too young for such excur-sions, Jim had decided, wise after the event – he had resolved that this time he was going to bring the children straight back to Kate's house. He had bought some toys and games they might enjoy, and in spare moments was making a doll's house which he intended as a surprise for them. It was hidden in a cupboard during their visits. Today, roast chicken with all the trimmings, followed by ice cream, had been decided upon as a safe choice for lunch, and before that, if the weather was fine when they arrived back, all four of them would go to the park.

Kate set about preparing the vegetables and calculated when to put the oven on.

One of Jim's difficulties, when he took the girls to a public place, was the lavatory problem. You couldn't take two small girls into the gents', and they were very young to go into the ladies' alone. Other men – widowers, for instance, apart from those like himself – must encounter this problem too; he hadn't yet discovered how best to solve it, and as for swimming – it was out, unless Kate came too, to cope with the changing rooms. Luckily she liked swimming. Some pools had family changing rooms, and time would ease these difficulties. Children grew up fast, these days.

So far Lily and Rose hadn't stayed overnight, simply coming for a day on either Saturday or Sunday when Jim was in the country and not working, but soon they would, on alternate weekends; however, no routine could be maintained, if he was suddenly sent off to cover a story.

It would be wonderful to have a whole weekend without them; just her and Jim. Kate wondered how long it would be before it happened.

Jim had to stop for petrol; he liked to start these expeditions with a full tank. If he needed a refill when the children were with him, he would never leave them on their own in the car while he paid; always, he laboriously unbuckled them from their little child seats in the rear, taking them with him. He'd once covered an accident where a child, briefly left, was seriously injured when a lorry ran into the back of the stationary car. He was a nervous parent, he admitted to himself as he drove towards Rotherston; too nervous; he had seen too many accidents, too many avoidable disasters. It wasn't good for the girls to have such a fearful father, especially when their mother was so timid and uncertain. They must grow up brave and confident; Kate, who was both, would set them a good example.

He started to allow himself anticipation of the children's warm hugs and joy at seeing him. Before their births, he had not known that such unconditional love was possible, and after Lily was born, he and Debbie had been happy – almost euphoric – but it hadn't lasted. The demands of his job and the fatigue of broken nights had proved damaging, and Debbie, who before Lily's arrival had been an assistant manager in a hotel, part of a chain – they had met when he stayed in one of them while covering a political conference – had lost her former professional assurance. He supposed it had been a veneer; a role she had learned to play. Poor Debbie; Jim felt so guilty about what had happened. She had found out about Kate in a cruel way; a call at home, telling him to cover a breaking story, had come for him while he was in the garden with the children. Debbie had answered the telephone and the voice at the other end had said, 'Hi, Kate,' lapsing into a moment's shocked silence when she said that she was Debbie. Yes, they did want Jim, the voice had said, sorry, he'd got muddled.

After taking the call, Jim had behaved evasively. His caller had been brave enough to warn him of the blunder, and there was time to invent a story, but Jim couldn't do it. It turned out that Debbie had already been suspicious; he'd been different, she declared, kinder, more patient, and she'd thought things between them were improving; then she began noticing how eagerly he set off for work and how he told her much less about what he was doing and about his colleagues. When he returned from this assignment, she challenged him, and he confessed to the affair, so she insisted that he must go. She couldn't live with this, she'd said, weeping bitterly. She'd never trust him, even if he swore he'd never see this Kate woman again – and he couldn't, as they often worked together. He couldn't leave his job; he enjoyed it, and he was doing well. There was no question of his making a career change.

Rain had fallen all night but now it had stopped and a strong wind was blowing as Jim left the motorway at the turning for Rotherston.

When they got married, Debbie hadn't wanted to live in London, and property outside the London area was much cheaper, so they had looked for a house within easy commuting distance and had found this one on an estate on the outskirts of Rotherston. It was well laid out, attractive to young families, and they could afford the mortgage. Jim was sent all over the place and was happy to drive to distant locations, wherever there was work. He was increasingly sent overseas as various reporters asked for him.

He knew they shouldn't have married. They should have settled for a relationship which would have worked itself out in time and then they could have parted, doubt-less wiser for the experience but with no lasting damage. Before they met, Debbie had had a couple of affairs, the second, as he discovered later, serious on her part; the man had walked away and she had not got over it when she met Jim. When it was too late, he understood that she had been on the rebound, and he had let himself be flattered by her instant and unquestioning devotion. It wasn't difficult; she was a very pretty young woman, small, with silky dark hair cut in a swinging bob, and large brown eyes which Lily had inherited. He had felt protective towards her, chivalrous and knightly, and it had landed him in a paternalistic role. Kate was different; she was spirited and she was mature, a true partner.

Every time he went back to Rotherston to collect the girls, his anticipation was tinged with remorse and guilt as he neared the town. He tried not to remember his and Debbie's shared excitement when they moved into the house as only its second owners. They had decorated it with enthusiasm and gradually improving skill, and had redesigned the garden; looking back, he felt that they had been like children playing house. Then Debbie had become pregnant with Lily. This had not been the plan; they had not meant to start a family for several years and she was on the pill, but something had gone wrong. She'd had a stomach upset and been sick; that could have been the explanation.

So after Lily, it had seemed sensible to have another

child. Jim was glad there were two of them; they would be friends for each other and diversify their mother's attention. And share the looking out for her.

She might remarry. He hoped she would, but wisely this time: she needed a more reliable man than he had proved to be, one who wanted a dependent wife and who would appreciate her domestic skills, for she was a good cook and took a pride in keeping the house spotless. Even though Jim favoured this possibility, he was uncomfortable with the idea. The man would be Lily and Rose's stepfather and they would be living with him most of the time; he would have more influence over their lives than Jim did.

With these thoughts in his mind, when he arrived at the house ten minutes later than the appointed time, and the door was opened by a short man with wispy greying hair, dressed in brown corduroy trousers and an Aran sweater, Jim had a shock.

'You're late,' said Martin, adding, 'I'm assuming you are Lily and Rose's father?'

'Jim Grant – yes,' said Jim, cursing himself for his ingratiating tone. Hell, the man was standing in Jim's own hall and using his stocky body as a barrier to prevent Jim's entry.

'They've been waiting for you,' said Martin. 'Now they've gone upstairs.'

Rose, finally out of nappies, had wet herself with either excitement or dread – Martin had the wit and the recall to know it could be either – and Debbie was having to change her clothes.

'Yes – well, I had to stop for petrol,' Jim said lamely.

The man was still blocking the doorway. Jim, who was much taller, thought of forcing his way past; normally he came into the house, though with some awkwardness, but not when he brought the girls back. Then, Debbie would be watching for him; as soon as he arrived, she would open the door and run down the path to fetch them, whisking them away at speed. It was always awkward, always painful.

Who are you, Jim wanted to ask, but at this point Lily came racing down the stairs, brushed past the man and lifted up her arms, calling, 'Daddy, Daddy!'

Jim stooped to pick her up and hugged her as the man was forced to take a backward step, but he still stood there until Rose and Debbie appeared while Jim and Lily edged towards the car.

Staking his claim, marking his patch, thought Jim angrily, after he had buckled the children into their seats and was ready to drive off. Debbie, as always, stood in the road to wave them out of sight, and the man was still in the doorway watching them.

'Who was that man?' Jim asked Lily as he turned out of the estate on to the main road.

'What man?' asked Lily, who had forgotten Martin in her delight at being with her father.

'The man who opened the door. The man at—' Jim

had been about to say 'at home,' but he stopped himself. 'At Mum's,' he amended sadly.

'That's Martin,' Lily said, not interested. Then she stirred herself to add, 'He's Mum's boyfriend. He said so.'

Jim closed his lips firmly together. He would not ask another question, though his mind was full of them. Was this Martin living in the house all the time? He had obviously been there the night before. Had he a job? If so, what was it?

It was only much later that he realised if Martin were living permanently with Debbie, he could cut her maintenance, for the state, in its wisdom, would decide that she was being kept by this other man.

When he took the children back that night, there was no sign of him, but Debbie looked exhausted. Haunted by the image of her bundling the children indoors, Jim left promptly, aware that all three females were in tears.

After the children had departed with their father that morning, Martin had walked the short distance into town to buy a paper; he'd also bought some beer. While he was out, Debbie tidied up and put the washing machine on, weeping over the children's crumpled clothes. Each time they went away was like a little death. When Martin came back and saw her pale, sad face, he gave an inward sigh but made an effort, hugging her, hiding his revulsion, and suggested that they should go out somewhere.

They had driven to a pub some fifteen miles away, near the river, where they had had lunch and Martin had drunk several beers. Her mood lightened in the warm, cheerful atmosphere of the bar, and after their meal, arm in arm, they had walked along the river bank while Martin described his trip to Venice, mentioned some of the buildings his group had visited, and explained some of his duties.

'What were the clients like?' Debbie asked. 'Were they nice? Were some of them difficult?' She had experience of awkward hotel guests.

Martin did not have a lot to say about them. Most were middle-aged or older, he said; out-of-season guided tours did not appeal to younger travellers. He mentioned the woman who had forgone Torcello in favour of the Rialto.

'That was all right, though, wasn't it?' she said. 'It wasn't a school trip, where you have to stick to the programme.'

'I suppose it was her prerogative,' he allowed. 'She was upset about the Fenice burning down.' He explained about the opera house that had been gutted.

'How dreadful.' Debbie tried to imagine a visit to Venice with Martin. It would be interesting because he would know a lot about the city. She and Jim had been to Provence on their honeymoon, and had had several holidays in France, touring with the car. Debbie spoke very good French; during her training she had specialised in it, and had also learned some Italian; the languages were useful in her career. It had occurred to her that she might make use of them again; perhaps they would help her into an interesting job. The supermarket, where part-time work was easy to get, was a temporary stopgap to help pay for the car; perhaps she might later be more ambitious.

They'd had a good day. Martin's conversation had taken her mind off the girls; after all, they were safe with Jim; she knew he loved them and would take care of them. She wanted them to spend time with him whilst also resenting it. They'd be back at eight o'clock. At their age, that was late enough, but they would fall asleep on the journey and would not want to settle when she put them to bed.

Martin had turned on the television and was soon asleep in front of the racing after they returned to the house. Luckily he hadn't wanted sex; he didn't want to be at it all the time, which was a big relief, for she didn't really enjoy it with him. She didn't like his beery breath, and he did not make her feel special, as Jim had done; she sensed that any cooperative woman would have been all the same to Martin.

He was still there when the girls came home, and he roused himself, making an effort to greet them, wanting them to kiss him goodnight before going upstairs. Rose obeyed but Lily was tearful after saying goodbye to her father. Debbie was shaking when she came downstairs again after they had finally fallen asleep.

'You need a drink,' Martin said, and he went to the kitchen to fetch the bottle of brandy he kept there.

He stayed again that night. He was too drunk even to take a taxi back to Bishop St Leon.

The estate agency was busy that day. Susan looked after the office while the others took clients round viewing houses. It was rare, now, for prospective purchasers to go unescorted, though the vendors, at weekends, were often in when they called. Going home, there was fear in her heart about Martin. Would he be there? If not, would he be back soon, and if so, in what mood?

It was never a good idea to try to talk to him about his conduct; he would twist the conversation round, putting her in the position of the accused so that she was left trying to defend her own rights, in vain asserting that he had a duty towards her.

'What duty?' he would sneer, and would pour himself another drink.

He had not returned. With huge relief, she made certain, checking every room. Then she went out into the garden. Brian had told her to go home soon after four, so it was still light. She walked across the long lawn to the willow near the fence. It had grown tall since the day it went in as a slip taken from an established one in the Field House garden. She remembered that as clearly as if it had only just happened – treading soil in round its slender stem, watering it and several others, staking them to prevent them from blowing over. They soon struck; willows grew easily like that from slips. Later, she had thinned them out as they had been planted very close to one another; she kept the strongest. The wind was rustling through its leafless filament branches now, sighing, like a ghost. She shivered, drawing her coat collar closely around her neck, then turned towards the house, where friendly lights beckoned from the lower windows.

Though he wasn't in, Martin might soon come back, but if she was lucky, he would spend the night away again. Perhaps this woman would find in him the goodness that had once been there and now was deeply buried. It wasn't too late for him to reform; it was almost never too late for that.

Nearing the house, Susan heard the telephone and hastened to answer it. Mary Church had seen the lights come on and had rung to ask her to supper.

Susan had not been to their house for some time. She instantly accepted. If Martin came back later, she wouldn't be there. He could drink himself silly until he passed out. She wouldn't let herself think that he might sit up waiting for her return, like a stern father with a wayward daughter.

In Chapel Row, Adam had been busy in his room which, though superficially clean, was far from spotless. Before driving over to move in, he had bought cleansers and cloths. He had found the vacuum sweeper in a cupboard under the stairs, emptied its bulging bag and used it on the worn blue carpet. Then he swept the curtains with the hose attachment. Afterwards, with the windows wide to air the place, he washed surfaces and polished. Finally, he made the bed up with his own sheets.

That was better. Now the place was his. For how long? As long as it would take.

8

Roger's day had been successful. The fraud suspects had been arrested in their various residences while they were still in bed; with their solicitors present, they had been interviewed throughout the day, and charged. Bail was refused, lest they try to flee the country – which, even with their passports confiscated, was possible – and they would be brought before the magistrates on Monday. They'd be bailed then, almost certainly. Roger's part of the process could not be spun out any longer. What followed would be up to the Fraud Squad and the Crown Prosecution Service; if all went well, the wrongdoers should be behind bars for several years.

Roger was reluctant to go back to Bishop St Leon, but what options were there? He had no wife or family now, no girlfriend, and no desire to look for easy sex. He'd tried that, and it was degrading. In Rotherston, he picked up several films from the video shop; they'd help pass the evening, and if necessary Sunday, though with luck he'd get a call to an incident. Passing the Grapes, he decided to stop there for a meal; he felt more at home at the Grapes than in the Crown in Bishop St Leon. Perhaps he had made a mistake in choosing to live in a village, but his youth had been spent in one and he liked gardening. In his married days he'd been a keen gardener when the job allowed, and it had kept him out of Elaine's way. Even before the accident, things had been difficult between them.

He didn't want to think about it. He sat in the corner of the bar eating roast pork; the Grapes served a varied menu which included good honest fare, and they sold crisps. Three girls sat at the next table; from habit, because a good policeman has trained his powers of observation, Roger glanced quickly at them. He recognised one of them but could not recall where he'd seen her before and cast them from his mind. Before leaving, he bought several packets of strongly flavoured crisps to take home. He'd had a few beers by the time he left, but it wasn't far to drive. He'd be very unlucky if he were stopped on the way back.

He'd had nothing to drink, that other time. Life was a bitch.

The Crown was busy; cars were parked all along the road outside, and it had its own yard at the rear. Roger turned into Chapel Row, where most of the houses had garages or off-street parking. Since space at his workshop was limited, Christopher used their garage as a store for extra timber and furniture waiting for repair. He ran his van in off the road, and Roger, who might be called out at night, left his Mondeo outside. Now an unfamiliar car, a black Toyota, stood on the spot he usually occupied. Roger was obliged to park further up the road.

Carrying his rented videos, his bags of crisps and a six-pack of beer, he let himself into the house, awkward with his packages, transferring his keys to his mouth as he shut the door. The kitchen door was closed, but a savoury smell permeated the hallway and Roger remembered the new lodger. His must be the Toyota. He opened the door and went in, still clutching his burden.

A thin, dark man was standing at the stove, turning a stir-fry mix of vegetables and meat in a large pan. He turned, smiling, ready to introduce himself.

Even before Roger dumped his crisps on the table, Adam recognised him as the oafish crisp-eater from the train two nights before, and Roger identified him as the man seated opposite him, with the laptop computer.

Both of them, instinctively and instantly, decided to ignore the fact that they had previously encountered one another, but while Roger had formed no opinion of Adam, since he had sat there working, unassumingly, Adam already had a very strong antipathy towards Roger. However, he hid it, smoothly.

'Hi. Adam Wilson,' he said, and held out his hand. 'I moved in today.'

'Roger Morris,' said Roger.

They shook hands, each measuring the other, Adam's gaze shrewd and assessing, the sharpness of Roger's perceptions marred by alcohol.

'I'm cooking. It will stretch for two,' said Adam, ready to chop up more vegetables. 'Like some?'

He learned later that it was rare for Roger to turn down an offer of food, even when he had already eaten, but that night, he did, gesturing towards his videos, also now sitting on the table.

'Going to catch a video. And the football,' Roger said. 'Thanks, though.' He hesitated, collected up his crisps and videos and left the room.

Thankful that he had decided against eating his crisps while in the kitchen, Adam dished up his meal. While he ate it, washing it down with a glass of wine, he heard Roger go out again, but he didn't hear a car start up. He wouldn't see a lot of Roger; the policeman, like Christopher, would be out most of the time. Anyway, he would not be living here for ever.

Roger had remembered what had been said in the Crown about Susan Trent. It wouldn't hurt to postpone the video and walk past Cedar Cottage once again. He set off along North Street, passing the pub. Tonight the wind was blowing, gusting down the road. Leaves swirled around his feet as he trudged along. When he reached Cedar Cottage, Roger saw that there was a light on above the porch. He walked past, crossed over, and returned on the farther side, pausing on the pavement opposite Susan Trent's house. Behind him was the Churches' house; they were the couple talking anxiously about her in the Crown; he knew where they lived. Standing there, he could hear the murmur of voices. They were a responsible pair; they would have made sure, during the day, that there was no cause for concern over their neighbour.

When he arrived back in Chapel Row, he went straight upstairs. He did not want to see that quiet man again just yet; he had plenty of crisps and beer in his room to pick at while he watched television.

Much later, he remembered where he had previously seen the girl in the Grapes. Like Adam, she had also been on the train on Thursday night, sitting next to Adam, grimly reading a large book.

Roger never read books, just the sporting news in the paper, and the endless reports that came his way at work.

In the morning, he hoped for a call from the station. There would certainly have been violence in parts of the area during the night; every night, something happened, and more on Saturdays when the pubs emptied. But no call came.

Roger lay in bed for a while. He had had several hours of merciful oblivion but he was still tired; unless he drank, he could not sleep, and though he was seldom badly hung over, he often woke feeling nauseous, with a sour taste in his mouth. This morning he got out of bed and went to the basin in the shower room, where he drank several glasses of water, smacking his lips, belching, scratching his heavy, hairy body. He peered at himself in the mirror, then turned away from his displeasing reflection. Best have a shower and go to the village shop to collect the paper, or several papers; they'd help to pass the time while he decided how to spend the day.

If it didn't rain, he might get out in the garden. You could always find things to do out there, fiddling about, even when the broad beans were sown and everything else that could go in at this time of year. It was too windy to sweep up the fallen leaves; they'd only blow about again. He wished there was a greenhouse; that would have given him an interest during the winter. But there'd be some big crime needing his supervision before long; he could be sure of that.

Roger showered and cleaned his teeth; there was no need to shave, as it was Sunday and he was off duty unless an incident intervened. If it did, he could soon run his razor over his jaw. He rubbed his hand over his stubble. Elaine used to complain about what she called his spiky chin; it brought her out in a rash.

Those three at the next table in the Grapes last night had been all right. They were enjoying their meal and the bottle of wine they'd had on the table. He did not recognise the others, only the one from the train, which she'd left ahead of him. He hadn't seen her leave the station.

She probably worked in an office in London. He'd no chance of getting a girl like that to take an interest in him. He'd no chance of getting a decent woman at all, let alone a young, sweet one like that.

But maybe she wasn't so sweet. Appearances were very deceptive, as twenty years' experience in the police had taught him.

Roger picked up his black leather jacket and put it on; there was cash in his pocket. He made sure his mobile telephone was also there, and went down the stairs, letting himself out of the front door and setting off up the road towards the cluster of shops that formed the heart of the village.

Christopher and Adam were in the kitchen, where Christopher had brewed a large pot of freshly ground coffee. Both had frozen as they heard Roger's steps outside, and when they heard him leave the house, both relaxed.

Christopher made a wry face and said, somewhat sheepishly, 'You've met, then?'

'Barely,' said Adam. 'But he was on the train on Thursday night, when I came down from London.'

'You said "but",' Christopher pounced. 'Why so?'

'He was eating some rather smelly crisps,' said Adam. 'Scattering crumbs,' he added.

'Onion rings as well, perhaps,' said Christopher.

'Mm.'

'He's partial to them.'

'Oh.'

'He'll have gone to get the papers. It'll be the *News of the World* and the *Mail*,' said Christopher. 'And I think he'll have bought a *Times* for me. He does, if he's here on a Sunday. I wonder if he'll have chosen anything for you.'

'He's all right, then,' said Adam. 'It's just the crisps?'

'And similar,' said Christopher. 'He's a great gardener. Have a look outside, later on. It's all down to him.'

Adam had already seen, from his window, the orderly beds. The wind had got up during the night, and the lawn was carpeted with leaves from two tall trees by the end wall.

'He grows vegetables,' Christopher went on. 'He wasn't here in time to raise sprouts and potatoes, but he assures me there will be plenty next year. There'll be no need to buy any; Roger will keep us self-supporting. Free, too; he says it's his hobby. Well, it is, I suppose.'

'He must have been married,' said Adam.

'I suppose he must. He's never said.'

'No – well, you don't, do you, to strangers, when it's gone wrong,' said Adam, putting bread in the toaster. 'Does this thing work?' he asked.

They were both eating toast to the accompaniment of Classic FM on the radio, a programme which was playing music with romantic associations for various listeners who had written in with their stories, when Roger returned.

He looked healthier than he had done either on the train or the previous evening, with a faint glow in his flabby cheeks and a film of damp on his sandy hair.

'Have some coffee, Roger,' said Christopher hospitably, adding, 'Oh thanks,' as Roger handed him his paper.

'I didn't know if you'd like one,' Roger said, turning to Adam. 'I got you the *Express* and the *Telegraph* but you needn't take them. I'll have what you don't want. Sometimes on Sundays there's nothing else to do except read the papers.'

'Thanks very much,' said Adam. 'I'll have them both.'

Christopher got up and went to a plastic wipe-off board which hung on the wall near the door. It was blank. On it he wrote the money now owed by him and Adam to Roger for their papers.

'Roger never chalks up any debts,' he said, and poured coffee into a very large mug. 'Here you are, Roger,' he said.

Roger hesitated, still standing, and Adam thought he was going to turn and leave the room, but then he began taking off his jacket. At that moment the toast popped up.

'Have some toast,' he invited, and as Roger hung his jacket over the back of a chair, Adam took a plate from the cupboard, put a piece of toast on it, found a knife, and set the lot down on the table. He put more bread in the toaster, and soon all three men were eating toast and marmalade while reading their papers, with the radio, its volume turned down, playing softly in the background: a peaceful, domestic scene. No one spoke.

*   *   *

At Field House on Sunday morning, breakfast in the big kitchen was also relaxed. Hannah revelled in being at home with the children; time enough later to think about tomorrow, when she must catch the early train from Rotherston and return to her city office after the Florida holiday. It had been wonderful to spend time with the children, not to have to rush off after handing them over to Linda, returning only when it was almost their bed-time. Unless she rang to say she had missed her usual train, Linda kept them up, in their pyjamas, until Hannah arrived, and then she could put them to bed.

Linda was efficient, reliable and kind; and she remem-bered the funny things Georgie had said during the day to tell Hannah in the evening, but the day before they went on holiday, it was to Linda that Georgie had turned for comfort after a tumble, not her own mother. That had hurt.

You couldn't own a house like this one, with a mort-gage the size of theirs, on one salary: not even one as high as Edward's, when your husband had another family to support. Edward had an older son and daughter; the son was at Manchester University; the daughter was doing A levels. Their mother had recently remarried, but several years of heavy expense for them still lay ahead. By the time Hannah's salary was less essential, Georgie and Henry would be at school; perhaps, then, she could earn enough by working from home, thus being around to help with homework and go to school events. She hadn't mentioned it to Edward, but it was her dream.

You can't have your cake and eat it too: Hannah accepted that. Her life was good. She was career-oriented and ambitious, but she had begun to fear that marriage and children were going to elude her when she met Edward at a conference in Geneva. Here they were, six years later.

This morning, Edward had walked up to the shop for the paper. He did this every Sunday, and while he was out, Hannah pretended that she spent all her time at home and was simply waiting for his return, but the fantasy was short-lived, for she had work to sort out for tomorrow. Yesterday, she had dealt with most of the waiting e-mails, and unusually on a Saturday Linda had been there till the afternoon; she had taken care of Henry while Hannah had taken Georgie with her to do the weekend shopping. Edward had gone to his older daughter's school to watch her play in a hockey match, and then he had brought her home for the night. Jackie was still asleep upstairs.

Hannah thought the girl must resent her, though she did not blame her for it. If it were not for her, Edward might still have been living with Jackie's mother, a complete, original family, though he had discovered, during the divorce proceedings, that his wife had been having an affair for years. She was lonely, she had said, married to a workaholic whom she never saw.

Probably it was true. His demanding job involved

demanding hours, but Hannah, working in the same area, understood, for it was something they shared.

Hannah hoped the girl would, in time, accept her; Jackie was very fond of her little half-sister and brother, and that might help toleration.

She looked up cheerfully when Edward reappeared, his greying hair wisped with moisture for though it was windy, the air was damp.

'It's raw out,' he said, putting the paper down. 'I don't know when I'll have time to read this. I'm going out now to see what's happened in the garden while we've been away. No sign of Jackie yet?'

'Not a murmur.'

'I'll go and wake her up,' offered Georgie, eagerly.

'Not yet, sweetheart,' said Edward. 'She's tired. We'll let her sleep a little longer. You can come and help me in the garden.'

He bore her off to get her ready, garbing her in a waterproof suit and boots, and they went out through the kitchen door. Soon Georgie was scuffling through the leaves that covered the lawn while her father went to the shed to get out the machine he had recently bought which would sweep them into a container. He hoped it would operate despite the wind; anyway, he'd give it a try.

Upstairs, in the pretty room that was solely hers – not even Linda, the nanny, used it when she stayed overnight – Jackie watched her father from the window. It gave her a shock to see that he looked quite old, pushing the lawn sweeper over the grass. From her high vantage point, she noticed a bald patch on the top of his head. She thought he must be about fifty; her mother was forty-five. Hannah was much younger, only thirty-four. Jackie tried to imagine her own mother living here, and couldn't; the village was too small and scattered. Her mother liked living in London, and so did Jackie; it must have been Hannah who chose to live here, out in the sticks. Surely it wasn't Dad? They'd moved just before Henry was born.

Her father seemed to like it here; she watched him pushing that silly machine; he'd quite taken to gardening, and there was a lot of laughter when he and Hannah were together.

There hadn't been much laughter around when he lived with Mum.

She decided to get up and go and help him. She didn't mind Georgie being around. She was sweet.

Jackie pulled on some clothes, tugged a comb through her curly dark hair, and went downstairs.

9

Susan's Sunday paper, like her daily one, was delivered.

Few of the commuters had a daily delivery because they left before the rounds were made; they picked theirs up on the way – sometimes at the filling station on the outskirts of Rotherston, more often at Rotherston Halt, and in a few cases at the village shop. These were among the customers who walked up to fetch their Sunday papers; the Saturday shopping trip, which was routine for most of the commuting families, included buying that day's paper at the supermarket.

It affected local trade. Stan Finch, who ran the shop, was a cynic and a realist; he benefited from the Sunday customers who bought minor groceries that had been forgotten earlier, or chocolates, and the magazines they did not receive by post, but it was a struggle to keep the paper delivery service going because so few children would take on the job. A theory was that they were given too much pocket money, but one boy had told him he could make more nicking radios from cars and selling them. Stan hoped that he was joking. An elderly man delivered Susan's paper on weekdays; the *Sunday Telegraph* was delivered by his grandson, a seventeen-year-old schoolboy working for his A levels, who was saving to finance a gap year travelling.

Unable to sleep late, Susan was up and dressed, drinking coffee in the kitchen when the paper came. She heard the boy, Owen, start pushing the thick wodge of newsprint through the letter flap and hurried to open the door.

'Morning, Mrs Trent,' said Owen cheerfully. 'There you go, then.'

Susan took the paper.

'Thanks, Owen,' she said, and watched him walk down the path back to the small cart supplied for the deliveries. The Sunday papers, with their supplements and extras, were now too thick and heavy to be carried in a bag, though the weekday deliverers mostly managed. Owen's grandfather, however, tugged a little cart along. Owen had cut Susan's lawn for her for several weeks in the summer after she had sustained a cracked rib. Martin, drunk and argumentative, had pushed her across the kitchen so that she had fallen heavily with her arm against her chest; she knew instantly what had happened as the sharp pain caught her. Martin's father had injured her in exactly the same way, when Martin was a baby, but he had pushed her harder and had kicked her when she lay on the floor.

The injuries were worse then, although because she was young, she mended more quickly. This summer, she'd told Owen that she'd fallen, which was true. She hadn't gone to the doctor; broken ribs were not strapped up these days but left to mend themseves, unless there were some internal injury, but Susan knew there was no damage to her lungs.

Now she called after the boy.

'Owen, there are piles of leaves to sweep up, if you want a bit of work. I'd be glad of your help.'

Owen halted, hand on the gate.

'Oh, right – yes – thanks,' he said.

'It's no good in this wind,' said Susan. 'Come any time you like, when it dies down. The sooner the better.'

'Right,' said Owen again. 'I'll be along. Cheers.'

Susan waved as he went out. He was such a nice boy. You heard so much about vandals and hooligans these days, and not enough about the kind, hard-working, well-mannered youngsters who were the majority.

Heartened, she went inside with her paper.

Martin had stayed out all night. It was possible that she would have a peaceful day without his presence in the house. It would depend on his current romance. The women with whom he became involved always had a house, and they always had children; they were always vulnerable. Martin was probably charming in the early stages; that was his true nature, after all; it was the alcohol that brought out the brutal side, just as it had with his father. Susan's reactions, as each new affair began, were always mixed; she was thankful that he was happy and emotionally fulfilled – if he was – but she dreaded the moment when the woman discarded him, as was inevitable when he revealed his darker side. Perhaps, one day, he would meet someone who had such a good effect on him that his baser nature never surfaced; Susan repeatedly nourished this hope until the day of reckoning arrived and Martin returned, white with rage, rejected yet again and ready to take it out on her, the one he blamed for everything.

She wouldn't think about that now. She'd enjoy the day.

She wouldn't go to church. If Martin were at home on a Sunday, she sometimes went to the morning service, for it offered her an hour of peace and safety. Not a believer, she nevertheless approved the rules, liked the hymns – though so few now were familiar – and found the ancient building a soothing place – in fact, a refuge. She didn't need one today, or not yet. She heard the bells, however, a distant sound, wafting across the river in her direction. Some of her neighbours would be going to the service, but not others. She didn't know if the family at Field House were attenders; they had two small children; perhaps the elder one went to Sunday School. The baby had arrived soon after they had moved in; Susan had gone along with flowers for the mother, Hannah, and a soft toy for the baby. There'd been a nanny there, a pleasant, smiling girl.

Community spirit in the village was weaker now than in the past, when fewer mothers had careers and the population included a higher proportion of retired people; few of the younger people had time to help with fundraising events, or even to play cricket, though some managed it. A trend had developed for older couples, on retirement – or particularly if one partner died – to move to smaller houses but remain within the village, while younger families moved into larger ones. Brian had not sold Field House, but he had conducted several transactions where, with financial adjustments, there had been exchanges.

Susan would not contemplate down-sizing – a descriptive phrase – herself. Brian had suggested it, saying that she would make a tidy profit if she bought a smaller house, hinting that it would be a way of getting Martin out. She could even give him some of the proceeds to set him up.

But Susan knew he would only drink away the money. Besides, Cedar Cottage was not a large house, and there were other reasons why she could not move.

While she dawdled over breakfast, glancing through the paper, the wind had dropped a little. Owen might decide to return and tackle the leaves. She slipped a jacket on and some strong shoes, and went down the garden, as she had done the night before. Now, in the grey light of a dull, damp day, there was no ghostly aura; around and below the willow, the slender yellow leaves lay thickly on the ground, with those from other trees – apples, a plum

tree and a copper cherry – spread over the grass. Perhaps
Owen, when he'd swept them up, would run over it with
the mower once again; if it dried out enough; a final cut
now would keep it neat through the winter and stop it
from getting straggly in the spring. Snowdrops carpeted
the ground under the willow from late January and
through February. They had spread and multiplied, and
were much admired. Field House had even more, and a
fine display of naturalised daffodils and narcissus.

Since she had lived at Cedar Cottage, Field House had
changed hands several times. In those early years, it had
been the doctor's house, with the surgery held in a part
of it; later, the surgery had moved to a new building in
the High Street and Field House was bought by a property developer who did a great deal to it, putting in
two more bathrooms – there had been only one – and a
swimming-pool. He and his wife and children had lived
there for about ten years; then his company had gone into
liquidation and they had been forced to sell up, though
the house, which was in the wife's name, was safe from
seizure.

The next owner was an industrialist whose factory, near
Slough, made plastic containers; he sold his company and
moved abroad. For the past nine years the occupants had
been an architect and his wife, who did interior design;
the two often worked in partnership, so it was all the
more of a shock when, after nearly thirty years of
marriage, with their three children adult, they separated.

The husband now lived in London with a new partner; the wife had moved to Bath, where she was running her business as successfully as before.

Susan had been acquainted with all these previous owners. She had been very fond of the last couple, and particularly the wife, who had several times invited her to visit her in Bath. Susan thought she might accept when Martin was away on a trip. She didn't like his being at home without her. Who knew what might happen if she left him there on his own?

She fetched the secateurs from the shed, and an old wooden trug – you seldom saw them now – and set about dead-heading the withered late-flowering roses. A few brave buds still held out the hope of blooms, but some were mildewed round the edges. When her basket was full, she tipped it on the bonfire pile; there was a mound of rubbish waiting to be burnt. Susan did not put rose clippings in the compost heap, for the diseases to which they were prone might fester and survive the breaking-down process. Some of the roses were badly afflicted by rust. Quietly occupied, she was content. The previous evening with the Churches had been good, apart from when they told her they'd heard Martin banging on the door the night before, and when they questioned her about her bruise. She'd repeated her story of the fall, and said that he'd forgotten his key and she had not heard him. These were familiar tales; Mary and Bill had heard such stories many times. She knew they weren't deceived, but if she once admitted to the full horror of her life, she feared she might not be able to bear it any longer. Last night, Bill had seen her across the road to her door, and made sure that Martin wasn't there.

'Do you really think he'd be waiting up for me, armed with a rolling-pin?' Made brave by several glasses of good burgundy, she had mocked him.

'I want to make sure you suffer no more tumbles, tonight, at any rate,' Bill had replied.

In a way, it was a comfort that they knew, even if they did not understand. If Martin lost all control and really tried to kill her, and they heard the commotion, they wouldn't simply turn away. She wouldn't mind his killing her, as long as oblivion came quickly. But he'd pay the penalty. He wouldn't get away with it; there would be no one left to help him.

She'd learned to count the good moments, the periods such as this one, peacefully snipping roses in the garden.

Owen came round again at two o'clock; the wind had dropped, and he would make a start at sweeping up the leaves.

In Rotherston, Debbie had crept out of bed early, as soon as she heard the girls' voices from their room. Martin was still asleep. Through the night his loud snoring had kept her awake, but he was quieter now. Probably he'd spend the morning in bed, but if he woke, he'd want her there, too. He saw no reason why she shouldn't settle the children with the television on; cartoons were provided for this very purpose, liberating parents to spend time together, intimately, but Debbie couldn't go along with this; if she were alone on Sunday mornings, the girls would bring their books and climb into her bed where they would all snuggle down, enjoying the stories and the pictures, but when Martin was there, though he pulled on a pair of shorts when he went to the bathroom, and he hugged them and was friendly, Debbie wasn't comfortable about his being there with the children. Most mornings, Martin smelled unpleasant; once, Lily had mentioned it and Debbie was repelled by this consequence of heavy drinking.

Today, she gathered up her clothes and left the bedroom, closing the door quietly behind her; she showered quickly and dressed in the bathroom, then collected the girls and took them downstairs in their pyjamas. After their breakfast, eaten in the kitchen, she turned on the television cartoons and sat Lily and Rose in front of the set; then she fetched the ironing, putting the board up in the sitting room, and started on the pile of waiting garments while a new load was being washed in the machine. She liked the girls' clothes, and her own, to be crisp and fresh; some of Martin's were now being laundered.

If he hadn't woken by the time she'd finished, and if the rain held off, she'd take the girls down to the park; they both loved the slide, and Lily liked the climbing frame. Debbie would talk to the mothers, fathers or grand-parents who would be there with other children. The girls would come home with a good appetite for their Sunday lunch; she managed a roast most weeks, setting the oven to come on automatically if they went out.

It was quite windy today when they set off. That would blow the rain away, Debbie thought, and it might have brought more conkers down, though most had already fallen from the chestnut trees which bordered the park. Sure enough, they found a few to add to their collection. When they returned, Martin was up and had put the vegetables on to cook.

Debbie was deeply touched. Though Jim had always helped with every task, Martin rarely did, and the irritation Debbie was harbouring because of his snores and other irksome habits dissipated. She smiled warmly at him, thanking him, and began dishing up the chicken.

Lily, who hadn't witnessed it going into the oven earlier, said, 'We had chicken yesterday at Dad's. Kate cooked it. There were little sausages and bacon, too.'

Debbie, on the instant, answered bitterly.

'I can't afford sausages and bacon,' she said. 'And I'm sorry you've got the same meal two days running but I had no prior knowledge of your father's menu.'

Lily stared at her, her lower lip trembling. Debbie's voice had been so hard and sharp.

'The child wasn't accusing you, Debbie,' Martin said. 'She was simply making a statement, not a protest.'

But it had seemed like a complaint to Debbie, and his reproof was too much for her. She burst into tears and ran out of the room.

Martin sighed. Then he started mashing the potatoes; he'd already drained the carrots. He carved the bird, and sat down to eat it with the girls, cutting up Rose's portion so that she could manage it with her spoon.

'What's wrong with Mum?' asked Lily, in bewilderment.

'She thought you didn't want chicken because you had it yesterday,' said Martin.

'But I like it,' Lily said. 'So does Rosie.'

Indeed, Rose was already tackling hers with gusto.

'And we'll be having it tomorrow,' Rose prophesied. 'Maybe the next day, too.'

She meant, if enough were left, Martin realised.

'You can't have too much of a good thing, can you?' he quipped cheerily, fetching a can of beer from the fridge.

Although not fully comprehending, Lily laughed, and Rose began to chuckle, too. Soon both little girls were collapsing into giggles.

Upstairs, Debbie, weeping, heard them, and her tears fell all the more copiously, while Martin congratulated himself on his skill at child management. He hoped Debbie would calm down before too long; he didn't want to be on duty all the afternoon. Besides, he should get back to Bishop St Leon, write up his reports on Venice and see if any of the companies he worked for had left messages wanting him as stop-gap courier for a future trip. At the moment, he had none booked till March and the winter stretched tediously ahead.

As an afterthought, he carved several chicken slices for Debbie and put them, with vegetables and gravy, on a plate, covered with another, in a low oven.

When she had not reappeared after half an hour, he found a video of *Bambi* for the children and put it on. Then, deciding not to telephone for a taxi, as its arrival might cause Debbie to come down and make a scene, he shut the children in the sitting room and left the house; he'd walk into town and get one there.

Debbie, lying on her bed, and wakeful through the night, had wept herself into an exhausted sleep and did not hear him go.

Lily was sad at the end of *Bambi*. The screen flickered and the tape rewound as Rose, sad too, began to cry. She'd wet herself. Lily also began to cry as the noise of a motor race on the television channel that was now automatically on the screen filled the room. Lily had forgotten about the chicken and her mother's tears, and she'd forgotten Martin, and now she began wailing for her mother. Soon both little girls' cries grew hysterical. Lily opened the sitting room door and took her sister's hand, standing in the doorway, sobbing. Were they alone in the house? Daddy had gone; maybe Mum had, too. What would become of them?

Rose, though, needed changing. The clothes their mother had ironed earlier had all been put away. Lily knew there would be clean knickers in their bedroom. Still crying, she set off up the stairs, tugging Rose by the hand. Step by step, Rose could manage the stairs, though now she was wailing loudly. Debbie, through her closed bedroom door, at last heard them; her sleep had been so deep that rousing herself was like trying to surface from a sea of treacle. She hauled herself off the bed and opened the door just in time to see Rose lose her balance, and tumble down the flight, pulling Lily with her.

In Chapel Row, Christopher put his paper down and asked Adam, 'Have you any plans for today?'

'Not really,' Adam answered. 'What about you?' There was the girlfriend Christopher had mentioned the day before.

'No social plans,' said Christopher. 'I might go to the workshop. I often do, on Sundays. Would you like to come along?'

'Won't I get in your way?'

'I shouldn't think so,' Christopher said. 'I might get you doing some sandpapering or varnishing. You never know.'

'I'm quite willing,' Adam said.

They drove off together in Christopher's van.

'Shouldn't we tell Roger we've gone out?' said Adam, buckling up his seat-belt. It seemed unfriendly not to leave a note.

'He's a detective. He'll work it out,' said Christopher.

Adam suspected that Christopher's invitation was a means of saving him from spending his first Sunday cooped up in the house with Roger.

He'd have to get some outside interests going, join a gym, take up golf. Meanwhile, however, he'd be interested to see Christopher's workshop.

10

Roger soon grew bored with the newspapers. He noticed that the wind was dropping and decided to tackle the fallen leaves. Very few were left now on the trees; it had been a windy autumn, and a wet one. The soil was too waterlogged to work on, but he had dug over most of the beds during the few fine spells there had been when he was off duty.

He wanted a summons to the station or a crime scene. He wished the telephone would ring to call him to a murder site or one of suspected arson, but, off duty, he would not be sent for unless everyone else was already out. He was not popular with his team; his history had followed him to the area, and an officer who had killed a child in a road accident carried an aura of disaster with him, however much it was the child's fault for running into a busy street between two parked cars when the driver had no chance to see her in time to stop, as witnesses had established beyond doubt, and even though the child was his own daughter.

No one liked to mention the tragedy, but awareness of it had hung in the atmosphere to the extent that one day, in the briefing room, before sending off a team to mount an observation of some suspected drug dealers, Roger had brusquely tackled the assembled officers.

'You know why I moved out here, and you don't know what to say,' he said. 'I'm telling you, say nothing. I killed my own daughter but I was exonerated of all blame. That's it. You may be thinking, shit, poor bugger, could happen to anyone. Well, it happened to me. It's over. End of story. Now, here's the plan for today,' and he swept on to give an exemplary briefing for what turned out to be a successful operation.

After that, his wishes were respected, and some of his colleagues admired him for making such a statement, but his prickly attitude and his manners – uncouth even in the perception of police officers who were accustomed to far worse from those they dealt with on the streets – were not endearing. He never went out drinking with them, though it was known that he liked a drop. One or two whispered that he might have been over the limit at the time of the accident, but others said that he was clear. Someone wondered how the little girl – not three years old – had been able to run into the street. Where was her mother? No one seemed to know.

The truth was that she had been upstairs in bed with

the builder who was putting up their new kitchen exten-sion. The child had gone into the garden through the unlocked kitchen door and wandered towards the front gate, which the postman had left unlatched. A chain of circumstances, which Roger had discovered but most of which he had not revealed, had proved fatal.

Within minutes, the builder was back in his overalls, and Elaine, in her dressing-gown, had said, amid hyster-ical tears, that she had been in the bath. The builder and Elaine, between them, bore official censure for not ensuring that the back door was kept closed but it was implied that Elaine should have been responsible for the safety of her own child.

The builder had sent someone else to complete the extension, and after the inquiry, Roger had moved out. He did not know or care whether the builder had returned, or if Elaine had found a substitute. He hoped she had; he bore her no ill-will. Her guilt was as great as his; some would say hers was the greater. No one measured the extent of either's grief, and the house was now Elaine's.

He tried not to think about it now, but it was difficult, except when he was working. Daisy had loved being with him in the garden, toddling along wheeling her tiny barrow, in her little red wellingtons, pulling out plants in the belief that they were weeds. He still found solace outside, digging, planting, weeding, and pretended sometimes that a small figure would appear, saying, 'Daisy's come to help Daddy.'

Sweeping away, Roger sternly directed his thoughts towards the acquisition of a cold frame. Planning permission was not required for one, and it would not be expensive. He could bring on seedlings for the vegetable bed, and grow lettuces. Christopher and the new man, Adam, would appreciate them. Roger had had no strong feelings about the departed Jeremy, who had left soon after his own arrival, and he had not suspected that the one was the result of the other. From his own point of view, moving from the one-roomed flat he had rented in Reading to this area had been a good decision. He had an excuse for avoiding his colleagues in off-duty hours, and he had regained a former interest. As far as possible, he kept out of the other tenants' way. He didn't look too far ahead, except when necessary where work was concerned, and, now he had the garden, planning future planting. How long he would remain in Bishop St Leon was anybody's guess.

There were several garden centres in the area. Roger went to the one thought of as having the best range of equipment; he wanted choice. He might have shopped more thriftily elsewhere but that was not important; he wanted the frame today.

As it was Sunday, the place, three miles beyond Rotherston, was busy with weekend customers buying bulbs and compost, and bundles of wallflowers. On impulse, Roger put some wallflowers in his trolley. The frame came in pack form. He bought the one that seemed the most suitable – larger and likely to be steadier than another type. Perhaps he'd better get some bulbs; even if he were not in Bishop St Leon in the spring, others would be at the house and would benefit. At this centre, you were invited to pile them into buckets and pay so much for each one; he filled three of the small plastic pails provided and loaded them with the rest of his purchases. When he could spin out his browsing no longer, Roger paid and wheeled his trolley to the car. The bulbs were now in plastic bags; he put them in the boot, with the frame and the plants, then set off for home. He'd forgotten how short the days were; he must hurry or the light would go before he'd assembled the frame, much less planted the wallflowers; the bulbs could wait.

Roger drove back through Rotherston. As he approached the Grapes, whose bar was closed on Sunday afternoons, a man was getting into a taxi. It pulled out ahead of him, and Roger, unable to pass it, drove behind it all the way to Bishop St Leon, where it turned down North Street and continued past Chapel Row.

Curious as always, and with nothing better to do, Roger followed it and saw it stop outside Cedar Cottage. A man got out, and Roger, driving slowly by, had his first sight of Martin Trent.

Martin paid off the taxi at the door of Cedar Cottage. Sometimes, coming back the worse for wear, he would have no money left and would demand the fare from his mother, but today he had enough. The taxi driver knew him of old; Martin had been a frequent user of the service over the years.

Martin was in an argumentative mood, and he walked about looking for his mother, but he could not find her in the house. Though he did not want her company, he wished to know her whereabouts in order to provoke a quarrel. He'd been kind and amenable all the time he was at Debbie's; now he would revert to what had become normal conduct here.

Through a window, he saw a youth in the garden clearing leaves. He had raked up several orderly heaps of them and was now piling up another. His mother, her back towards the house, was sweeping more into smaller mounds with a besom broom. Most were down now; only a few hung starkly here and there on bare branches.

Martin went out through the kitchen door and approached the pair. He wavered slightly as he walked silently over the damp grass. Neither of them noticed him until he came up behind his mother and said, loudly, 'I want tea.'

Susan started, almost jumping with fright, and clasped her hands, besom and all, to her chest as she heard his voice, menacing and so like his father's. Owen was also startled. Later he told his mother, 'You should have heard how he spoke to her. Poor Mrs Trent. I tell you, he didn't say much but the way he said it was scary.'

However, though her companion was only a boy of seventeen, Susan was less easy to bully when she was not alone.

'I'll make some when I come in. Owen and I want to finish this before the wind gets up again.'

'I want it now,' said Martin, who didn't, but had determined to exert control.

'Make it yourself, then,' said Susan, steadier now, and she went on sweeping, turning her back resolutely towards her son. Her heart was pounding and her vision blurred, but she swept on.

After a few moments, Martin gave in and turned away. She had achieved a little victory.

Martin scowled as he went back to the house. Bloody woman. She'd fouled up his whole life, been the cause of all his problems. His father hadn't been there when Martin needed him in the years of adolescence; there was simply his ineffectual mother and his bossy sister who ordered him about and was, in other people's eyes, a perfect child. He never communicated with her now; her move to California was the best thing that could have happened, from his point of view.

Even if he'd wanted it, because she had told him to, he wouldn't have made tea now. He went upstairs to his room and checked his e-mail, but there was nothing waiting, nor had there been any post for him. There had

been no message for him on the answerphone, either. His
mother was reliable about writing those down, but he
could get at her about it, challenge her, accuse her of
failing to remember or of not giving him his letters. She'd
soon be getting doddery and forgetful – or worse than
she was already; if she became incapable of coherent
thought, he could have her sectioned and take over the
whole house. It would be his anyway, on her death. He
looked forward to that event; he might have to buy out
Patricia's share, assuming half the value would accrue to
her, which would be hard, but it was worth a lot, and
then Martin could take his place in society, sell up and
move away from this narrow, gossip-ridden village to a
university town or even overseas; yes, that might be best
– Florence, perhaps, or Rome, somewhere property cost
less and the climate was better.

Martin doodled on his computer, logging on to internet
images of Italy, fantasising about the future he would have
when his mother was not in his way.

After a while he settled down to write the report on
Venice, which he should have done the day before. He
ought to get it in before the clients sent their complaints.
There were always some who found fault, no matter how
much he put himself out for them. Any grievances which
were justified were not his responsibility but that of the
organisers of the tour; he merely carried out their direct-
ives and followed their itinerary, though he could set up
a better one himself, if his advice were asked.

He'd go along to the Crown this evening for some company; it was the landlord's job to treat him well and listen if he wished to talk. But first, he'd have a reckoning with his mother, when she came in from the garden and sent that useless boy about his business. Martin did not want a witness to his actions.

Susan spun out her leaf sweeping for as long as she could, but eventually she and Owen completed their task. The grass was too wet to cut, and it was agreed that Owen would come round another time to do it after school, on a day when there had been some sun to dry it out. Even if it didn't rain, the dew was heavy now. Susan could mow it herself, perfectly well, and enjoyed seeing it looking neat after its trim, but having something done for her was a rare pleasure, and she wanted to encourage Owen and his fund.

Owen didn't suggest that Martin, now that he was back, might undertake the task, which a son might reasonably be expected to do. He had been shocked by Martin's glowering face and belligerent manner with his mother; it worried him as he put the broom, rake and barrow away and closed up the shed. Among the leaves there had been a few small branches from the willow and twigs from other trees; the winds had not been strong enough to bring any major boughs down, but one afternoon the previous week, a sudden gusting gale had blown up like a small tornado. Owen had been walking home from the school bus and for a few minutes it had been quite difficult to stand up against it; some of the girls had pretended to be alarmed.

In the house, Susan had put the kettle on and cut him a slice of sponge cake; when he came round, he always had cake if there was any, or biscuits, with a mug of strong tea. They'd sit at the table and he'd tell her about his plans. She was always interested. She'd told him she had a grandson much his age, but she never saw him, and Owen thought that sad.

Upstairs, Martin heard their voices as they came into the house, but when the kitchen door was closed, the sound was lost. He knew she'd be feeding that boy; wouldn't she even bring him up a cup of tea and a slice of cake? He waited, but she didn't.

He'd let her know about it when the boy had gone.

Lily and Rose were crying loudly. Even in her shocked state, Debbie knew that meant that they would not have broken their skulls.

They lay in a mass of limbs near the foot of the stairs and Rose was screaming. Lily's cries were deep shuddering sobs, shaking her body as Debbie gently pulled her away from her small sister.

They hadn't fallen the full length of the staircase for they were only halfway up when Rose stumbled, but Lily had not been holding the banisters, only her sister's left hand. She slithered down on her stomach, and somehow managed, with her free hand, to clutch at a banister post, clinging on, and arresting her own descent so that Rosie's also slowed and they did not hurtle to the bottom. Debbie gathered them to her, trying to hush them, while part of her mind was wondering if she should instantly call an ambulance, but she could not release them to reach the telephone. And where was Martin? He must have heard them. Why didn't he come and help?

After a while, though still crying, they began to move, and Lily's sobs diminished, while Rose wailed on.

'Rose, hush, where does it hurt? Tell me,' Debbie urged, and to Lily, 'Are you all right? Can you stand up?'

Lily did so; she was regaining her courage.

'I tried to hold her,' she said.

'I know you did,' said Debbie. 'Rosie, tell me where it hurts.'

But Rose couldn't; however, she was wriggling now, clinging to her mother, and Debbie, whose own heart was pounding so fast that it felt as though it would leap out of her chest, began to realise that probably neither of them had suffered more than shock and bruising.

Lily had remembered the reason for their ascent of the stairs.

'She's wet. Rosie's wet. We were going to get some knickers,' she told her mother, and her voice caught on a sob.

'Well, let's do that now,' said Debbie. 'Can you manage, Lily?'

Lily could. She stood up and gripped the rail.

'We'll go slowly,' Debbie said. 'Hold on to the banisters, and you go first.'

She picked Rose up and carried her, following behind Lily's small and now cautious figure as she stepped upwards, one step at a time, her left foot being joined on each tread by the right one before she moved on, and eventually the little procession reached the top.

In the bathroom, Debbie undressed Rose first. There were no cuts, and, as yet, no bruises on her little body nor her soft, dimpled limbs. By now her crying had eased, and in response to Debbie's request, she moved each arm and leg and, when asked to wiggle her fingers and toes, began to giggle as she did so. The same ritual was then carried out with Lily, whose front was rather pink where she had tobogganed on it, but her limbs were also all intact. At this age, they were so soft and pliable that this protected them when falling; Debbie knew that, but there could have been a broken arm or collar bone.

She put them both into a warm bath and let them play there, with their toy boat and ducks. No longer crying, their faces had returned to their normal colour, and both were laughing. Best forget about it, Debbie thought; distract them, it was just a tumble. In their pyjamas, they went down again for supper, with Debbie carrying Rose, for safety. But she might fall herself, she thought, terrified again.

Mothers mustn't fall, she told herself as they went into the sitting room. The television was still on. She turned it off, and it was not until later that night that she realised the *Bambi* video was in the set and understood what Martin had done.

The fault was hers. She should not have rushed upstairs in tears, just like a child.

And none of it would have happened if Jim hadn't left them.

11

Adam and Chris returned to Chapel Row on Sunday evening to find that Roger's Mondeo had been reversed into the driveway and was now standing on the spot where Chris normally left his van.

'That's OK. I don't mind, and anyway I'm off out again,' said Chris, stopping in the road. 'It's not my place of right, but you've parked where Roger does.'

'I'll move,' said Adam. 'I don't want to cause an incident.'

'Leave it this time,' Chris advised. 'He may have been out shopping for the garden and be unloading compost or something.'

'Let's go and see,' said Adam, who had had an interesting afternoon in Chris's workshop and had been useful, first sweeping up shavings and sawdust, and then planing bits of wood to Chris's instructions. Chris's girlfriend, Melanie, had telephoned while they were there, and the pair had made a plan to meet that evening. Chris had brought Adam back and had arranged to pick her up after changing his clothes and smartening himself up.

'You carry on. I'll grab the shower,' said Chris.

Adam walked round the side of the house to where a bulky figure could be seen crouched on a patch of concrete which might grandiloquently be described as a patio, grappling with some lengths of plastic.

'Need some help?' he asked.

Roger looked up.

'I can manage,' he said, between gritted teeth. 'No need for you to be the friend of all the world.' This new guy was just too helpful to be true, first offering food, then helping Chris, and now this.

'No need for you to be so hostile,' said Adam calmly, also bending down. 'If I hold this piece, won't it be easier for you to slot that other one in?'

In seconds he had seen just how to fit the parts together, and another pair of hands certainly made the task simpler. Roger, about to make a sharp retort, swallowed both the sentence and his pride and suffered Adam to assist him. The job was finished, silently.

'There,' said Adam, satisified. 'I've always found self-assembly to be a major challenge, but you'd cracked this one. What are you going to grow in it?'

He hadn't referred to their meeting on the train, deeming it tactful not to do so. Perhaps Roger had not recognised him; he'd been intent on his drink and crisps, oblivious, it had seemed at the time, of anyone else's comfort and therefore, probably, of them.

'Lettuces,' growled Roger. 'Maybe start off sweet peas,' he muttered.

'Great,' said Adam heartily, then added, 'Sorry if I took your parking spot, but I didn't know about it. I'll leave my car further down the road in future.'

'Sometimes I need to leave in a hurry,' Roger managed. 'If I get an urgent call.'

'Sure,' said Adam. 'Must be tough, your job. Interesting, though. Worthwhile. Catching criminals.'

'Not when they get off because they have a sharp brief,' said Roger.

'No. That must be discouraging,' said Adam. 'Well, I'll leave you to it.' He turned to go, anxious not to push his luck, then added, 'Fancy a pint at the Crown?'

He saw that Roger, as a reflex response, was about to refuse, and then changed his mind.

'I don't mind,' Roger said, ungraciously.

'Right. Give me a shout when you're ready,' said Adam, and went into the house.

Roger put the finishing touches to the frame, then carried it to the sheltered sunny spot beside the garden shed, where he intended it to rest. He secured it in position and slotted in the glass. He could not sow any seeds until he had prepared the soil, so, in the gathering dusk, there was no more to be done. He wouldn't hurry; Adam might forget the whole thing.

But then how would he spend the evening?

Adam, too, was chiding himself for being a total idiot; what was he thinking of, suggesting a trip to the pub with a man who had a chip on his shoulder the size of a giant oak? As he went up to his room, Chris, all spruced up, emerged from his, ready for his date.

'What's Roger up to?' he asked.

'Fixing a garden frame. He's going to grow lettuces,' said Adam.

'That's good,' said Chris. 'We ought to buy them from him. We can't expect him to contribute to the larder from the goodness of his heart. If there is such a thing,' he added.

'There may be, and you're right,' Adam agreed.

'Perhaps he won't offer them to us. Perhaps he means to flog them down at the nick,' said Chris, and was gone, leaving a waft of expensive aftershave in his wake.

Debbie could smell the dried-up chicken in the oven when she went into the kitchen to make supper for the girls.

They seemed to have recovered from their fall, with no ill effects, and had decided that they'd like banana sandwiches as they followed her into the kitchen. She opened the oven door and saw the plate of food which Martin had left there, and her eyes filled with tears because he had been so thoughtful. She'd flown off in a temper; he had given the girls their lunch and settled them down with a film; it was unreasonable to expect him to stay with them all the afternoon while she sulked. He could not have known that she would fall asleep.

'Ugh,' said Lily, looking at the charred remnants on the plate.

'It'll wash off,' said Debbie, scraping what she could into the bin. 'I'll leave it soaking. It'll be all right in the morning.'

And so would all of them. A good night's sleep was what they needed. She set to work with a sliced loaf and made their sandwiches, then some chicken ones for herself; having missed lunch, she was hungry now. Martin had not cleared the table, nor put any of the food away. Why should he? She was the one who'd lost her temper and flounced off. Debbie piled everything on the drainer while they ate; then, leaving the girls to brush their teeth, she quickly changed the sheets on her bed; tonight, they'd all sleep together, but with fresh bedding.

She read them a story about a little bear, which Rose, in particular, enjoyed, then told them she would come up to bed herself as soon as she had done the washing-up. There was a gate at the top of the stairs, and she fastened it before going down. Surely it wasn't necessary to have one downstairs, too?

She wished she could discuss today's frightening accident with Jim, but if she told him, he might accuse her of not taking proper care of their daughters.

The washing-up took some time, for everything had

congealed. While she did it, Debbie wondered if Martin would come back that night. He had not mentioned any plans but she knew he had no courier work arranged for the immediate future.

Part of her wanted him to return, so that she could apologise for her behaviour; part of her hoped that he would stay away, just for a while: not long.

Martin had left the door of his room ajar, so that he would hear when Owen left. He heard his mother say, 'Goodbye, Owen, and thanks,' and Owen's cheery, 'See you,' before the boy rode off on his bicycle. Martin watched him from the window. He'd got no lights on the machine; serve him right if he got run over.

In this spirit of truculence, intent now on battle with his mother, Martin went downstairs.

Susan had not heard him on the stairs; he was good at moving quietly about the house, except when he was drunk and wanted to disturb her. She was washing up the tea things, but she sensed his presence the instant before he spoke.

'Why should you give that boy tea and not your son?' he demanded.

Susan dropped the mug she was holding into the sink. He sounded exactly like his father and the shaking she had been unable to control in those years began again, as it often did with Martin in this mood; she had been so frightened of his father that she had trembled whenever he came near her. Then, too, there had been sex to fear; that, at least, was not a present threat.

'You can have some now, Martin,' she said. 'I'll make some fresh.'

'It's too late,' Martin said. 'I'll have whisky.' He brushed past her, knocking her against the sink. 'And where's my post?' he asked. 'Where are my letters?'

'You didn't have any,' she said. 'Only those that came while you were away and I put them in your room.'

'I don't believe you,' Martin said. 'There must have been some post today.'

'It's Sunday, Martin.'

'Well, yesterday, then,' he snarled, wrong-footed.

'No,' Susan answered, fishing in the bowl to rescue the mug, which luckily had not broken.

'Look at me when I'm talking to you,' he said, and again she heard his father's voice.

She did not turn, carefully reaching out to place the mug on the drainer, her back towards him, and he caught her by the elbow, forcibly turning her to face him.

'Look at me, I said,' he repeated. 'Let's have some respect here.'

'Yes, let's,' said Susan bravely. 'It's time you showed some for me.'

Quick as a flash, he slapped her hard on both cheeks, then again, and again, her head wagging to and fro like a punchball on a spring. Susan dropped the mug which shattered on the tiled floor and she caught at his hands, crying out.

'No, no, Martin. No, no,' she wailed, and somehow managed to kick out with one foot.

She caught him on the shin, not hard, but enough to pull him up.

'Bloody old bitch,' he said. 'Why can't you die?'

As suddenly as he had begun the attack, he stopped it, with one last blow to her head. Then he took the whisky bottle from the cupboard and stormed off upstairs. She'd cry now, stupid cow that she was. She made him sick.

He did not realise that the attack of nausea he felt was due to inadmissible shame.

Susan staggered into the sitting room and collapsed on the sofa. Her head was ringing from the battering she had received, and sobs choked her as she drew her knees up, curling herself into the foetal position.

How long could this go on? How much longer could she endure it? He didn't really mean to hurt her, she consoled herself; life had been too hard for him. If he were to see a doctor, would that help?

But he would never agree to consult one; she'd never persuade him. If only he would find somewhere else to live, move to a simple flat in a university town or city where he might be able to return to the academic world, his life would improve. He had taught successfully for years before things started to go wrong, and he wasn't yet too old for a teaching post, though younger teachers were a better economic proposition because they were paid less, but he could coach exam students, and he could teach English as a foreign language, as he had done before.

Susan knew his book would never see the light of day. While he was in Venice, she had looked in his room and found very few typescript pages; greatly daring, and with only limited computer skills which she had acquired in the office, she had even dared to turn on his computer to see if there was more material, but could find nothing substantial. There was no book; it was a fantasy.

And was this romance also a fantasy? Surely not; he had just been away for two nights. Living here was free, so where would he have stayed except with a woman? Perhaps this one, unlike his mother, brought the best out in him.

Some of these thoughts went through Susan's head as she lay there in the dark, too upset to turn on any light, and subconsciously afraid that if she did so, when he came downstairs on his way to the Crown, he would come into the room and vent more anger on her.

Perhaps his woman friend had broken off with him; that would explain this last attack of rage. If anything went wrong for him, there had to be the scapegoat, and who better to fill the role than his mother? While she was available, any woman he was mixed up with would probably be safe.

Her uneven breathing grew easier, but her head was still ringing. Susan knew she could not safely move; not yet. She stayed where she was, very quiet, no longer sobbing. So often she had lain like this, on another sofa, long ago discarded, whimpering with pain and terror, and sometimes, in those years, she would be holding Martin tight against her body, stifling his cries, sheltering him as well as herself, while Patricia crouched behind the sofa, all of them hiding from her children's father.

She knew that later on, at opening time, just as his father used to do, Martin would go along to the Crown.

He did.

He was there before Roger and Adam arrived.

They walked along the road in awkward silence, while Adam strove to construct some neutral comment, but it was difficult to think of an appropriate topic as they stepped out together.

'The rain held off,' he said, at last. 'The wind seems to be getting up again, though.'

It was. They could hear it sighing in the trees.

'Yeah,' said Roger. He'd brought a torch, a large, heavy one, which Adam supposed must be official equipment, suitable for investigating crime scenes. He had a small pencil torch in his own pocket. Coming back after a pint or two might be tricky in the dark, and he was not yet familiar with any hazards on the route. He wasn't going to make a night of it, and had no idea if that was Roger's habit. Perhaps it depended on the company.

'Do you know many of the locals, apart from those that go to the Crown?' Adam ventured as they turned into North Street.

'No,' said Roger.

'Do you go there much?'

'Now and then.'

A three word answer: that was progress. Ahead, the pub was visible a hundred yards away, its sign board swinging in the breeze. Cars were parked along the kerb.

'Seems popular,' he said.

'Food's good,' said Roger. 'Not pricey. Folk enjoy something cooked for them.'

'Yes.' Now it was Adam's turn to be monosyllabic. Then he decided it was wise not to have unnecessary secrets. 'Chris and I ate here on Friday night, after I'd seen the room,' he said.

He wondered if Martin Trent would be in the pub tonight, or, if he wasn't, whether anyone would mention him and point him out. At this early stage, he was not going to reveal that he had an interest in the man, and in his mother; the two, it had been suggested, had a difficult relationship, and he meant to learn about it, but discreetly; there was no hurry.

That night, however, he was to meet the man.

Roger, not commenting on Adam's having eaten at the pub, led the way through the door. Adam reflected that he would be a good person to have on your team if you were in any trouble, and resolved, however difficult it might become, to maintain his conciliatory attitude towards the other man. Besides, it would aid domestic harmony.

He spotted Martin at once, without needing to be told his identity. He was sitting in a corner with a half-empty pint glass in front of him, and a chaser beside it – whisky, probably. Though seated, he was obviously not a big man; he had greying, slightly wavy hair curling round his ears, and a drinker's florid complexion. He was staring at the table top, intently. His face was exactly like those in the photographs Adam had so recently discovered.

Roger, recognising the taxi passenger dropped earlier at Cedar Cottage, waxed suddenly communicative and said, 'Watch that bloke. He gets pissed regularly and can be trouble.'

'Oh,' said Adam, adding, 'What sort of trouble?'

'First sentimental, then angry.' Roger hesitated before saying, 'Argumentative.'

'Thanks for the warning,' Adam answered. 'I'll keep out of his way. Who is he?' he remembered to enquire, for he must not seem to know.

'Martin Trent. Lives with his widowed mother along the road.'

'Oh.' Adam decided not to mention that he had heard Martin being discussed in the pub on Friday night. 'Not married, then?'

'No more than you or me,' said Roger enigmatically. He drank up, almost smiling, and Adam hastened to do the same, so that he could buy his round promptly. This mood of comradeship must be encouraged.

Des had remembered him.

'Settled in then?' he asked, pulling their pints.

'Yes. I feel quite at home already,' Adam said.

'Roger showing you the ropes?'

'He's a great gardener,' Adam replied.

'Is he, then? I didn't know,' said Des as he handed Adam his change and turned to serve another customer, a young woman. 'Evening, Linda,' he said. 'And Jo. This is Adam. He's new to the village. Jo's family have lived in Bishop St Leon for generations, and Linda is a friend of hers.'

'Hullo,' said Adam, smiling at the girls, and as he did so, recognised one of them; she had sat beside him on the train from London, with Roger facing her, threatening to scatter crisps over the book that she was reading.

'Hi,' said Linda, hesitating, looking at him curiously, and then she, too, remembered. 'The train,' she said. He was the quiet man with the laptop who had sat next to her. She'd taken very little notice of him, glad only that he was unobtrusive.

'Yes,' he said. 'As the landlord told you, I've just come to live here. I must take my new house-mate his drink. Would you like to meet him?' He nodded towards Roger, who was looking away from them at the fire. Though no longer wearing his ginger brown tweeds, there was no mistaking the crisp-eater from the train.

Linda cast an astonished glance from one man to the other, and gasped, 'No!'

'Yes,' said Adam. 'I haven't mentioned it,' he warned. 'Too embarrassing. Maybe now's the time.'

'Right,' said Linda, on the brink of an attack of giggles. 'Let's go for it. Thanks, Adam. We'd like to join you for a while, wouldn't we, Jo?'

They crossed over to the table where Roger was sitting, carrying their glasses, and Adam made the introductions.

'Roger, you remember Linda? She was on the train last Thursday night,' he said. He couldn't have explained why he still hadn't mentioned that meeting to Roger, but then the other man had not spoken, either, and Adam was sure he had been recognised. 'And this is Jo,' he added, as the second girl, looking somewhat puzzled, came forward.

'Can't say I do,' said Roger, not getting to his feet, but he gave Linda a sharp look. She was just an ordinary young woman with brown hair cut in a sleek bob, and grey-blue eyes. They were memorable eyes; he'd not have forgotten them if he'd noticed them. Linda, however, had kept them fixed firmly on her book and had not looked directly at him. A woman had been sitting opposite him in the train, after he had had a long and wearisome day in London, tying up details for the prosecution before the following day's arrest. He recalled seeing a woman walking ahead of him to the parking lot, but other passengers also left the train when he did. Then he remembered: he'd seen her in the Grapes the night before; the girl Jo and another girl were with her.

'Doesn't matter,' Linda said, sitting down.

Jo took the fourth chair at their table, setting down her glass.

'So you're new in Bishop St Leon?' Linda asked Adam. She remembered how quietly he had sat there in the train, moving minimally as he used his laptop.

'Yes.' Adam felt cheered at meeting the two young women. 'Do you live here, too, then?' he asked.

'No. In Rotherston,' said Linda. 'I work here, though.'

'We're both nannies,' said Jo, before he could ask.

'And you look after children in the village?'

'Yes,' said Linda. 'My family live at Field House. Do you know it? On the way to the church.'

'I've been along there,' said Adam.

'My family live in Chapel Row,' said Jo.

Adam remembered the renovated chapel with the children's play equipment in the garden.

'In that house that was once a chapel?' he asked.

'Yes.'

'We live in Chapel Row too,' said Adam. 'Well, I've only just moved in, but Roger's been there a while. Number seventeen,' he added.

'Oh – right.' Jo nodded. 'I know it.'

Linda realised that he must be the new tenant Amy had mentioned. He seemed nice enough, but her low opinion of Roger had not improved as he sat silently drinking his beer, not contributing to the conversation. At least he wasn't eating vinegary crisps tonight.

Adam asked about the children she and Jo looked after and learned about the playgroup their older charges went to several mornings a week. Linda might have been the woman he had seen on Friday at Field House, unless that was the children's mother. As the garden bordered that of Cedar Cottage, he was just wondering if he could frame a question about the neighbours when Jo said, beneath her breath, 'Oh dear,' and there was Martin, standing right beside them, swaying gently to and fro.

'Well, Jo,' he said, leering down at her. 'Aren't you going to introduce me to your friend?' and, ignoring the men, he gave Linda what she described later as a dirty, leching look.

'Oh, hi, Martin,' said Jo. 'Roger, Adam, Linda. This is Martin Trent.'

Her tone made it obvious to the two men that Martin was not a favourite of hers and it was clear that he had had a lot to drink. This was the man who was notorious for bullying his mother, and Roger's big hand tightened round his glass. Adam looked up at the red face which wore a silly, vacant grin. He found he could not speak, but Linda did.

'We met the other morning, when you nearly knocked us and our prams over,' she said, in a crisp voice. 'Friday, it was. You were in a hurry.'

'If I'd seen you, I'm sure I'd have stopped,' said Martin.

'I expect you were hurrying to catch the bus,' said Jo. 'When do you get your licence back?'

Martin's mood altered instantly.

'You pert miss,' he said. 'You'll get what's coming to you one day.'

He took a swallow from his glass, almost overbalancing as he did so, and gripped the back of Linda's chair to steady himself.

'Martin, stuff it,' said Jo, undaunted. 'One day you'll go too far.'

He ignored her.

'I'm sure you're not sarcastic, like Jo,' he told Linda. 'You're different.'

Adam had recovered his composure. Ignoring Martin, he turned to Linda. 'Rotherston, you said,' he prompted.

Linda took up his effort at distraction, but she did not want to let Martin know where she lived.

'I share a flat with another girl, Amy,' she said. 'She works in Marsh's estate agency. She mentioned sending someone to look at a room here. Maybe it was you.'

'Maybe it was,' said Adam. 'A very nice girl did look after me.'

'Not my mother, then,' said Martin. He had reached

round behind him to take a vacant chair from the adjoining table and sat down, trying to join their group, but none of them would move to let him.

Now Adam turned and looked him in the eye.

'Your mother?'

'My silly old mother,' Martin said, and tittered. 'She should be put out to grass but she still goes into that office, pretending to do a day's work. Brian keeps her on out of charity.'

Adam had seen an older woman in the background in the office on his first visit, but she had gone into an inner room while the younger woman dealt with him; she had not been there yesterday when he returned. He was absorbing this while listening, amazed, to Martin.

'If you think so little of her, why do you live with her and make her life a misery?' said Jo hotly. 'My dad's told me about you. You're a shit, Martin Trent. Come on, Linda. Let's move.'

'No,' said Roger. 'This man – Martin – joined us without an invitation. You move, Martin Trent. We don't want you at our table.'

His voice carried; there was a frisson reaching to the neighbouring tables, and Des, behind the bar, began to take notice. Rows weren't allowed to happen in his pub, or not major ones.

'Who do you think you're talking to?' said Martin, his voice now petulant.

'You,' said Roger. 'You, Mr Martin Trent. Move.'

'Who'd want to talk to you anyway?' said Martin. 'You're a waste of space.'

Roger had not risen. He merely sat there, quelling Martin with what Adam described to Chris, the next day, as a basilisk stare, but it had effect. Martin pushed back his chair and got up, turning away. He went to the bar and bought another pint, with a chaser. Des let him have it; he was in the trade to make money, and Martin was not driving.

There was a brief silence among the four he had left. 'What has your dad told you about him, Jo?' Adam broke it.

Jo was now looking rather sheepish.

'Sorry – I didn't mean to cause a scene, but he's trouble,' she said bluntly. 'My dad went to school with him and he was useless then – clever, a bit of a swot, but always running to his mother if things went wrong, and she was always complaining to the school. She was a teacher herself, but not there. When he grew up he expected her to wait on him hand and foot, my dad said. But he went away to university and then got married.'

'He's back here now,' observed Adam.

'Yes. His wife left him years ago. Dad said he lost his job soon after.' She paused, then decided, as she'd said so much, she might as well go on. 'He goes after girls – women – he can get quite nasty when he's drunk. He had a go at my aunt – my dad's sister. That's why Dad's got no time for him. It was years ago and it didn't amount to much,' she added. 'But he wouldn't let her go when she dumped him, which was pretty quickly after they first went out together. Kept phoning and calling round and pestering her. He goes for younger women now. Ones he thinks he'll impress. He's got one in Rotherston. I don't know who she is.'

'Hm.' Roger's grunt was apt comment.

Adam gazed down at the beer mat on the table.

'What happened to his father?' he asked at last.

'Went off. Just left,' said Jo. 'Martin was only two or three at the time. His sister's a bit older. Dad liked her. I think he may have fancied her.'

'Didn't they see their father?' Linda asked. 'The children, I mean?'

'No. He never came back. Settled in New Zealand, it was said.'

Roger rose to his feet. 'What are you having, Jo? Linda? Adam?' he asked, and went off to get more drinks.

While he was away, Linda looked at Adam.

'No vinegar crisps tonight,' she said.

'Maybe Des doesn't sell them.'

'Maybe not.'

They exchanged conspiratorial grins and Linda told Jo she would explain later.

'He did well with Martin,' Jo said.

'Yes, he did.'

Adam was wondering what sort of mood Martin would be in when he left the pub and went home. He was still there when Roger and Adam left, having eaten. The two girls had departed earlier; Linda had her car, and took Jo home. Adam was sorry to see them go.

'I hope Martin Trent's mother locks her bedroom door when he's out on the booze,' said Roger, as they walked home.

'I hope so, too,' said Adam.

'If he'd left the pub, I'd have followed him,' said Roger. 'Just to make sure things were all right. But he's a fixture now till closing time. He'll be expecting sympathy from the barman, as none of us have been too friendly.'

'Must be tricky, being a barman,' Adam said.

12

In the morning, Roger left the house early. Adam heard him overhead, but the big man moved quietly; it was the water pipes and flushing that made the noise.

How damning first impressions can be, he thought. If he hadn't sat opposite Roger on the train, and witnessed him behaving in what was, if not an antisocial manner, at least inconsiderate, he would have had a better opinion of the man. Adam had travelled widely; he had been at close quarters with people whose behaviour was far more offensive than Roger's on the train. There was no reason for a hungry passenger not to eat while travelling; it was his apparent unawareness of anyone else's comfort but his own which had been so repellent. Meeting Linda, the staunch reader, was a surprise, and her friend Jo's attack on Martin Trent had been startling. Roger had revealed anxiety about Susan Trent; was she really at risk of violence from her son?

It was time to engineer a meeting with her. Adam had been thinking of a cold call – ringing her bell – finding some excuse – but thanks to last night's conversation in the bar, he now knew that she worked in the estate agency.

He'd do it today. He might look out for Linda, too, and Jo; surely the nannies would be wheeling their charges round in prams? He'd meet the two of them quite easily.

Adam had reckoned without the modern nanny's lifestyle. Later, he learned that intercepting them on their way to or from the playgroup was the one sure way to catch them, and even then they often went by car, with their young charges anchored in the back.

There was no sound from Chris's room, and the van was not outside the house when Adam came downstairs. He must have got it together with Melanie last night. As it was more comfortable than the van, he'd offered Chris the Toyota for the evening if they were going out to dinner, but Chris had said she had to take him as he was, or not. Good sentiments. Adam did not hurry over showering and shaving, deciding that his and Roger's new chumminess had better not be tested too vigorously by break-fasting together so soon. It was obvious, though, that Roger had gone out without so much as a cup of coffee, unless he brewed up in his room. The kitchen was as tidy as it had been the night before, and there was only cold water in the kettle.

He decided to walk up to the shop to buy a paper. As he turned into North Street, he glanced along the road towards the Crown and saw an elderly man pushing a paper-delivery cart; proceeding on his way, he met a pale middle-aged man with a desperate expression on his face as he laboriously jogged, and an old woman walking a small dog. A plump woman runner, a Walkman plugged into her ears, overtook him, coming up behind him on her rubber soles; he heard her pounding feet and made way for her. Various children, in ones and twos, were making their way towards the school bus's collection point.

As Adam arrived back from his errand, a small red car drew up at the former chapel. The driver waved at him; it was Jo, arriving for work. Adam waved back and went indoors. He was curious enough to look out of the window and saw, moments later, a blue Saab leave the house; one of her employers, going off to work, no doubt. Some time later, when Adam left himself, the little car had gone.

In the meantime, Chris had returned, dashed indoors to change from the tidy clothes he had worn to take Melanie out into working jeans, and dashed out again, barely pausing to say 'Hi!' to Adam, who emerged from the kitchen as he passed through the hall.

'Someone's happy,' Adam said.

'Yeah,' said Chris, hurrying on.

Long may it last, Adam thought, returning to the paper. It was too early to go into the estate agent's office.

He did not take the direct route into Rotherston, driving first along North Street, past Cedar Cottage. The house looked quiet, the curtains drawn back at all the front windows. Martin Trent might have a thick head this morning; though, as Roger had reminded him on their way home the night before, it being Sunday, the Crown would have closed at half-past ten. Adam went slowly on, passing Field House, and there he saw Jo's red car parked on the gravel sweep. Beside it was the small Fiat he had seen before. The nannies were getting together. Talking to them had been good; they were attractive, friendly girls. He wondered about inviting one of them out, but which one? Jo was the livelier of the two, but Linda's quiet charm was appealing. He wondered if Chris knew either of the girls; a foursome would be the way to go, but as Chris seemed serious about Melanie, he might not want to risk it. Better not: he didn't want to get emotionally involved with anyone while he was here, and they probably both had boyfriends anyway, so it would be a pointless exercise and might deflect him from his purpose. That, however, could not be hurried; he must go very steadily and carefully or he would fail.

Adam drove on into Rotherston and left the car in a long-stay park. He needed to do some shopping; he must think ahead a bit, stock up with some clothes and food. His task might take only weeks, but it could last months. And he must seem to be busy; if his days appeared to be spent in idleness, people – and Roger in particular – might get curious.

It was half-past ten when he went into Brian Marsh's office.

The girl who had given him the details of the house was alone, behind a desk. She looked up when he entered, recognised him, and gave him a big smile.

'Hullo,' she said. 'I hope there's nothing wrong with the house?'

'Not at all,' he said. 'I came in to say thanks very much for fixing it up. It's fine.' He paused, and added, 'I think I met your flatmate last night in the pub.'

'Yes. She mentioned it,' said Amy. 'It was quite an evening, I believe.'

'Full of surprises,' Adam said.

Linda had described her train journey with Adam and with Roger. Last night, talking to them for the first time, she'd liked Adam, and admitted that Roger improved on acquaintance, though his manners left something to be desired.

'Would you like some coffee?' Amy asked.

'Thanks – if you're making it,' said Adam, pleased. With luck, Susan Trent might come in at any minute.

'Sue's got the kettle on,' said Amy, and she went to an archway behind her desk. 'One more, please, Sue,' she said, to someone who was in a room beyond the office. 'Milk and sugar?' she asked Adam.

'Milk, please. No sugar,' Adam said. Sue: that was different from Susan; friendlier, somehow. He added, as Amy returned, 'I'm interrupting your work.'

'That's all right,' said Amy. 'Take a seat. I expect the phone will start to ring quite soon.'

It was amazing how easily someone's confidence could be won. Adam was aware that all these new acquaintances were taking him at face value, even Roger; he had produced cash up front and had the ability to get along with people. It wasn't difficult to start your life again, establish a new identity; he knew the truth of that.

'Are you very busy?' Adam asked. 'Are lots of people moving?'

'The market's slowed up a bit,' Amy said. 'Steadied, I should say. To sell, you need just one person to want your house, really want it, not dozens. Are you staying in the area? Might you be buying, later on?'

'I'm not sure,' Adam said. 'I'll see how things go.'

'What's your line?'

'I'm freelancing at the moment,' Adam said. 'Research.'

As he spoke, a woman came through the archway bearing a small tray on which were two mugs and a cup and saucer. She was intent on watching the tray, carrying it carefully, and did not look at him or Amy, setting it down on the desk.

'Oh, thanks, Sue,' said Amy. 'Meet your new neighbour, Adam Wilson. This is Susan Trent, Adam.'

Susan Trent started back, automatically putting a hand to her face, and Adam saw that beneath her heavy makeup there was a yellowing bruise on one side of her face, and a newer, purple one on her forehead, which was slightly swollen. He tried to control his reaction, standing up and saying, 'How d'you do?' Not well, would be the truthful answer.

Susan did not extend a hand. She looked him in the eye, but only briefly, before averting her head to hide the marks and taking one of the mugs from the tray. As she did so, she muttered, 'Good morning,' and slunk, mug in hand, to one of the other desks.

'The cup's for you, as you're a client,' Amy said. 'Susan took a tumble yesterday,' she continued. 'I think she ought to see a doctor.'

'Oh dear.' Adam, shocked at her appearance, was at a loss.

'I'm sure Mr Wilson doesn't want to hear about my silly ways,' said Susan, and, picking up her mug, she went out of the office through the aperture again.

Amy made a face at Adam.

'I know you've heard about it,' she told him. 'Linda said Jo's really worried. So am I, to tell you the truth.'

Adam shared their disquiet. He'd just seen a very frightened woman who had been beaten up.

'She should go to the police,' he said.

The telephone rang at that moment.

'Will you tell me about her? Will you meet me for lunch?' he asked, and expected her to say that it was no business of his. But she didn't.

'Yes,' said Amy promptly. She picked up the handset and said, in a crisp voice, 'Marsh's. Amy speaking. Would you hold for just a second?' and put her hand over the mouthpiece. 'Not the Grapes,' she said. 'He might be there.'

'Let's meet outside the town hall,' said Adam, mentioning a landmark that he knew.

'Half-past twelve,' said Amy and turned back to the telephone, uttering apologies to whoever was on the line. She waved at Adam, who gulped down his coffee which, though instant, was excellent, and as he left another of the telephones began to ring. Business was hotting up.

Adam filled in the interval by buying wellington boots, some casual shirts, a thick sweater and a pair of corduroy trousers. He had his dark suit for formal occasions, but he needed something warmer than jeans for casual daily life in Bishop St Leon in the winter. There were two men's outfitter's in the town; one, an old established firm, had everything he wanted. He wondered if Roger had bought his ginger-brown tweed suit there; it was a curious outfit, the sort that he associated with gentlemen of the turf rather than plain-clothes policemen, but it was a perfect disguise; no one, seeing Roger wearing it, would guess his occupation.

He wasn't sure why he had suggested lunch to Amy. He had been horrified by Susan's bruises, and Amy had seemed so worried, that he had acted on impulse. It was significant that when Amy warned that 'he' might be in the Grapes, neither of them had mentioned Martin's name.

He put his purchases in the Toyota and walked back to the town hall, wondering where would be a good place for lunch. Amy might have a suggestion; he guessed she would not want to be out of the office long. There were a few cafés and restaurants in the town. Waiting for her, he stood in the lee of the Victorian building that was still the town hall; did they have council meetings inside its sober premises? Was much administration done locally, or did it come from the county town? How had it changed and developed in past decades?

His musings ended when Amy came into view, walking briskly along from the office which was at the further end of the High Street. She saw him and waved, walking faster. She wore a scarlet coat, warm against the strong wind which was still blowing, and a fluffy black hat. She was older than Linda and Jo, who must be in their early twenties; Amy might be thirty.

'There's no fear of Sue seeing us,' she said. 'She's having sandwiches in the office. Doesn't want to be seen anywhere. We take staggered lunch-hours and often I have sandwiches, but sometimes I come out.' Often, too, she was with a client at this time of day.

'Where shall we go?' said Adam. 'I'm afraid I haven't had time to discover the best places.'

'There'll be a nice fire in the Country Nook,' said Amy. 'It sounds twee, but it isn't, and quite a few guys go there who aren't off to pubs and such. It's just round this corner.'

She led him down a side street to a timbered building with a bow window, set between a solicitor's office and a hairdresser's. The whole row was old, and many of the shop fronts had been restored as closely as was possible to their original appearance. The Country Nook was warm; as promised, there was a fire at one end.

'Only gas, but very comforting,' said Amy, leading the way to a table in the corner where there was a reserved sign. 'I rang up,' she confessed. 'I knew you wouldn't know where to suggest we went. They know me here,' she added, unnecessarily, for a young man wearing an apron had hailed her as she entered, and an older woman gave her a smile.

Adam realised that in this small country town people really did know each other; some of them might have lived here all their lives. He helped Amy take off her bright coat, and the young man took it and Adam's wind-proof jacket, removing them to a rack near the entrance.

There were several hot dishes on the day's menu; Amy didn't dither, saying that she would have fish pie and then she needn't bother this evening. She and Linda were going to the cinema. Adam felt like asking if he could come too. Instead, he said he'd have the same; they promised themselves blackberry and apple crumble afterwards. The Country Nook was licensed, but Amy said she wanted only water; Adam asked for lager. The young man took their order, and Amy told him this was Tony, son of the owner, a widow.

'So not all the sons of widows turn into bullies,' she said. 'Tony's going to train as a chef. He's done a catering course already.'

'You think Susan Trent's injuries were caused by Martin, do you?' Adam decided to tackle the subject directly.

'It's slanderous to say so, I suppose,' she answered, 'but yes, I do. He's just come back from a trip – he's a travel courier – and while he was away, she was so much calmer and happier. He's only been back a few days and look at her. I can't think why she doesn't chuck him out. He's living off her, a middle-aged man. It's disgusting.' Amy's face was pink with indignation.

'Jo said last night that the father just went off,' Adam prompted.

'Yes. When Martin was very young,' said Amy. 'There's an older sister – Patricia – Pat, Brian calls her. She lives in America. Brian – my boss – has known them for years. Susan taught him at primary school.'

'Where did he go? The father?' Adam asked. New Zealand had been suggested.

'No one knows – except there was a postcard from Australia or somewhere. No, New Zealand – that was it. He beat her up, too, it was said. So it was good riddance, really. But she's had a tough time. Being a single mother then was far harder than it is now. In those days, unless you were respectably a widow, you could be a social out-cast.'

Their order arrived, steaming individual pies in small pots, with crispy brown potato on the top. There was a pause in the conversation while they helped themselves to mixed vegetables from the large dish which Tony set in front of them.

'Looks good,' said Adam.

'It'll taste good,' Amy said.

The pie was delicious.

'So the message is, like father, like son?' Adam returned to the ostensible reason for their meeting.

'It doesn't have to be,' said Amy. 'After all, Susan's genes are in him too. But she must have lost heart while her husband bashed her up, and I suppose she wasn't firm enough with Martin. I think he was all right as a little boy. I don't really know, but Brian has talked about it a bit, recently. She broke her arm, you see – that was some time ago – said she fell over. If she's telling the truth, she's always falling over, but she hasn't in the office – not since I've been there.'

'How long's that?'

'Two years. Susan's been there since the beginning. She was Brian's only assistant, when he started the business. He won't let her go unless she wants to leave. Or unless—' Amy didn't want to say it aloud, but Adam nodded.

'Circumstances dictate,' he said. 'If she orders Martin to leave, I suppose he'd refuse to go.'

'I don't think she'd order him to leave, because he's her son, you see.'

'Yes, but he should be looking after her, not treating her like this.'

Adam was forgetting to eat his fish pie. He turned his attention back to it. When he came to Bishop St Leon to look for Susan Trent, though he hadn't known what to expect, he hadn't anticipated this situation.

'I agree, of course,' said Amy. 'But I don't see what we can do about it.'

'Someone who knows her well, like this Brian, your boss, could talk to her, surely? What's her legal position? If it's her house, couldn't she get an injunction to keep him out?'

'No one quite likes to interfere. It's her business, after all.'

'"Am I my brother's keeper?"' said Adam, and when Amy looked bewildered, went on, 'Never mind. But it is someone's business, if she's in danger. Not especially yours, though, unless she decides to tell you about it.'

'She won't. She might tell someone nearer her own age, if it got too much,' said Amy. 'But it's too much already, isn't it? You think so.'

'I think it is, but I'm new to it – a stranger,' Adam said. 'I can be objective.' But that wasn't strictly true. 'Anyway, at least I know about it, which is something, seeing that I expect I'll be in the Crown quite often, and Martin Trent might be there, too.' Then he went on, 'Did you rent out Roger Morris's rooms, or did he fix that up privately?'

'We didn't do it. Yours was a special, because of Jeremy wanting to leave and Nigel – my colleague – knowing him. We said we'd head enquirers that way. It's mostly done by adverts in the paper.'

'Well, Roger is a police officer. He's noticed Martin's behaviour.'

'And he was the one who saw Martin off last night?'

'Yes.'

'Linda said. The man from the train. And you were the other one, the quiet one she barely noticed.'

'Thanks,' said Adam ruefully.

'Well, you didn't take much heed of her, did you, but you recognised each other last night,' said Amy.

'I don't know about not noticing her. I could tell you what she was reading,' Adam said defensively. 'Well, not the title, but it was by someone called Maeve Binchy.'

'I know, and she's finished it and now I'm reading it,' said Amy, gathering the final morsel of her fish pie on to her fork. 'Strange you met again, after being on the train, isn't it? And this Roger. You might never have known any more about one another.'

'That's true,' said Adam. And I might not have had lunch with you, either, he thought, but did not say. She had a deep dimple in one cheek; it showed when she smiled.

'And you and Linda might have gone on thinking what

a rude, unpleasant person Roger was, if you hadn't seen him putting Martin down last night.'

Adam knew that Roger could still be rude and unpleasant.

'Everyone has their good points,' he said.

'Do you believe that? Even people like Hitler?'

'Even them,' said Adam, unable, however, in the face of this challenge, to think of any redeeming feature attributable to that man.

They spent a little while, over their blackberry and apple, thinking of hate figures and trying to recall what softer sides were known about them. This led to laughter. Both were sorry when Amy looked at her watch and said she must fly. She wanted to pay her share of the lunch but Adam wouldn't let her.

She almost said, 'My turn next time,' but didn't. She mustn't assume that there would be a next time, and anyway, she had a regular boyfriend who at present was serving his country in Bosnia.

She sped off, and Adam paid the bill. He saw that there was a more elaborate dinner menu, and wondered if Tony took over the cooking then. It was a good place. Had Chris and Melanie tried it? He must ask.

13

Back in his room in Bishop St Leon, Adam switched on his computer and looked at the information which had brought him here. He had stored the scanty material away, dates and names, what he had learned in London, not much. Now he had more to add, but very little. The disappearance of Susan Trent's husband had not been featured in the press; he had never been reported as a missing person, and eventually he had written from New Zealand.

There must be people still living in the village who had known Norman Trent. Susan was in her sixties – Adam knew that before he set out on his mission – so Norman was probably much the same age, maybe in his early seventies. He needed to find senior residents who would remember the Trents as a young couple with small children, perhaps even their arrival in the village. His plan had been to try to find Susan Trent if, as he expected, she had moved. Des, in the Crown, was a comparative newcomer; frequent career moves meant shifting population and these days few people spent their whole lives in one area, but some did. Where could he start?

He could begin with Linda. He could ask her about former owners of Field House; if she did not know much about them, her employers might. Or Jo's parents; he had learned last night that they had farmed in the area for generations. With this thought, he looked out of the window at the Old Chapel, but Jo's car wasn't there. Maybe she was still visiting Linda. He could go and see, and if he met an aged local, he could strike up a conversation and try to extract some information. He wanted to know if there had been much talk when Norman left, suggestions of his having gone off with a woman, even rumours about Susan. But she had gone nowhere, nor had she remarried. He had not been able to find any record of a divorce, but, searching, he had guessed at dates.

It was still very windy; as he left the house, a gust caught him, and, glad of his jacket's warm lining, he turned up its collar. He walked along North Street, down to Field House. The red car was where he had seen it this morning; the other car, a Fiat, was not there. Were the two girls out somewhere in the Fiat? It seemed a reasonable deduction. Adam loitered. Surely the children had to come home for their tea? Or were the nannies visiting a third nanny somewhere else?

In fact, they were, but the third nanny had to collect

an older child from school, and when she left to do so, Jo and Linda returned to Field House. It was dusk now, and the car's lights were on; it overtook Adam, who, at its approach, in case it was their car, had turned to walk their way. He hoped they would think he was in mid-tramp, not hanging about looking for them.

They saw him. He followed the car through the gates of Field House and in no time at all was sitting in the kitchen having tea with them and their small charges.

Honesty was the best policy. He told Linda that he had had lunch with Amy.

'We talked about Martin Trent. Susan Trent was in the office and she looked as if she'd been in a fight,' he said. 'Do you ever see her, Linda? She lives next door, at Cedar Cottage.'

'Not really, because she works in the week and I'm not here at weekends, unless Edward and Hannah are away, which isn't often – not both of them, anyway.'

'I wondered why she stayed here, after her husband left,' said Adam.

'Why leave?' said Jo. 'She'd got friends here. Though she didn't socialise much, except parties for the children when they were little, my Dad said. He went to them.'

'Who lived here then?' Adam asked. 'At Field House?'

'It was the doctor's house at one time. They had the surgery here,' said Linda. Hannah had gleaned the house's history from the deeds and had told her this. 'His old brass plate is still in an outhouse among a lot of clutter which has to be sorted when Edward gets around to it.'

'What was the doctor's name?'

'I couldn't tell you,' Linda said. 'But the plate's still there. Hannah and Edward are going to get a skip. There's masses of junk to throw away. The previous owners never got around to it, and I don't think the ones before had done it, either. They just added their own rubbish.'

'Could I see it some time?' Adam asked, keeping his voice very casual. 'The plate, I mean.'

'You can see it now, if you like,' said Linda. 'Jo will keep an eye on Georgie and Henry, won't you, Jo? I'll get a torch.'

She did not bother with a jacket, leading the way out of the back door and round the side of the house to a row of what must once have been stables, part of which now formed a double garage. Attached at the side was another building in which there were old trunks, an aged pram, and other clutter.

'Edward and Hannah moved here just before Henry was born and they haven't had time to sort this. The house was in good shape and didn't need much done, though they're having a new kitchen later,' she said.

Adam hadn't seen much wrong with the old kitchen.

'Oh,' he said, inadequately.

'Why do you want to see the plate?' Linda asked.

'I collect old brass plates,' Adam said, the best excuse he could come up with, for this was a reasonable question. 'If it looks interesting, maybe I could buy it.'

'What a strange hobby,' Linda said. 'I should think Edward would be glad to get rid of it for nothing.' She opened the door to the outhouse, a brick building attached to the side of the garage. It was solidly built, the door secured by a latch and a strong bolt. 'This place should be locked before Henry starts walking. Georgie hasn't got round to doing much exploring so far, and it's too cold now for them to play for long outside. But I'd better mention it. You can't be too careful. I don't let them out of my sight.'

'They're out of it now,' Adam pointed out.

'They're safe with Jo.'

'Of course they are. Sorry. I was being pedantic,' Adam said.

The shed smelled musty. Linda fumbled for a light switch beside the door. Inside, there were old crates and boxes, some rusted sheets of corrugated iron, an old tennis net and its wooden posts, a mildewed cabin trunk and several boxes full of books.

'It's in here,' said Linda, opening a wooden box with metal corners. 'It's an old tuck box. The doctor's child's, I suppose. Cleaned up, it could be useful as a toy box or for tools.'

The initials painted on the box were impossible to read

because it was so grimy, but inside, not wrapped up in any way, just dumped among some old diaries and a photograph album, was the plate, very tarnished now, the legend worn but legible.

Martin had gone to Debbie's house on Monday afternoon.

When he returned from the Crown on Sunday night, Cedar Cottage had been in darkness, apart from the porch light left on for him. Susan shouldn't have provoked him. No wonder his father had lost his temper with her; that he did so was folklore in Bishop St Leon, though not spoken of now in his hearing. He avoided people who had known his father. Jo's parents were only a little older than Martin but they had heard about it. Gossip: Martin preferred to believe that that was all it was; he could remember nothing about those early years. Memory, for him, began with walking up the road to school with his sister, and discovering that he was cleverer than she was. Susan had been proud of him then.

He did not examine why this had changed. He'd been dogged by ill luck; that was all. It wasn't fair.

He had hit her really hard yesterday. She'd show marks today, but she bruised easily and he knew she would pretend that she had walked into a door or fallen over yet again. Clumsy cow. Anyone who saw her, like her colleagues in Marsh's, would think the same – that stuck-up Amy, and Nigel with his poncy ways. Martin knew all about him; indeed he did. One day she might have a heart attack, she got so scared. He liked seeing her afraid. He'd liked that with his wife, too, only she didn't frighten so easily and she had hit him back.

How would Debbie react if he hit her?

She'd cry, and apologise for whatever had upset him. He could try it some time, as an experiment. But she was not rebellious; Debbie was soft and gentle, needing his protection and advice; he felt good when he was with her. The problem was the children, because they were what came first with her. He knew that. He'd understood her being upset about the chicken, with Lily seeming to be critical because Debbie's cooking wasn't as good as Kate's. Of course poor Debs was jealous. Lily hadn't meant to be unkind; she was just thoughtless.

He might go round and see if she had calmed down. He'd nothing else to do today. If she wasn't in, he'd buy the paper and take it to the Grapes to read. And he'd go to the library to consult *The Times Educational Supplement* and other publications which might have job advertisements for which he could apply.

Martin set off to catch the bus. They ran infrequently between Bishop St Leon and Rotherston, and he'd missed the mid-morning one. He stood by the stop, ignominiously gesturing with his thumb at passing vehicles, hoping for a lift: a short man with a florid face, wearing an anorak, his unprotected head exposed to the strong east wind.

Eventually, his ears aching with the cold, he pulled a base-ball cap from his pocket and put it on. Someone must stop for him.

But they didn't. Car after car went past, and in the end he called a taxi from the telephone box outside the post office.

Debbie was out when the taxi dropped him at her house. He supposed she was at the supermarket. If it weren't for her kids, he might move in permanently. That would get him away from his miserable mother. He'd once suggested it to Debbie, but she had told him, tearfully, that if he did, her maintenance from Jim would be affected and she couldn't risk it. Remarriage would offer her security, she had said, hastily adding that her divorce was not yet through so she couldn't think of it just now, and she knew that he had other responsibilities. She didn't mention his uncertain career; she meant that he had to support his mother. Martin had concealed the true facts from her.

Frustrated and cold, Martin set off into town. At the Grapes, he could rely on warmth and company. Among those at the bar would be strangers, passing trade, whom he could engage in conversation. You met interesting people in this way, and he had tales of his own to tell.

On the way to the Grapes, he made a detour to the library, but his brief positive action in consulting *The Times*

Educational Supplement was foiled because, as it was Monday, the library was closed.

How was one supposed to manage when vital public services failed to function? Martin, once again frustrated, turned away and walked up to the newsagent's where he bought a copy of the paper. He took it to the Grapes, settled in a corner of the bar, and started to consult its pages. While he was there, the playgroup which Rose attended telephoned Debbie at the supermarket saying that Rose seemed lethargic and unwell; she was due to be collected soon in any case, but they thought that Debbie should come for her as soon as possible, and if she couldn't get there quickly, they would call an ambulance. The principal of what was an excellent playgroup was thinking in terms of meningitis, that terrifying enemy of little children, but Debbie, hurrying to tell her supervisor that she had to leave at once, was remembering Rose's tumble.

Roger had spent a boring morning doing paperwork in his office. Needing a distraction, he asked a constable to run a check on a vehicle licence number – that of Adam's Toyota. Quite quickly she came back with the information that it was registered to a car hire firm based at Heathrow airport.

He ran a check on Adam then. Nothing, however, was recorded about his past.

*   *   *

Adam, unaware of Roger's interest in his history, had spent the day in Oxford. He had not been there for years. The day was wet and windy, and he was glad to duck in and out of buildings.

Parking had not been easy. In the end he had found a space in a residential street to the north of the city and had walked into the centre. The colleges were closed to visitors, but he went into the cathedral and wandered around there for a while, then walked across the meadows to the river. The rain lifted as a crew rowed past. Your golden years, he thought, but were they? For some, perhaps.

He had come to Bishop St Leon with only a sketchy plan, a need to find out about the past, to learn why his father had suddenly left the village and had never set foot again in England. Adam's father and mother had parted when he was six. His mother had remarried; his step-father, a kindly but remote man, was a diplomat who was posted to new appointments every few years. During that time Adam had seen very little of his father, and after his mother's death in a road accident when he was thirteen, he had been sent to school in Switzerland. Later, he went to Harvard, and subsequently became a company lawyer. Busy with his own career, Adam had not seen his father for several years and had been unaware of his failing health – he had had heart surgery – until he was summoned urgently. Adam had arrived in New Zealand to find him in a final coma, and, sorting through the papers he had left – there was no one else to do it, no other family – he had come upon three postcards, all addressed to Mrs S. Trent, Cedar Cottage, Bishop St Leon. They bore trite messages about the weather and hoped she and the children were in good health. They were undated, and none had been stamped. Why were they never sent? It was a mystery.

There were other papers, too.

Jim got Debbie's message on his mobile telephone in Italy, where he was covering a conference. He had flown out the previous afternoon.

She told him, in cold, calm tones, that she was ringing from the hospital. Rose had had a fall the previous night, tumbling down the stairs, and had seemed perfectly all right afterwards, but today had become drowsy and unwell and was in hospital, where the result of tests would be through soon. Now, more aware of what might be the situation, she uttered the dread word meningitis.

Jim felt a sick shock of dread; then professionalism took over. However fast he moved, he could not get to her for hours; Debbie was to call him back as soon as there was any news and meanwhile he would make arrangements to catch the first available flight. Somehow a substitute for himself must be found; there might be a local technician who could be employed, at least until another could be flown out. Debbie wouldn't be on her own; that fellow, Martin, would be with her. But Rose was his child; he was the one who should be there. What if she were to die? If it was meningitis, she could be dead before he arrived. As he made plans, Jim's anxiety was beset by other thoughts, including pangs of guilt, which he endeavoured to repress.

Rose had not got meningitis, nor a fractured skull; the diagnosis was mild concussion after her fall, and as vacant beds were scarce in the hospital, she was sent home, to be kept quiet for the next few days. Another mother had taken Lily back with her from the playgroup, while Debbie went in the ambulance with Rose; now they were marooned in the hospital without transport. Why wasn't Jim there to help? Debbie telephoned him on his mobile again, and caught him at the airport.

Her main purpose in ringing him was to berate him for his absence, not to reassure him, but when she heard his voice calmly asking her if it was meningitis, Debbie told him that it wasn't, and that she was taking Rose home. Jim felt a huge surge of relief; she did not know that he was about to board the aircraft as he told her that this meant he need not return; he'd be back anyway when the conference ended three days later.

He could return to work; he'd lost very little time.

He'd rung off. Debbie stared at the dead instrument of the hospital public telephone. How could he cut her off at such a time? The money hadn't run out. She thought of calling him again but what was the point? He didn't care that Rose had almost died. Her imagination ran away with her as she stood there, slowly taking in her situation and wondering how to get home.

Martin would have come for them, only he'd lost his licence. He'd had to tell her that to explain why he wasn't driving, trying to win her sympathy by complaining that he'd had too much to drink because he'd had an argument with his mother. Debbie had formed an impression of a demon witch almost equipped with a cauldron of spells brewing in a corner of her cottage and a broomstick parked beside the hearth. Poor Martin, cruelly misunderstood.

She would have to get a taxi. Debbie had just reached this conclusion when Yvonne, the mother who had taken Lily home, came walking across the corridor towards her. She was alone, and for a moment Debbie thought something must have happened to Lily now, but Yvonne grasped her by the arms and asked her about Rose.

Debbie promptly burst into tears, so that the other woman feared the worst, and it was some time before she learned the reassuring truth.

'And now we can't get home,' wailed Debbie.

'Of course you can, silly. I'm here, aren't I? I can take you,' said Yvonne.

Later, she told her husband that it was like having

another child in her temporary care as she brought Debbie and Rose back, collected Lily, ran all three home and stayed with them until Rose was in bed. By this time her husband was home from work himself and had collected their children from a neighbour's where Yvonne had left them and Lily while she went to the hospital.

'She needs another husband,' Yvonne said. She knew there was a boyfriend, a shadowy figure who was absent this evening, just when he was needed.

'Sounds as if she needs a nanny. For herself, not the children,' said Yvonne's husband unsympathetically.

'She's been badly hurt,' Yvonne reminded him. 'She adored Jim. Probably still does.'

They had liked him, too. They'd met when the parents got together to organise a fund-raising sale for the play-group.

'They weren't a couple, more a pair,' said her husband enigmatically. 'Ill matched, I always thought. But she's very pretty. Or she was,' he added. For in her abandoned state, Debbie had lost some of her prettiness, exchanging it for a wounded, woebegone air. 'Some men might find that waif-like look appealing,' he went on reflectively, not sure whether he did, himself. 'Is she really all right now?'

'As all right as she can be, under the circumstances,' said Yvonne.

'Hasn't she got a mother? Mothers come at such times.'

'No,' said Yvonne flatly. 'Her mother's dead. Hence, perhaps, rushing into marriage.'

'Well, you've done your bit. She'll ring you if she has another crisis, won't she?'

'I told her to,' Yvonne admitted. 'She doesn't seem to have a network of friends.' Most women had, in her experience, though they could have been drawn together through circumstances, not necessarily mutual liking; you were friends with the parents of your children's friends. If Debbie had been part of such a ring, she might have stood up better to Jim's absences; on the other hand, there were women who could have regarded her as a problem, someone who might need the help of husbands or partners, a fragile person who could pose a threat. 'Maybe the boyfriend will go round there later,' she added.

Having done her bit, Yvonne directed her attention to the needs of her own family.

While Debbie was at the hospital, Martin had left the Grapes and returned to her house, to find it deserted. There was no note left to tell him where she had gone. Surely she expected him to come round today? How inconsiderate of her.

He inspected her fridge and found the remains of the chicken. It looked unappetising; otherwise he might have eaten it. Instead, he decided to go back to Bishop St Leon and let his mother cook for him; then he could go up to the Crown and in the morning he would follow up some job advertisements he had marked. He'd get his career back on track, he resolved. Before he left Debbie's house, he contemplated leaving her a curt, reproving note, but decided not to; she needed to be taught a lesson, but he'd make it one of silence.

His mother could give him a lift home; it would save the taxi fare. But perhaps not; belatedly he recalled the events of the previous evening and the fact that even before that, she had bruises on her face. He might visit another pub in Rotherston, not the Grapes, before he went home; the Angel was a friendly place with a young clientele; he'd try it.

That night, it rained heavily and in the early hours, when it stopped, the wind got up. Susan had been woken when Martin came in at around midnight; she heard the taxi in the road outside, its engine idling interminably, as it seemed to her; Martin would be looking for money to pay the driver.

At last she heard the door bang, and the taxi drove away.

14

Susan's bruises faded.

Martin avoided her in the days following his most recent attack. Returning from the Angel on Monday night, and without enough money for the driver, he had raided a drawer in the kitchen where she kept some cash to deal with charity collections at the door and other irregular demands; latterly, she had taken to making sure, while Martin was at home, that there was enough in it to meet a taxi fare he might require. She topped it up from time to time; it was better than being roused in the night with a demand for funds, or leaving her handbag downstairs for him to rifle. Both had happened.

On Tuesday, she had gone to a solicitor in Rotherston to ask about her legal position concerning Martin: could she force him to leave her house?

The solicitor, Caroline Barker, looked at her yellowing bruises and expressed controlled dismay. She had seen worse, though never inflicted by a son upon his mother.

'But can you prove your son injured you?' she asked. 'If he denies it, and says you fell, it's his word against yours.'

She explained that Susan could not take out an injunction against Martin unless the police were involved and his violence could be proved. Eviction was the alternative, and unless he left voluntarily, it would be difficult. The law would say that Cedar Cottage was his home because he had lived there for years, more or less since the break-up of his marriage, establishing a right of residence. Were he to attack her again, however, and she called the police, and if they charged him, the case for an injunction would be strong.

She had established the fact that Susan worked for Brian Marsh and her colleagues had seen her bruised face. She had also learned that each time Martin hit her, Susan had pretended she had fallen.

'So they can't confirm your allegations,' said the solicitor. 'If it happens again, my advice is that you call the police.' She had suggested that Susan should try, during a moment when Martin seemed to be sober, to talk things over with him and attempt to reach an acceptable solution, but Susan replied that she had tried, more than once, and he had flown into a rage, demanding to know where else he should live but with his mother, and who else would look after her when she was too old to look after herself?

There was not the slightest possibility that he would ever do it. He would commit her to a home at the first chance he got.

Both women felt frustrated when they parted, Susan because there seemed to be nothing she could do, and the solicitor because she was powerless to help her client. It was like a case of wife-battering; the victim blamed herself and became less and less able to resist or to change her situation. But Susan was not financially dependent on her son; indeed, even when he was working, the reverse seemed to be the case. And how could she call the police while she was warding off Martin's blows? Outside intervention was required. Caroline had asked if her neighbours were aware of what went on, and Susan admitted that Bill and Mary Church had their suspicions.

Caroline was acquainted with Mary, who taught her children; in this small town, many people knew one another; client confidentiality, however, would prevent Caroline from discussing Susan's problems with her.

Years ago, after a particularly savage outburst, Norman used to bring Susan a bunch of flowers and express penitence, saying it wouldn't happen again. There would be a brief, sometimes ecstatic, period of reconciliation, and then it would all start once more. She believed that Martin, also, felt ashamed, but he could not bring himself to apologise. The best that he could manage was a period of comparative calm, and now there was such a spell of peace, during which he made a number of telephone calls and wrote several letters. Susan kept out of his way; they had no meals together as he left the house each evening, but because he came home after closing time, she feared his new romance had failed. Perhaps he would answer one of the advertisements he circled in the paper and acquire a new interest. Or perhaps a job would surface. Meanwhile she made the most of the period of calm. It would not last.

When she was out, Martin was content enough at home; he got up after she left the house, went up the village for the paper, came back and read it, had some lunch and a beer or two – he made sure there was always a good supply in the house – and spent time at his computer making notes, drafting sentences that pleased him, whether or not they bore any relevance to any of the projects he maintained that he was working on, and he logged on to the internet, starting by looking for work and ending up chasing rainbows while Susan's telephone bill mounted. A good idea would be to join a chatline, he decided. That might be entertaining and productive.

On Thursday afternoon he went round to Debbie's. He'd punished her with silence long enough.

Since the weekend, Roger had been busy. Among other incidents, varying in their seriousness, his team was investigating a series of armed robberies, attacks on small shops and post offices in the region, where the staff were held up at gunpoint and ordered to hand over all the money on the premises. The pattern was that two men, in combat gear and wearing animal masks, entered the shop while an accomplice stayed in a car, stolen earlier, that was parked outside. On Monday afternoon, a customer in a village shop where there was also a post office, present during the raid, set off in pursuit of the robbers as they fled with their takings. Before they reached the waiting car, he clutched one of them, grabbing him by the arm. The other robber turned and fired his sawn-off shotgun at the man, who staggered back, wounded in the shoulder. Fortunately, his life was not in danger.

The robbery had taken place near Chris's workshop, and that neighbourhood was agog with talk about the incident. He and Adam were discussing it at breakfast the next day, by which time rumour was rife about how much had been stolen and the extent of the hero's injuries. Roger had come in very late the night before; likely suspects were being interviewed about their activities at the time of the robbery, and filed records were being consulted. The same gang were probably responsible for five similar robberies carried out in the past eighteen months; their *modus operandi* involved at least two stolen cars, one used at the scene and abandoned a mile or so away, where another had been waiting. The robberies all took place within a twenty-mile radius of Reading.

Local radio reports had given these details.

'You don't have to be Sherlock Holmes to deduce that

the thieves must live in Reading,' Chris surmised, over his toast and coffee. 'Do you agree, Roger?'

'It's a theory,' Roger said. He was first down and had cooked himself a fry-up, which he was now tucking into heartily.

Adam was rather envious of his feast, wishing he had fried himself some bacon.

'Brave chap, that guy who chased them,' he remarked.

'Could have been killed,' said Roger.

'True. But we can't all just stand around and let the villains have their way,' said Chris.

'The only thing necessary for the triumph of evil is for good men to do nothing,' said Adam, adding, as both the others stared at him, 'Or words to that effect, as Burke said.'

Roger was not one to philosophise.

'It should be left to the police,' he said. It was up to him to utter the official line.

'Whosoever shall save his life shall lose it,' Adam said, to his plate. 'One's life isn't worth a lot if one's a coward, is it?'

'We don't encourage heroics,' Roger declared, stoically. He had an idea Adam was quoting from the Bible.

'Will you get these guys?' asked Chris.

'I hope so. We were quickly on the scene – the alarm went and someone called on their mobile phone, describing the getaway car, even giving part of its registration number, but they dumped it very quickly.'

'And they wore those masks,' said Chris. 'A tiger and a leopard.'

That hadn't been in the paper or repeated on the news, just that the robbers were masked, but Chris had heard it locally.

'You might catch them with the masks in their possession,' Adam suggested. 'That would be good, wouldn't it? Proof positive.'

'Yes,' said Roger, getting up to go. 'But we should be so lucky.'

He bundled up his crockery and cutlery, taking them to the sink.

'Leave them, Roger,' Adam said. 'I'll see to them. I'm not going anywhere very early. I'll do yours, too, Chris,' he added, as the other man also rose.

'You're quite a little mother, aren't you?' Roger said, but not maliciously. He left without waiting for an answer.

'Roger's getting almost human,' Chris declared. 'He nearly smiled.'

'He'd be a good bloke to have around if you were in a tight corner,' Adam said.

Roger, driving off, pondered briefly on Adam's remarks about good and evil, life and death. He was a strange chap. Whatever research he was doing didn't seem urgent or demanding. Why had he hired a car? There could be plenty of innocent explanations – his own had been in an accident, he was waiting for a new one, he found it economical. Plenty of companies hired cars for their staff, but not from self-drive car hire firms. So far, Roger had resisted a prying visit into Adam's room; a man was entitled to his privacy unless he broke the law, and there were no signs of that in Adam. If he were a fraudster or was planning a major scam, he would hardly be renting a room in a house shared with a police officer. Besides, the comments he had made about the courageous witness to the armed robbery, if weird, were very much on the side of virtue.

Roger put the mystery out of his mind while he returned to the business of the robbery. The next steps in the investigation would be routine, but it was to be hoped that they would produce information of some sort, or that further witnesses would surface. Someone might have seen the cars used by the thieves in the period between their being stolen and the robbery. The injured man would be interviewed in hospital; he might remember more about the robbers than he had been able to reveal immediately after the incident.

Roger was glad to have some active policing to do. These were real villains; so were fraudsters, but they were rarely violent. The shot fired at the brave bystander could have killed him; as it was, there could be a charge of attempted murder. He went into his office with his energy renewed, forgetting Adam, eager to inspire his team to fresh efforts.

*　　*　　*

Adam went out on foot on Thursday afternoon. The nannies had been at The Old Chapel this afternoon. He'd seen Linda's Fiat parked outside and several children had been playing in the garden. He'd heard their raised voices when he went out earlier. He'd been working in his room, and he'd gone to Rotherston to collect mail which was being sent to him at the post office. He didn't want letters addressed to someone with another name arriving at the house. Most of his communications could be carried out by computer links and e-mail, but there were some things that could not be managed in this way. Having dealt with his letters, he set off to the post office to buy stamps and post them, and then continued round the village. It was a bleak, grey day; the wind that had been blowing all the morning had dropped. Suddenly the air was very still. Adam had experienced this phenomenon before. He was nearing Field House when there was suddenly a swirling sound and all the trees within sight, in the various gardens and bordering the road, began to sigh and bend as a mighty gust of wind blew towards him.

It lasted for several minutes. Adam stood close against the boundary wall until it had passed. He could see the tall willow in the Field House garden bending and swaying; bare lacy branches of other trees tossed to and fro, like wild dervishes.

Then it was over: a tiny tornado or miniature hurricane. Adam walked on through what was now a normal minor gale, and then the rain came.

Soaked, he was glad to get home. The nannies' cars were still outside The Old Chapel.

Martin was in Debbie's house when the storm struck, but Rotherston was on the fringe of it and the impact was much less.

She'd been out again when he arrived but as it had begun to rain, he let himself in and made himself at home. It was pleasant here, more so than in Cedar Cottage where his mother's furnishings were of the old-fashioned chintzy sort, though he conceded that she had some nice antique pieces. Debbie and Jim, with a sizeable mortgage, him freelancing and funds uncertain, had gone in more for modern warehouse stuff but Martin liked the clean lines and plain colours. The large sofa was extremely comfortable. He spread himself over it and put on the television. In a moment of insight, he realised that his intellect was shrinking; nowadays, he never read anything challenging, nor wrote more than stark reports about the tours he led. And at the moment there was no prospect of another, not for months. It was too soon for unfavourable reports, if any, about the Venice trip to have consequences, but in sober moments Martin knew there had been complaints from clients on other journeys.

They were just sour whinges from stupid sods who would moan about anything, but even so, they could wreck his prospects.

He'd brought some beer.

Debbie and Rose had gone to collect Lily from Yvonne's, where she was at a party. Balloons were hung around the gatepost, and in the house, twenty small children had had an early lunch and were now playing in the self-contained way of those who have not yet learned to interact. Oliver, Yvonne's son, was three today, and he was enjoying driving around in his new pedal car; he was not pleased when forced to surrender it to other children so that they could take turns.

Debbie had considered that Rose, although much better, still needed to be kept quiet and had not let her go to the party, but Lily was quite happy to be there on her own. The party was to end at around two-thirty before older siblings who were at school had to be fetched. Debbie and Rose stayed while the other guests old enough to be there on their own – which was most of them – were collected. Yvonne gave the mothers cups of coffee. She was so well organised, thought Debbie enviously. They went home at last, Lily flushed and excited, both children clutching a bag of sweets and a balloon.

As soon as she opened her own front door, Debbie

realised that someone was in the house and for one wild moment she thought it might be Jim, who still had a key, but it was Martin.

She had not seen him since the scene on Sunday when she had left the table so abruptly, and the day had ended with Rose's tumble.

'Well, have you missed me?' he demanded, all smiles, looking up as they came trooping into the sitting room.

'Look at my balloon, Martin,' said Rose, approaching him, and, benevolent, he took her on his knee, but Lily hung back. Something bad had happened the last time he was in the house and she wasn't sure quite what it was; she thought it was her fault, but somehow it was linked with Martin, and, as he stretched out an arm for her, she smelled his breath: part of the smell she didn't like. Reluctantly, she let herself be enfolded, and Martin made much of the children, ignoring Debbie, who dithered on the fringe of this domestic group, wanting to take the children's outdoor clothing off. Both wore little snowsuits, zipped up the front.

Martin began undoing Rose's zip, and at that point the doorbell rang. Without waiting for it to be opened – he had used the ring as a preliminary warning – Jim marched in. What he saw in the sitting room was the man he knew to be Debbie's boyfriend, unzipping the suit which encased his younger daughter, about to extract her from within its folds.

On the way there, Jim had been imagining dire things.

He had telephoned Debbie to say that, now back from Italy, he was coming over to see how Rose was, but there had been no reply all day and he had begun to panic that she was ill again. He had last spoken to Debbie on Tuesday night, when she had said that Rose was all right and there was no need to worry; as a result of this, he had not rung again until today.

'Put my daughter down, you – you—' he was about to call Martin a pervert, but as the children saw him, Lily scrambled off the sofa, going towards him, and Rose began to cry because she was pinioned half in and half out of her snowsuit and could not do the same.

Jim plucked Rose out of Martin's clutches and clasped her, while also grasping Lily.

'Get out of here,' he said to Martin, who stood up and snarled at him.

'How dare you speak to me like that?' he demanded, squaring up to Jim, clenching his fists.

'Jim, don't,' said Debbie. 'Martin's my friend.'

'He is, is he? Well, he can take his hands off my children, that's what he can do,' Jim said. 'Rose, are you all right?' and he began gently completing the removal of Rose's suit, while scrutinising her small features.

'Of course she is,' said Martin, still unaware of the dash to hospital and the scare.

'I'm sorry, Martin,' Debbie was saying. 'Jim doesn't understand.

'No, I bloody don't,' said Jim. 'I just know what I can

see. And smell.' He, like Lily, had caught the alcoholic fumes. 'A bloody drunk pawing my daughters.'

'There's no need to swear, Jim,' said Debbie, and she reached out to take Rose from him, fearing that at any moment the two men might start to fight.

'I'm not staying here to be insulted,' Martin said. Jim was younger than he, and bigger; a fight would be extremely ill-advised.

Jim handed Rose to Debbie.

'I'll help you on your way,' he said, looming over the other man. 'Get on with it.'

He took Martin by his jersey collar and marched him to the door, thrusting him through it and banging it behind him.

'My coat!' came a shout, and Jim, glancing round, saw a grubby anorak hanging over the banisters. He opened the door and flung it out after Martin, who let out a further yell.

'I'll sue you for assault,' he cried.

'Just you try it, and see how far it gets you,' Jim threatened, banging the door again.

All three females, Debbie, Rose and Lily, were now in tears.

15

It was dark when Susan arrived home that evening. The funnel of wind that had swirled so suddenly and fiercely through Bishop St Leon in the afternoon had missed Rotherston; by evening it was blowing steadily, and tales of gusts around the area had reached the office. It was said that someone's greenhouse had been shattered by a hurricane, and Susan was warned to watch out for fallen trees on her journey.

She met none, but as soon as she entered the house she knew that Martin was there. She could sense his presence, even though he was nowhere visible downstairs. He must be up in his room. Perhaps, she thought forlornly, he was working. Perhaps the book would take shape after all – perhaps it was, indeed, written and stored on secret disks, away from prying eyes like hers.

Should she call out to him, be friendly? It would be a

normal action, but her relations with Martin were anything but normal.

The safest thing to do was to pretend she thought he
was still out. There was no evidence in the shape of his
anorak or baseball cap hanging in the cloakroom or beside
the boiler in the kitchen. If he had been caught in the
rain and did not want to have his presence in the house
acknowledged, they would be draped over the radiator in
the bathroom.

She tiptoed about, pouring herself a glass of wine as
she unwrapped the shopping she had done on the way
home; the supermarket stayed open until half-past six
which was very convenient. She'd bought some chops and
fresh vegetables – broccoli and ready-washed imported
new potatoes. She hated sprouts, healthy harbingers of
winter, and resisted them. There were plenty of apples;
she'd picked them, helped by Owen, and they were stored
in boxes lined with newspaper in the garage. There was
enough food for two; she'd cook it, gather up her courage
when it was ready and call Martin down, then see what
he would do. He might storm past her to the pub. She
rather hoped he would; it would defer a confrontation.

Upstairs, Martin had heard her return. Soon she'd put the
radio on and that would be a barrier to stop him noticing
her presence.

Routed by Jim, he had walked through the driving rain

into the town where the bars were shut – even the Grapes closed in the afternoon – at first determined to go to the police and lodge a complaint. However, by the time he reached the main street, his false bravado had diminished and he saw that this might provoke a scandal. People were swift to believe the worst of you, especially where children were concerned, but how wicked to accuse him of abusing those little girls he had treated as his own. Why, he had given them their lunch on Sunday while their mother had hysterics. Where would she be without him to comfort her? That man, her husband, must feel very guilty, turning his own neglect and adultery into accusations against an innocent, caring individual. Soon Martin's wrath had metamorphosed into a fresh surge of self-pity at how gravely he was misunderstood. This time, however, he felt a tiny stab of fear. Jim could make a lot of trouble for him, simply by his accusations, blameless though Martin was. He was not a paedophile; was every man who helped his girlfriend with her children to be suspect in this way?

Needing sanctuary, Martin sought it where it was always to be found: in his mother's house. But not in her company. He took a taxi back, pausing on the way at the off-licence. Martin managed well for money; he contributed nothing to the upkeep either of himself or Cedar Cottage, or of any woman he was involved with, so that he lived free except for what he spent on drink, meals in pubs and rare occasions, such as when he had taken Debbie out on

Saturday. His income was extremely small, consisting of his fees as travel courier and any other jobs he managed to secure, which were very few, but an insurance policy he had started when he was working regularly had matured recently, so that he had some money in the bank and small monthly payments. Sometimes he signed on when out of work, but drawing unemployment benefit was no longer very easy; you had to be prepared to work at almost any job authority selected, despite being overqualified for most of them. When his mother left her handbag around, he helped himself from her purse; she didn't miss the odd ten or twenty pounds, and there was the emergency cash supply she kept in the kitchen. He could usually find funds, but whisky was very expensive and a bottle lasted such a short time; Martin frequently had to make do with beer, which gave you more volume for your money.

In the taxi, Martin's resentment against Jim and his accusations increased. He planned revenge: neglect of Debbie was the most obvious strategy but there might be other, devious ways in which he could attack Jim directly. He could devise a scheme for setting the little girls against their father; it should be easy for one of Martin's intelligence. Critical remarks about him, saying that as he had deserted them, he could not love them, blaming Debbie, would be effective; there were ingenious ways in which he could make things difficult for Jim, and for Debbie. She must take her share of the punishment.

Martin raided Susan's money cache to pay the taxi;

then he went upstairs, still in his rain-drenched jacket and his sodden baseball cap. He hung them in his bathroom. The cottage had two bathrooms; Susan had had the smallest bedroom turned into a large one for herself some years ago while he was working on a cruise liner. He remembered that now, and how he had come home to find the deed done. It suited him; he no longer had to put up with seeing her toothbrush, sponge and flannel every day. He hated to think of her ageing, flabby body and his own helpless, bloody emergence from it.

He'd liked that cruise. There was plenty to drink, and he'd had a brief fling with a desperate divorcée. That was a thought; he'd apply to the shipping lines again. A trip to the Caribbean would be delightful; he'd escape the British winter with its damp, penetrating cold, and the wind. A gale seemed to be blowing now; gusts had caught him as he walked from the taxi to the house and he could hear the wind sighing round the eaves. Sometimes when it blew hard it whistled past the house, catching at the trees, bending them, making the silver birches bow and curve, their long thin fronds and the willow's filaments writhing. He'd never liked that willow, hating it in summer when its branches made a green cavern in which his sister loved to hide.

He drew the curtains in his room and turned on his computer. He'd seek a chatline friend to talk to, someone from overseas whom one day he might meet, preferably an unhappy woman.

Quite a long time after he had heard and ignored his mother's return, she spoke from outside his door.

'Dinner's ready, Martin. Are you coming down?'

Her voice was steady, calm. He hated her composure; it challenged him.

He stood up, crossed to the door and opened it, standing glaring at her. She had often seen him angry and she had often felt afraid of him, but tonight there was something very fierce in his expression. His eyes were wild.

'I'll bring you up a tray,' she offered, and now her voice shook.

'I'll – I'll—' Martin had been going to declare that he would eat with her, intending to sit in silence at the table, but he was swaying in the doorway and had enough wit left to know that he might not manage to get safely down the stairs without falling. He turned back and shut the door.

Susan went down and made him up a tray. She put it on the floor outside his door and called out that it was there.

He might not take it in, might leave it. But when, hours later, she went upstairs to bed herself, it had gone.

In the night, the wind got up again. Susan woke and heard it yowling round the house. She pulled the covers up to her ears and snuggled down in bed. At least she'd had a peaceful evening.

*   *   *

A few miles away, in Rotherston, Jim and Debbie were curled up in bed together.

After Martin had gone, the children's tears had ceased quite quickly; Debbie's, though, took longer to abate. First she was angry, raging at Jim for insulting her friend, and eventually he took her in his arms, easily beating down her physical resistance, telling her they could not talk if she would not calm down.

'We'll discuss this when the girls are in bed,' he told her firmly. Suddenly, somehow, he was kissing her, and gradually her body found its former compliant softness in his arms. He drew her and their daughters round him on the sofa.

First he had to hear from Lily about the party, then, in detail, about Rose's trip to hospital and finally the garbled story of her tumble. Lily remembered how they had been alone downstairs, after Martin left, but loyally she did not mention Rose's need for dry pants. Mum had been upstairs in bed, she said; she'd got a headache, probably.

'Wasn't Martin here?' Jim managed to utter the dreaded name.

'No. He left,' said Lily. 'He isn't always here,' she added.

'Didn't he go with you to the hospital?'

'No,' said Debbie. 'He doesn't even know what happened. He hasn't been here since, until today.'

They left it then. Jim rang up to order pizzas for their supper and went to fetch them, buying two bottles of red wine while he was out. Then he helped put the girls to bed, reading them a story. Afterwards Debbie, emotionally exhausted, sat beside him on the sofa, telling him about that night and how she had flipped when Lily seemed to prefer Kate's cooking to hers. Jim's arms somehow went around her as she talked.

'But you're a far better cook than Kate,' he told her truthfully. How could he be loyal to both of them at once? 'She'd made a terrific effort that day to get it right.' He poured more wine into Debbie's glass.

Debbie wasn't going to be appeased so quickly.

'You didn't come back. Rose needed you. I needed you,' she said.

'I thought that fellow was with you,' Jim replied, then added, after a pause, 'If I've got it right, you were upstairs in bed and he went off leaving Lily and Rose downstairs on their own without telling you.'

'He put a film on for them,' Debbie said, defending Martin.

'So?' said Jim.

Debbie was about to say that he wasn't used to children, he had none of his own, but he had a son somewhere, and he had been in the house often enough with Lily and Rose.

'He's fond of them. He reads to them,' she insisted.

Jim knew that paedophiles befriended lone mothers because it gave them access to their children. Now was not the time to mention it.

'He sleeps with you here,' he stated, flatly.

'You sleep with Kate.'

Jim was going to say that the children had not yet stayed overnight with them and so had not been exposed to the intimacies of their bed, but it would happen.

'I don't like to think of them being in bed with him and you on Sunday mornings,' he said, thinking of cuddles in the past.

Debbie hadn't liked it either, but she wouldn't say so. She turned her head towards him. They didn't discuss what would happen next. It just took place. Clasped together in the big bed, familiarity took over, and when the wind got up outside, neither of them heeded it.

Lily woke during the night. She had a bad dream, and came looking for her mother. Like a miracle, Daddy was there, too; she snuggled in between them both, smelling their funny, sweet, accustomed smells.

Dan and Fiona, in the house next to Cedar Cottage, had both returned to work that week. On Thursday night the gale which had blown during the day, bringing the mini-tornado to the village in their absence, got up again. Dan got out of bed to shut the window, which, in a healthy way, they liked to keep open if it was possible. Not long after he returned to bed, they heard an alarming cracking sound, a loud crash.

'Something's blown down.' Dan thought of the garden

shed, the fence, even one of their cars being picked up and swept away. 'I'd better take a look,' he said.

'Can't it wait?' Fiona asked, shivering. The noise outside had been alarming. 'What can you do in this weather, in the dark?'

'I'd better find out what it was,' he insisted. 'You stay in the warm.'

He pulled on jeans and a sweater, and collected his big powerful torch. In wellingtons, he left the house, and as he did so an external light came on. Dan instantly saw a black mass straddling the fence separating their garden from Susan Trent's.

The big willow had blown down, and much of it lay across their garden.

Dan walked over to it, stunned by how vast it looked, sprawled over the roses they had inherited, crushing the small pergola. Luckily it had missed their garden shed.

At least it hadn't hit the house.

Carrying the torch, he made a circuit past the shattered tree. A silver birch that had grown near it had been brought down too, and was tangled in its branches. Dan played his torch over it. It spread across almost the whole width of their garden and rose high into the air. He could not get around the top of it; at the base the bulk was less, and he straddled the shattered panels that had formed the fence, trying to get round that way. The huge globe of the roots was exposed, and there was a cavity in the ground where it had been torn up.

Dan looked towards Susan's house. No light showed. Hadn't she heard the noise?

There was no point in waking her if she had slept through it. The wind still blew and the rain was lashing down. He turned back towards the house just as Fiona appeared in the kitchen doorway.

'It's that willow,' he said. 'We can't do anything now. It's wrecked the garden, but nothing else. Might as well let Mrs Trent find out what's happened in the morning.'

They went back to bed, and Fiona fell asleep again at once, while Dan mentally rehearsed how to deal with things the following day. Since it was still dark when they left the house these mornings, perhaps action could be postponed until the weekend. Susan, after all, would not be much affected; the damage was on their property. Who was responsible for the removal of the tree?

Susan had taken a sleeping pill. The doctor had provided them when she broke her arm and she had been able to repeat her prescription from time to time. She had taken one every night since Sunday's scene and tonight, with Martin home and silent, she had felt very tense. She must somehow find oblivion.

It was still dark when she got up and drew back her bedroom curtains before she went downstairs. She did not see what had happened overnight, making her breakfast, moving quietly, leaving at her usual time, not looking outside.

Owen's grandfather, after delivering the papers, walked back from the end of North Street and noticed something different about the skyline. He saw that the tall willow at Cedar Cottage had been flattened.

Susan would have left by now. She would glance at her paper before departing, then take it with her to read at lunch time. Goodness knew whether that layabout Martin was at home or not; he'd go round and make sure there was nothing that needed attending to right away, and maybe leave a note; he and Owen could cut the tree up into logs and stack it neatly. There would be no need for her to look for other help.

He walked round the side of Cedar Cottage and down the garden. The tree had been plucked out from the ground and it lay across the other garden, covering the major part of the lawn; the smashed pergola was invisible beneath its branches. Poor young couple, thought the old man; but there'd be work in clearing it all up. He knew that they had a wood-burning stove; his son, a jobbing builder, had fitted it for the previous owners. Clearing up the mess would be a nice little job for grandfather and grandson, and then there would be the fencing to replace.

Plans safely made, the old man set off home, and on the way he met the newcomer to Chapel Row.

'Morning,' he said to Adam, who was on his way back to the house with his paper.

'Morning,' Adam answered. 'It was a rough night.'

'Yes,' the old man replied. 'Big tree down at Mrs Trent's.'

'Oh dear. Much damage?'

'Only to the neighbours' garden. New people. Young folk. Smashed the roses.'

'Nothing structural, though? No one's hurt? Mrs Trent's all right?'

'No harm to the houses. She's gone off to work as usual,' said the grandfather. 'Me and my grandson will go round when he gets back from school and see what's what.'

'Sure there's nothing needed now?'

'No. I had a good look round. My grandson and I help her in the garden,' said the old man.

Adam nodded.

'That's good,' he said.

The two parted. Adam's impulse was to go and take a look, but that would be trespass. He'd never met Susan Trent. It was lucky she had this sturdy old man and his grandson to deal with the problem for her.

Linda and Jo were more inquisitive.

After they had left the older children at their playgroup, both the nannies saw that a silver birch and an apple tree had been blown over. On Linda's drive from Rotherston, there had been one-way traffic along a stretch of the road where a tree had fallen; by the time she passed, it had been dragged to one side of the road and was being dealt with by a gang of men, but elsewhere there had been fallen branches. Before entering the house, with the smaller children and themselves still in their outdoor clothing, the two nannies set forth to inspect the damage. It wasn't serious; the birch was tall and slender, and had been totally uprooted; the apple tree had broken at the point on the trunk where it branched. However, just across the way they saw the fallen willow. As far as they could tell from where they stood, it hadn't struck the house next to Mrs Trent's; it had simply spread itself across most of the garden.

'It could have been much worse,' they said to one another.

16

Owen, back from school that afternoon, was eager to accompany his grandfather to Cedar Cottage. He loved using the circular saw and it was a chance to swell his funds. They'd cost far less than some cowboy firm cashing in on the misfortunes of others, as the old man pointed out, and both were keen to help Mrs Trent. Off they went, in boots, and carrying the saw, just in case they could start at once.

There seemed to be no one in at Cedar Cottage. Mrs Trent was still at work as usual. Undeterred, they walked all round the fallen giant. It was a wide tree, its circumference vast, and it loomed over a large part of Dan and Fiona's garden. For convenience and their own pleasure, they sawed off a few side branches to aid passing between the two gardens. This made crossing the fallen fencing easy. They were cutting up some of the branches that were crushing the pergola and the roses when Dan returned;

he had come home early from the office, deciding that he must inspect the damage in daylight. He found an old man and a youth in his garden, already improving the situation.

Fred, the grandfather, was equal to the occasion.

'I'm Fred, and this is my grandson, Owen,' he said. 'His father put the stove in your house. We work for Mrs Trent. Thought we'd make a start.'

'Oh – that's very good of her to get on to you so quickly,' said Dan, who feared he might have to bear some of the expense.

Fred was not going to tell him that they were using their own initiative.

'Maybe you'd like the wood for your stove,' he suggested craftily. If they cut it up to sell elsewhere, there would be the problem of carting it away, not easy for an old man and a youth who was not old enough to drive. As it was, they would need ropes and tackle to deal with the higher branches.

'Good idea,' Dan agreed. 'I'll just change and then I'll come and give you a hand.'

Fred and Owen exchanged glances, the boy grinning. They'd got a nice little job here for the weekend, if the rain would just hold off. It had stopped some hours ago; however, there was a pool of water in the hollow left by the willow's roots.

Dan, booted and in a rough jacket, went round to have a look. The birch had fallen towards the willow; removing it would be comparatively simple, and its shallow root had not left much of a hole. He looked into the other, larger crater, peering into it with sudden intensity, then turned to break off a branch. Climbing a little way into the hole, he leaned down, poking about with it in the muddy puddle. When he lifted it up, a fragment of cloth adhered to it. Dan landed his catch and, frowning, fished about again. Then he climbed further down the side of the pit and poked about some more.

'Fred,' he called. 'Would you come here a minute?'

He was going to add, don't bring the boy, but it was too late. Owen arrived before his grandfather. He could see, rising up out of the muddy water, what Dan's branch had raised just above the surface: a skeletal hand.

'Cripes,' he said.

Dan waited for the old man to appear and see it too; then he dropped it back.

'Maybe there was once an ancient graveyard here,' he said.

But all three of them had seen a dull metal object caught around the wrist bones: a watch.

Fred, after his first moment of shocked surprise, knew immediately whose body it must be.

Norman Trent had left home about forty years ago. A few people had been aware that he had treated Susan badly: she was always in the wars, having, she said, fallen over or walked into a door; she never complained. Norman, company secretary to a firm in Slough and considered, at least by himself, to be a rising man, had smooth good manners in public; at village functions he was suave and smiling. Fred's wife, who helped in the house once a week, didn't like him, but they seldom met. Norman bullied the boy, Martin, she said. Usually Norman was at work during her weekly spell at Cedar Cottage, but once when he was at home with a cold, she witnessed him disciplining the small boy, who was less than two years old at the time. The child was made to stand in the corner for an hour because he had spilled some of his breakfast cornflakes on the floor, and Rita, Fred's wife, had seen bruises on his legs. She suspected the man of beating the child.

There had been some talk after Norman left. It was implied that he had gone off with a woman, though no particular one was named. There were a few jokes suggesting that maybe Susan had got rid of him, but these remarks were not serious; it was thought much more likely that he would have murdered her than she him. Those who knew her liked her; the gossip didn't last.

Dan was looking very serious, and, new to the village, knew nothing of the Trents' past history.

'We mustn't touch it,' he said. 'We must inform the police.' He turned away to go and do it. 'Maybe you'd best leave this now,' he said to Fred.

'We'll wait for Mrs Trent,' said Fred stoutly. 'We'll not go near the roots.'

Later, telling Fiona about the find, Dan said, 'The old man looked at me quite strangely. I suppose he couldn't have put the body there?'

'Where's Martin?' wondered Fred, when Dan had gone.

Martin had gone to London.

Debbie would be no good to him now; his angry thoughts of revenge against that husband of hers were as strong as ever, but the man could put a tale about and he would be believed, not Martin. He'd write her off, find another woman and another job, escape. He'd go round the travel agents and see what he could find; many, including cruise lines, had head offices in London. He'd bang on doors, assert himself.

He bathed and shaved, put on clean clothes and an ancient but expensive navy blazer over dark trousers and a blue shirt, with a restrained tie. Then he rang up for a taxi, taking the money his mother had put in the emergency store before she left that morning. He knew that she'd have restocked it. He could rely on her. While he was upstairs, he had pulled back his bedroom curtains, but his room overlooked the road so he did not see the fallen tree, and he never glanced out of the kitchen window. Martin was not interested in much beyond what affected him.

*   *   *

'Who do you think it is, Granddad?' Owen asked Fred.

He was amazed at what he'd seen, and fascinated, rather than dismayed. Just those few old bones balanced on the twig – it was weird. Creepy, in a way, but not repulsive. He didn't want to puke.

Fred, however, was perturbed. Susan must be warned.

Rita had retired long ago and Susan had employed no other cleaner. Fred and Owen both knew where she kept a spare key in case she locked herself out, which had happened more than once; occasionally they, or Owen's father, if he were working in the house – doing repairs or painting – needed to get in.

'I'll phone Mrs Trent at her office,' Fred decided. 'You keep an eye on things out here, Owen. You can cut a few of those branches off but be careful with the saw.'

He heard it whining as Owen set about this welcome task. Fred fetched the key from a nail where it hung under the eaves of the shed and let himself into the house.

He had to look the number up in the directory, and without his glasses, couldn't read it; he should have thought of that and got Owen to do the telephoning but the news would come best from him. It was no good calling the boy now; he wouldn't be heard above the saw. Then he saw a spectacle case on the dresser. Susan must have left her glasses behind, he thought, opening it and taking out a pair; maybe they would do.

They did. He got through to her at Marsh's.

'I'm ever so sorry, Mrs Trent,' he said. 'Your willow blew

down in the night and them young neighbours of yours have found what's under it. They've gone to call the police. Maybe you'd best get home.'

What would they do to her after all this time? He hoped she wouldn't pile the car up, driving back. And however had she managed it? He replaced her glasses in their case, locked the door again and put the key back. Then he turned towards the fallen tree, where he saw another man had joined his grandson.

Had the police come already? They were quick enough when you didn't want them but took hours, even days, when you really needed them. However, as Fred crossed the garden, he saw the newcomer was the tenant from the house in Chapel Row where the copper lived. Perhaps he was another copper, swift upon the scene.

Adam had approached through the Field House garden. He had been feeling restless and disturbed all day; the storm had been unsettling and his own plans seemed to be in a state of flux. Somehow he must make a move, must call on Susan, ask her what she knew, try also to discover what was going on between her and her grace-less son. Deciding this, he had gone out again. The nannies were not at the house opposite; if they were at Field House, he might go and talk to them, make a plan for asking about the brass plate. That would provide him with an excuse for calling.

He stepped along, looking forward to the company of two attractive young women.

Linda and Jo were in the garden with their charges. He heard the older children's voices as they ran about, and he went to join them, fairly confident that he would be welcome. Then a chain-saw rasped, quite briefly. It wasn't in their garden, though there was some gale damage evident.

'Hi, Adam,' Linda said, and added, 'There's something going on over there. They're already sawing up that tree that's fallen down.'

The noise of the saw had ceased as Owen, curious, had turned back, in his grandfather's absence, to look once more into the hole. He was standing staring down as Adam said to the girls, 'I'll see if they need help,' and was gone, not held up now by any fence as the Field House one was also smashed.

'Shame,' said Jo, watching him depart. 'I like that bloke.'

'It's the saw. Boys can't resist toys,' said Linda sagely. 'He wants a go.'

Adam was soon at Owen's side, in Susan Trent's garden. 'Hi there,' he said. 'Can I lend a hand?'

'My granddad's on the case,' said Owen. 'He's ringing Mrs Trent. There's a body down there. The guy from here' – he nodded towards Dan and Fiona's house – 'is calling the police.' He was bubbling with shocked excitement.

'A body?'

'Yeah. We saw a hand. That guy fished it up on a stick.

You can't see it now,' he added helpfully. 'There's water down there. Only bones, it was.'

So that was it. Adam stood stock still as a piece of the puzzle slotted into place. Then he took a deep breath and went towards the hole, gazing into it. As the boy had said, there was water, but now he saw why the man had taken a stick to explore the depths. He'd have done so, too, for there was something down there, visible only vaguely, as you would see shadowy trout or carp in a pool. A scrap of fabric lay across an exposed root, where Dan had put it.

Then Fred joined them.

Susan, driving home, had a feeling of inevitability about what she was going to see.

For nearly forty years, this discovery had been a possibility, but as time passed, she had ceased to fear it. At first, so long ago, she thought someone would wonder about Norman's sudden disappearance and might report him missing, but no one had. After a few days, she had pre-empted enquiries by telephoning his office to say that he had left home. She had tearfully admitted that they had had a row and he had gone. They hadn't been getting on too well for some time, she had revealed; she thought there might be someone else. His boss had come to see her; he had been sympathetic and had said Norman's salary would be paid for a further month. After that, unless they heard from him with an explanation for his absence, it would stop. At the time, they had had a joint bank account – she had to record every penny that she spent – and she had gone on drawing from it until it had been used; it didn't take long; she made sure of that. Then she closed the account and opened another of her own. No one had investigated; there was no other family to miss him for he was an only child and his parents had been killed in an air raid towards the end of the war. She was working in a bank when she met him and when she heard that he was orphaned at thirteen, just after he had started at a minor public school, she felt sorry for him. He had spent his holidays with a bachelor godfather, a parson, who, after Norman left school, had sent him to be articled to an accountant and had thereafter washed his hands of him, dying two years later. Most of what money his parents had left had gone on school fees and his expenses, accounted for by the godfather who had also deducted pocket money and the cost of his keep in the holidays. He'd genuinely had a hard time, and though Susan blamed her own shortcomings for provoking him to violence, she also knew that however difficult his life had been, there was no excuse for treating her as he had done. No human being was entitled to treat another in this way, and his upbringing was not an adequate explanation, for his parents had loved him; even he admitted that he had a golden childhood. Losing his parents was the catalyst, she supposed; he blamed them for deserting him, just as Martin blamed the loss of his father for all the troubles he had brought upon himself. She had done her best for Patricia and Martin, and she had loved them. Even so, Martin had turned into a domineering bully.

Her mind was numb as she turned into the drive and put the car away, calmly closing the garage. She went in. Was Martin here? There was no need to look upstairs; the money she had put in the dresser drawer had gone, which was her answer. At least he need not know just yet.

She drew a deep breath, then opened the kitchen door and went outside, walking steadily across the lawn to where Fred, Owen and Dan, the man from next door, were standing. Another man was with them, and as she approached, he detached himself from the group and hurried to meet her, intercepting her before she could speak to the others. He was slight and dark; she had seen him before.

'Mrs Trent. We met briefly in Marsh's on Monday. You kindly made some coffee. I'm Adam Wilson.' He looked her in the eye and said, 'I'm David Fraser's son.' He put his hand out and took hers, holding it in a firm, warm grasp. 'I heard about the tree. I'm here to help,' he added, pressing her hand before he let it go. 'Don't say too much,' he warned her softly. Then, as she swayed, he put his arm around her as they walked towards the others.

'I'm ever so sorry, Mrs Trent,' said Fred, coming up to her. 'That young fellow saw it.' He nodded towards Dan, who was out of earshot in his own garden, talking earnestly to Owen about which branches could be swiftly lopped and moved without bringing in the tackle they would ultimately need. 'You could say you don't know anything about it,' he suggested.

The truth was that she didn't, not really. She had not killed Norman. He had slipped on the kitchen floor after she had pushed him in the chest. He had been hitting her with a stick across the face and shoulders because she had placed herself between him and Martin, who, aged three, was used to being beaten about his legs and buttocks by his father. She had reeled across the room, and Martin, seeing his father on the ground, had picked up a shovel used for filling up the Rayburn cooker. Swiping out blindly, he had brought it down upon his father's head. Shouting, 'Don't you hit my Mummy,' Martin had begun to batter him with all his puny strength. Norman had been getting to his feet when David had come in.

David had grabbed the tool used for riddling the stove and had finished off what Martin had begun. And this was David's son.

How much of this did Adam Wilson know? And why was that his name, not Fraser?

There was no time to ask. A police car, fortunately without its sirens wailing, had drawn up outside Dan's house and Dan, hearing it, went off to meet the constables who now appeared round the side of the building.

Susan looked at Fred and Adam.

'They'll soon prove that it's Norman,' she said.

'I'll go and delay them, while you think of something,' Fred said, stumping off towards the other house.

'You can say you don't know how he got there,' Adam advised. 'You had help, didn't you?' For even when she was a young woman, would she have had the strength to dig a hole and drag the dead weight of her husband's body to it, for a necessary burial?

She couldn't tell this son of David's that she hadn't buried Norman, nor witnessed David doing it. All these years, through four decades, she had kept David safe by saying nothing. She must go on doing it.

'How old are you?' she asked him.

'Thirty-four,' he said, and smiled at her. Then she saw the likeness. 'I don't know what happened,' he told her.

'You've got his eyes,' she said.

'He's dead,' Adam told her. 'Six months ago.'

'He was wonderful,' she said.

17

A young policeman and a slightly older woman officer approached, with Dan and Fred.

Owen, aware that his chief emotion, excitement, was not appropriate, put on a solemn face and hovered, while the small procession crossed the damaged fence towards the fallen tree and the hole it had exposed. Dan, who had taken the lead, was mildly aggrieved as the woman officer bade him halt before they reached the brink, but he went near enough to see that most of the water had now seeped away, leaving just the bony fingers visible. Muddy earth hid the rest.

He pointed.

'You'll see there's a piece of cloth there, on the base of the tree,' he said. 'That emerged before the hand. I touched nothing, once I saw the hand.'

'I see, sir,' said the woman officer.

'There's the branch I used,' Dan indicated.

'It must have been there a very long time,' said Fred. 'Maybe as much as a hundred years,' he added helpfully. 'That tree's been there years and years.'

'Maybe so,' said the male officer. 'We must secure the scene,' he stated. 'Madam, sir, please stand back.' He began talking into his radio, summoning help.

Susan and Adam had already stopped, well away from the site.

'This has been a shock for Mrs Trent,' Adam said. 'I think she should go inside.'

'Mrs Trent. This is your property?' the woman officer confirmed, with a sweeping glance around her.

'Yes,' said Susan. 'I should like to go inside, now, please. I've only just come home to find this – this – disaster.' For that was what it was.

'That will be best,' said the officer. 'We shall want to talk to all of you, but you can all go inside.'

Fred had no intention of leaving; nor had Owen or Dan. Dan and Owen took several paces back into Dan's garden while Fred stayed on Susan's side, from which position he felt more able to defend her, for she might need it. This new bloke, whatever he was called, seemed sensible. He'd take Susan inside and make her a cup of tea.

'This is a very old tree,' Fred told the officers again.

He seemed very old, too; seventy at least. He'd know about such things, thought the male officer.

'How old?' he asked.

Fred calculated rapidly.

'Oh – near fifty years,' he said. 'Maybe more.'

'It might be a legitimate burial,' said the male officer. People did that sort of thing from time to time. There was no need to conclude that there had been a crime.

'CID will soon find out,' said his colleague crisply. 'Fetch the tape, please,' she ordered him.

The male constable went back to the police car to fetch the tape with which they would fence off the scene, while Adam led Susan back to the house. They went in by the back door, into the kitchen, the room where it had ended all those years ago, when one reign of terror had been succeeded by another, abstract this time, years and years of fearing discovery before the children had grown up and could make do without her.

'Your father came in here a lot,' she said, when Adam had closed the door behind them. How strange it was to be saying that.

'I want to hear about it,' he said. 'But not now. I don't know anything about what happened, and if you do, you must not admit it. They won't know who it is down there, not for ages. That old man said the tree had been there for maybe fifty years.'

'They'll tell by his teeth,' said Susan, thus banishing any doubt Adam had about the skeleton's identity.

But their dentist had retired long ago. Would the old records still exist?

'You've had an awful shock. How about some tea?' Adam said. 'Why don't you go and sit down and I'll make you some? I'll find everything – don't worry,' he went on. 'I'm quite domesticated.'

'So was David,' Susan said.

She started taking off her coat. Adam took it from her and went with her into the sitting room, where he put the lights on and looked at the fire.

'It's a gas one,' she said.

'Oh – good. I'll light it, then.'

Adam did so, and as the mock coals caught, Susan sank down on the sofa.

'Put your feet up. They'll expect you to be shocked,' he said. 'You're a woman. Be a little helpless,' and he smiled at her again.

Suddenly she felt completely happy. It wouldn't last; the reckoning must come, but for a little while, miraculously, David's son was here, an adult man, not a youth as his father was when last she saw him. Briefly, she could leave it all to him.

He soon came back with the tea, laid nicely on a little tray.

'I didn't know if you take sugar,' he said. He'd found some and put it in an eggcup.

She didn't. He poured her out a cup and Susan sipped it, gratefully.

'That is your husband down there?' he said, to make sure.

She nodded.

'And my father helped you?'

He meant, helped you bury him, but David had done it by himself.

The day it happened was a Saturday, hence Norman's presence in the house. Patricia was at a party in another village and Susan had been due to collect her later on. With Norman's body lying on the floor, David told Susan to fetch her, as arranged, and stay away as long as possible. He'd see to things.

In a total daze, she had obeyed. Martin had stopped crying very quickly; she had taken him upstairs, washed and changed him, changed her own clothes, and then, sitting him beside her in the car, as was common practice then, had gone to fetch Patricia, somehow chatting and laughing with the other parents. When she and the children returned, the body had gone, the kitchen had been cleaned, the bloodstains on the floor and elsewhere had been washed off. The riddler and the shovel bore no trace of what had happened. Both had been scrubbed and coke dust had been rubbed into them. David wasn't there, but he appeared a little later, in different clothes, shiningly clean himself. He played draughts with the children, partnering Martin against Patricia, until it was time to put the children to bed. Martin seemed untroubled; he was used to witnessing extreme scenes, though he had never before retaliated, and was too young to understand how this one had ended. Norman never beat Patricia and minimised his conduct in her presence, but she did not ask where he had gone. The next day, Susan told her he had gone away and she wasn't sure when he would be coming back. Patricia seemed crestfallen, as he hadn't said goodbye; in the mornings, when he left for work, he had usually remembered. She soon stopped asking when he would return.

Before he left that evening, David gave Susan a tablet.

'It's something to make you sleep,' he said. 'I took it from the surgery. I'll attend to all the rest of it tonight. Don't worry.'

She hadn't killed Norman. He and little Martin, between them, had done it. She must leave it to him to save them all. Perhaps he – and the fact that Norman must have slipped on something spilt on the kitchen floor – had saved her and Martin's lives that afternoon, for Norman had looked murderous.

She took the pill and went to bed. Neither of them ever discussed calling the police, trying to explain. In the morning, three willow slips had been planted at the bottom of the garden. The ground around them was quite smooth and flat, the turves that must have been removed had been neatly replaced. A nearby flower bed had fresh earth, the surplus from the grave, strewn across its surface.

David came round quite early. He did not tell her where he had hidden Norman's body during the hours until it was dark and he came back to bury it, but he said that willows grew easily from slips. She was to keep the strongest, and perhaps plant other trees nearby, when she'd time;

birches, for example. If none of the willows took – but he thought they all would, and he was right – she must plant a sapling in the spot. It would be safe to dig down two feet or more. Then he said that he would have to go away. He wouldn't leave at once; not till Norman's disappearance had been accepted as a fact, and he'd had time to get his parents to agree without their suspecting him of more than a desire to see the world.

'He'll write to you from somewhere. Norman, I mean. Australia, say, or Africa,' he said. 'Just to tell you where he is and that he isn't coming back. I don't know how you'll do for money,' he added, suddenly looking young and anxious.

'I'll manage,' she had said, knowing that she must. 'My parents won't let us starve.' How had he done it, unseen, unaided, in the night? What a chance he'd taken.

'Don't sell the house. Not until the trees are well established.'

'I'll never sell it,' Susan had replied.

'Never's a long time,' said David. 'Can you give me a sample of Norman's handwriting?'

She had given him the list of instructions for her routine which Norman had drawn up; it was kept pinned to the inside of a cupboard. She was supposed to carry out these tasks on the days and at the times he designated. Among them were the cleaning of his shoes, the ironing, regular polishing of various items, the hours for shopping. She had to adhere to the timetable even when, on the advice of David's father, Rita had been engaged to help with the housework. This was after she had sustained a broken collar bone following what she maintained had been a fall. She was overtired, Dr Fraser had told Norman.

When David left the village, the willow slips looked strong and healthy. He'd expressed a wish to study at a Canadian university and had somehow got himself provisionally accepted at McGill. Until then he was going to do some travelling. His parents, though surprised, were agreeable to this new plan and had helped to make it possible.

Dr and Mrs Fraser stayed on in Bishop St Leon for more than ten years and were very kind to Susan and the children. Occasionally, they gave her news of David. He had become an architect and was living in New Zealand, a country he had formed a liking for on his pre-university travels. After Dr Fraser retired, he and his wife moved to Spain.

Years after they left, when Susan's troubles with Martin had begun, she realised that they had suspected something, if not the truth, all along. That final summer and into the autumn when it happened, David, an only child, had spent a lot of time at Cedar Cottage while Norman was at work. He had helped her in the garden — Susan did most of the gardening even in Norman's lifetime — and he had encouraged Patricia to learn to read. He always came to the cottage, not along the road but across the fence.

What seemed to be a schoolboy crush on Susan had

worried David's parents, who told each other that it would soon pass and that friendship with an older woman could be beneficial; still in her twenties, she wasn't that much older than David. She had a dreadful marriage; they knew that. Though Dr Fraser was convinced that the accidents she was prone to were not accidents at all, he could do little unless she wished to help herself. When he asked if things were all right at home, she smiled brightly and said they were; in those days, divorce was regarded as a scandal, and, except for proven adultery, was difficult. Susan and the children might have been destitute if she left her marriage. The Frasers didn't want their youthful son developing quixotic ideas of eloping, jobless, with a ready-made family. Susan, growing older, began to guess at some of their anxieties and concerns.

How much did Adam know? Dr and Mrs Fraser were his grandparents. Did he visit them in Spain? Were they still alive?

'We'll have time to talk, no matter what,' he said, as the doorbell rang.

It was Mary Church. Back from school, she had seen a police car in the drive of Cedar Cottage, and another, with an unfamiliar Vauxhall saloon, in the road. Susan should have been at work still; what had happened? Had Martin finally gone too far? She hurried over to investigate and the door was opened by a man she vaguely recognised.

'Is Susan all right?' Mary asked. 'I saw the police car. I live opposite,' she added.

'Yes. Just shocked,' said Adam. 'Will you come in?'

As she followed him into the house, Adam supplied his name and told her where he was living.

'I was at Field House and saw a tree had blown down over here,' he said.

'But why are the police here? Was someone hurt? I thought—' But perhaps she had better not tell this newcomer what she thought.

Adam realised that news of the discovery of a body would soon be spread around the village, and there would be speculation, even though Fred would insist that it had been there for centuries. She'd have to know.

'There was a skeleton under the tree,' he said. 'It must have been there a very long time.'

This woman might not have known Norman. Modern forensic technology would be able to date the body, but until that had happened, he decided to follow Fred's lead.

'Oh, how dreadful,' Mary said, and went to find Susan in the sitting room.

'I'll fetch another cup,' said Adam, leaving them to it. He put the kettle on again. It wouldn't be long before the police came to talk to Susan. He hoped she wouldn't be tempted to tell this neighbour whose the body was.

When he returned, with hot water to top up the teapot as well as another cup and saucer, he found, to his relief, that Susan was saying very little.

'When I left this morning, I never looked outside,' she had said. 'I didn't know the willow had blown down.'

'Where's Martin?' Mary asked.

'I've no idea,' said Susan. 'He was here last night. He's probably at the Grapes in Rotherston.'

It was just as well, thought Mary; he'd be no help at all.

'I expect the police will sort it out quite quickly and leave you in peace,' she soothed.

'I'll go and see what's happening outside,' said Adam.

'That's Adam Wilson,' Susan told her, after he had gone. 'He's living in Chapel Row.'

'What a nice chap,' said Mary. 'I've seen him in the Crown. Susan, when I saw the police car, I was so afraid that something had happened here.'

'Well, it has, in a way,' said Susan. She was feeling better. Now, events would unfold without her taking any action. The police would discover whose body it was; they would ask her questions which, as Adam had advised, she would not answer. Silence had protected all of them through almost four decades; it might go on doing so, and in any case, David was dead. He could not be hurt, only his reputation – but, by association, this son of his could be harmed.

Adam walked back to the fallen tree. The ball of its roots, with snake-like tendrils spreading from it, reached high above the exposed cavity. The scene was fenced off by tapes and surrounded by a group of police officers, some in uniform, some in plain clothes. Seeing him approaching, Owen came up to him. The boy's face was eager, alert.

'That puddle's drained away,' he said. 'You can't see much. Just that hand. It's all covered otherwise. They'll dig it out, I suppose.'

'I suppose they will,' Adam agreed. 'It'll take a bit of time.'

Fred now came across to join them.

'How's Mrs Trent?' he asked.

'Better,' said Adam. 'A neighbour's come, from opposite. A woman.'

'That'll be Mrs Church. She's all right,' said Fred. 'Owen, where's that saw got to? Grab hold of it before the police do. Then we'd best think about going home.'

Owen went off, planning to arrange with Dan that he and his grandfather, and maybe also his dad, would saw the tree up in the morning. The police wouldn't stop them, surely, when the body was in Mrs Trent's garden, several metres away.

It was getting dark. Fred gave Adam a sharp look, jerking his head, indicating that they should walk away together.

'You know who it is, don't you?' he said. 'That body.'

'You tell me,' Adam answered.

'Her late husband. That's who. Good riddance, I say. Treated her something terrible, he did. He's got a watch on; that's the pity of it. Else they might think it had been there hundreds of years.'

Adam didn't tell the old man that science would prevent such a miscalculation.

'Maybe it won't have his name on it,' he suggested. Then he added, 'You must have lived here longer than most of the others round about. They won't know what went on. No need to say too much about it.'

'I won't, and nor will Rita – that's my missus. She used to work in the house. What she told me wouldn't bear repeating.'

'No need to repeat it, then, unless it's needed to plead self-defence,' said Adam, looking, in the gloaming, into the eyes of this wily old man. 'Whatever happened here took place so long ago, there may be no evidence.'

'What I can't understand is how she managed to do it – bury him and plant the willow,' Fred remarked.

Nor could Adam, but he was beginning to suspect that she'd had help.

'The boy hasn't a clue,' Fred said. 'I'll head him off from guessing.'

He might succeed, though Owen was no dullard.

'Good idea,' said Adam.

'Lucky you came along. Been chatting to them nannies, have you?'

'Yes,' said Adam, belatedly realising that his interest might seem excessive for a stranger to the village. 'I've met them in the Crown.'

'Nice girls,' said Fred. 'They get about. That Jo – her grandfather knew Norman. He's dead now, though.'

Adam realised that Fred was mentally reviewing who was still alive who might be called upon as witnesses in the inquiry that must surely follow.

'Let's hope it all blows over,' he said, adding, 'If you hear of any trouble, you'll make sure I know, won't you? I would like to help. I live in Chapel Row – number seventeen – but I expect you know that.'

'Not a lawyer, are you?'

'As a matter of fact, I am, but not that sort of lawyer,' Adam replied.

'Not working at the moment?'

'No. Having a long holiday.'

'I'll be seeing you, then,' said Fred, and walked away towards his grandson as the police began to erect a small tent over the site of the discovery.

Adam went back into the house, entering by the kitchen door just as a ring at the front announced the arrival of a uniformed police sergeant who, accompanied by a woman officer, wanted to ask Mrs Trent some questions.

Mary Church let them in.

She had not known Norman Trent. She might have heard some gossip, but no more, and Susan knew that she was an excellent person to be present at this time. Meanwhile, Adam faded away. So far he had not talked to the police; much better not.

The officers were meticulously civil. They took down

Susan's name and established that her son Martin, aged forty-three, lived with her but was out at present; he was a sometime college tutor, schoolteacher, and currently a freelance travel courier, she said. It made him sound so respectable.

When they asked, she told them that she had lived in this house for forty-three years, moving in with her husband and small daughter shortly before Martin was born. Previously, they'd lived in Pinner.

'Where's your husband now, Mrs Trent?' asked the more senior officer.

Of course, they knew nothing, these two servants of the state.

'He left me,' she replied.

'Left you? Deserted you?' The officer had expected her to say she was a widow.

'Yes. I had a postcard from New Zealand, four or five months later,' Susan said.

'And this was when?'

'Nearly forty years ago,' said Susan.

'And did you hear from him again?'

'Never,' she replied.

Mary, telling Bill about it later, heard warning bells then, but would not lend them credence. The officers made no comment, and they left soon afterwards, telling Susan that the site would be guarded throughout the night. Further examination and the removal of the body would take place as soon as possible.

Bill, hearing this, said that because the body had been there for a long time, there would be no hurry about the inevitable investigation; it was unlikely to provide the answer to a search for a missing person.

No one suggested that Susan should not leave home or that she should surrender her passport. After the police left, and Mary had gone home, she thought briefly that she might run away, but where to, and why? She'd come so far; she could go the rest of the way.

And Adam would come back. She was sure of that.

18

Martin had had very little luck in London.

He had visited several tour and cruise organisers, putting on his best manner, being as gracious as he could manage, and two companies said they might have something in the spring; one said that if demand justified an extra tour, there might be a last-minute coach trip somewhere at Christmas.

Martin would welcome that. He had no wish to be closeted in Cedar Cottage with his mother over Christmas, though the Grapes would offer him a partial refuge if he could get there when public transport did not run and taxis were booked up, and the Crown would be another. She'd cook a small turkey, a farm-reared bird specially bought, doing all the trimmings – bread sauce, the lot, as if he were a child to be placated with a treat. And she'd give him money; fifty pounds at least. Of course, Debbie might be free then; children of separated parents divided their time between both parties, didn't they?

Ready to give her another chance, he resolved to go to her place while Lily and Rose – a milksop if ever there was one – were with that father of theirs.

By now, after that scene, the father would have gone. She'd be on her own again and no doubt full of remorse for how Martin had been treated. On the train, returning almost penniless, Martin decided to visit her. It was after nine o'clock; the children would be in bed by now.

He walked there from the station, and when he reached the house, he took a good look round to make sure that man's four-wheel-drive vehicle wasn't there. He needed that, Debbie had said, for getting to locations in remote spots and all weathers. There was no sign of it. If he'd thought of it, a bunch of flowers would have been a good tactic; they needn't have been expensive for it was the thought that mattered. She would have been delighted; women always were, though he had rarely given them to anyone.

He took his key out, then changed his mind: maybe this time he should ring.

Hearing the bell, Debbie put the chain up. Whoever could it be as late as this? No one she knew would come round at such an hour. Perhaps it was a salesman or charity collector. She opened the door cautiously, peering round it, and saw Martin smiling at her. She was too far from him to notice if he smelled of drink, but she saw that he was neatly dressed, wearing his anorak, it was true, but with a shirt and tie on.

'Aren't you going to let me in, Debs?' he said, in a cooing tone, and she did. She had been bitterly upset and disappointed when Jim, after what she had thought was their reconciliation, had departed back to Kate. He'd said that it had been lovely, just like old times, but it changed nothing and they must forget about it. How could she? And how could he?

Martin laughed as he embraced her. It had been so easy.

While the police were talking to Susan, Adam went back to Chapel Row. There, he unlocked his briefcase and took out a slim envelope which he zipped into a big pocket of his jacket. Then he got into his car, drove to the super-market in Rotherston and bought a bottle of red wine, a bottle of brandy and a ready prepared meal – duck in orange sauce, and vegetables. He had seen a microwave in Susan Trent's kitchen. He drove back to Cedar Cottage with his purchases and rang the bell.

'It's Adam,' he said, before she opened the door.

She seemed to be alone.

'They've all gone?' he asked. He had wondered if Mary Church would take Susan over to her house for the evening, and in fact she had suggested it, but Susan had refused. She must be here when Adam returned.

'Yes,' she said, knowing that it was only for the moment. They'd soon be back.

'I've come to supper,' Adam said. 'I've got it with me. I didn't think you'd feel like cooking for yourself, or going out, if I suggested taking you somewhere – the Country Nook, for instance.'

'So you've found it, have you? It's nice.' She closed the front door behind him.

'Yes. I took Amy from your office there to lunch,' he said. 'I think you probably need a drink.' He had brought his packages in with him and now went through to the kitchen with them, taking charge.

Susan watched him, marvelling. When he suggested she should have a brandy, she did not demur, but insisted that it had better be diluted. He had some, too. They took their glasses into the sitting room where the fire still blazed. It was warm and snug.

'Funny to think my father came here,' he said.

'He was still a schoolboy,' Susan said.

But during that fatal night, while he dealt with Norman's body, he had turned into a man, and afterwards he became her lover. It seemed to happen very naturally. He had come round the next evening, when the children were in bed and asleep; there had been no Norman to fear, and as he was dead, it was not adultery. Both of them had needed comforting. David had said he loved her, and, in a romantic sense, he did; in a way she loved him, too. He was inexperienced, but she had never before known sexual tenderness; for each of them, it was an initiation, repeated several times before he left. She panicked in case she should be pregnant, but that calamity did not befall her. How strange, she thought now: she might have given birth to this man's half-brother or sister. She could have passed it off as Norman's child, she had decided at the time.

'Will you tell me about it?' Adam asked her now.

'Didn't David? Isn't that why you're here? Because he died and you were curious?'

'No. He kept your secret safe,' said Adam.

As I did his, Susan reflected.

'Why are you here, then?'

'After he died, I found some postcards addressed to you here, in Bishop St Leon, in writing that wasn't his, and signed N,' he said. 'They said things like, "Good weather. Hope you and children are well." Nothing much. He must have decided not to send them. Obviously he sent that first one – the one that's known about in the village.' There had been snapshots, too, faded ones of a young woman and two children, and there had been sketches, drawings of the same young woman: Susan Trent.

'I expect his parents – your grandparents – told him about the postcard when they wrote to him. It would have been a piece of news for them to mention in a letter. What did David die of, Adam?' Susan asked.

'He had a heart attack. He was in a coma when I got there, but he came round briefly, just before he died, and he muttered something like, "Susan's safe." I didn't understand it. Now, I do,' said Adam.

You don't, thought Susan. You think I killed Norman and David saved me from the consequences, when really he saved first Martin and me, and then all of us.

In the years since then, she'd often wondered whether the police would have believed the truth, if they'd told it at the time. There would have been fingerprints on the weapons: hers, because she used both tools daily; superimposed above them would have been Martin's tiny marks on the shovel and David's on the riddler. David had made the decisions, hastily, because there wasn't time to plan and she'd been so battered and bruised, and so concerned for Martin's safety after Norman's assault, that she was not capable of rational thought. Even if they had described what really happened, at the very least, a charge of manslaughter would have been brought against David.

The death sentence for murder was abolished soon after this. As it was, David might have gone to the gallows.

'David was at a loose end,' Susan said. 'It was his summer holidays – he'd finished his exams – and he'd been ill. He'd had rheumatic fever and his heart had been affected. They said he'd grow out of it. He'd been due to go on an expedition to South America – a bit like adventure expeditions these days – but he wasn't fit enough. He started coming round here to help me in the garden – he could do that – he was more than convalescent, he was really just supposed not to get overtired or stressed, as we would say today. He'd grown a lot, too, rather suddenly. It used to be said that such boys – it never seemed to be girls – outgrew their strength. We became great friends. He drew rather well and he sketched the children, and the house. It gave him an excuse for coming round, I suppose.'

'Did Norman object?' Adam realised that his father had fallen a little – perhaps even a lot – in love with her.

'He didn't know how often David came. He thought he was just a child. David didn't come when he was here,' said Susan.

But he had, on that last day. Norman rarely set about either her or Martin in the garden, but that afternoon Martin had been outside, riding his little tricycle, and he had pedalled behind Norman, who was polishing his car which was drawn up behind the house, crashing into first his father, then the car. Susan thought he had wanted Norman to admire his prowess on the tricycle. Martin often sought his approval; like her, he thought he could win affection if he could meet the standards Norman set. The car, a large Humber, was slightly scratched, and Norman had been furious. David, in the Field House garden, had heard the rumpus and saw Norman chasing Martin, who fled, screaming in terror, into the house. By now aware of the perils of their situation – she had never told him, but he had guessed, and he had seen unexplained bruises on her and on the child – David had rushed over to defend them.

'I failed to protect Martin,' Susan said. 'Norman abused him – beat him – and I didn't stop it.'

'He beat you, too, didn't he? You had no spirit left to fight him with,' said Adam. 'It happens. Then, at last, you managed it,' he added. 'I'm glad my father helped you.'

'Did he have a happy life? Your grandparents spoke about him sometimes, before they left the village. What about your mother?'

'They separated when I was six. My mother married again but she died when I was thirteen. My stepfather was kind and took care of me; he remarried later and had another family.' There was no need to mention his desolation when his parents parted, and again after his mother's death.

'That's very sad. You didn't go to live with your father when your mother died?'

'No. I don't really know why not,' said David. 'I was settled at school by then, and I didn't know him all that well. Things just went on.'

'Did he remarry?'

'No. Maybe he never met the right person,' Adam said. 'He must have been rather lonely. But he worked hard and was responsible for some good buildings – not just houses but schools, a hospital, even a marina. He liked sailing. I do, too, yet I never sailed with him. He had a boat. Funny, isn't it? I wish I'd known him better.' Adam had inherited everything his father left, which included his boat and a house in New Zealand which he had designed.

'Perhaps what happened here spoiled his life,' said Susan slowly.

'It affected him. Of course it did. It must have been a crossroads,' said Adam. 'But he knew he'd helped you, and the children. Saved you, even. That must have been a good feeling.'

Adam was thinking that it was a great pity they hadn't done the right thing and called the police, but David was very young and inexperienced, and Susan was probably hysterical. At the time, with both of them shocked and frightened, a quick fix must have seemed the best solution, and after that, soon it was too late to tell the truth.

'What happened to Norman's car? If he'd left, wouldn't he have taken it with him?' he asked.

'We didn't have two cars. I told people that Norman had deserted us but he had left me the car. It made him sound generous. No one questioned it. He wasn't officially missing, you see. I sold it in part exchange for a small Ford,' she said. 'Not immediately, but a few weeks after David had gone away.' She sighed. 'Nowadays people are so suspicious – there are so many crime stories on television – we wouldn't have got away with it today. I don't watch them,' she added. 'Martin does, sometimes, if he's here.'

'I see.' Adam wondered if Martin would come in at any minute. They'd better have their meal before he did. 'Shall we eat?' he suggested.

The various dishes he had bought were good; Susan

seemed to enjoy everything and was appreciative.

'You're like your father,' she said. 'He was kind and thoughtful. I expect he went on being like that.'

'Yes,' said Adam. But he had been remote, often with-drawn, not like his parents, Adam's grandparents, who had been warm and friendly.

Susan asked about Adam's life and work. No, he wasn't married – he had come near it once or twice but it hadn't worked out. His law practice was in Philadelphia, but he had also worked in Montreal and Paris.

She asked him why his name was Wilson, and he said it was his middle name; he had come to Bishop St Leon to find out who she was, and did not want to be identi-fied as the Frasers' grandson, but he told her about the brass plate, still at Field House amongst a lot of junk. He said that his grandparents had died, but he had often visited them in Spain and was very fond of them.

Adam had grown up thinking that his stepfather was paying for his education, until, when he was twenty-one, his father sent him a large cheque which, he said, was to cover the rest of his expenses and give him a start in life. It would be better than the monthly sums which had been paid into a trust fund for him hitherto. Adam hadn't known that this arrangement had existed. He thought the unexplained sums which came his way were somehow left him by his mother.

It was difficult, and sad, to think that this weary woman, Susan Trent, whom he liked, had probably wrecked his father's life by making him an accessory to her murderous act.

She hadn't had an easy time thereafter; that was clear.

'The early years were quite good,' she said now. 'While Patricia and Martin were still children. Things went wrong later. With Martin, that is; not Patricia. He blamed me for his father's having left us.'

'He'd forgotten about the beatings.'

'Yes. I was glad about that.' Because it meant he had blotted out all memory of that final scene. 'Patricia may have been more aware,' said Susan. 'She was almost two years older. But Norman never hit her. He spoiled her.'

'Daddy's girl.'

'I suppose so.'

Susan made coffee, and after they had drunk it and had cleared away, Adam left. He made her promise to telephone him if there was any trouble, either when Martin came back, or if the police became difficult.

'You can insist on having a solicitor present, if they ask you awkward questions,' he said. 'But I don't think that will happen very quickly.' Not until they had formed an accurate opinion about the identity of the body, and then she would certainly need legal help. After all this time, wouldn't the law treat her mercifully?

Nothing was certain. The press would love the story and would make a meal of it.

'I'll make sure David isn't mentioned,' she said. She'd done it for almost forty years; she could do it for a little longer. She looked up at him. 'I don't want you to be tainted by association. You stay as Adam Wilson while you're here. Now you know about it, you'll be free to go.'

'I won't leave you to deal with this alone,' he told her.

He was glad to leave the house, however. Suddenly, it had become oppressive. Driving home, he had a lot to think about.

While Adam was out, Roger had returned. The house was quiet; Chris was not yet back. Neither his van nor the Toyota was parked outside.

Roger opened Adam's door and looked into the empty room. He saw a briefcase on the table, and his curiosity became too much for him. He stepped across, wrapped a handkerchief round his fingers, and tried the lock. It was open.

Inside was a passport. He inspected it, and saw that Adam Wilson was, in fact, Adam Wilson Fraser.

He also saw some photographs and sketches.

19

The next morning, Susan woke early, as she always did. Unusually, she felt rested, without the feeling of dread that haunted her so frequently.

Martin hadn't come back last night; one way or the other, either by hearing him, or sensing he was in the house, she'd have known. Slowly, the recollection of the previous day's events came back to her, and she realised that her main emotion was huge relief. Then there was Adam; an echo from the past, but not a threat. A wave of sadness came over her as she thought of David, who, though he had a fine, successful son, had not had a happy and fulfilling marriage, and who had died too soon; he wouldn't have been sixty.

She got up and had her bath, lying in it, enjoying the warm water into which she had poured bath essence given to her by her colleagues on her recent birthday. She would make the most of these small hedonistic pleasures while she could, for she was sure to be arrested before long on a charge of murder, and there would be very little comfort in a women's prison.

She would take Adam's advice and say very little. Safety lay in silence; she had proved that throughout four long decades. There was just a chance that, after all this time, there would be too little proof to justify her being charged. She didn't really mind, either way, but Patricia would be upset if she were convicted, and there was Paul, Martin's son, who might not like to have his grandmother – if he owned to having one – labelled as a murderer, even if she did not strike the fatal blow. After all, only she knew that.

It was Saturday, when she never went to the office early, though she worked most weekends. Leisure time was not much use to her; she had few hobbies except reading and the garden, and was better keeping busy. Would the police let her go to work today? It was still dark; they'd soon be rooting round beneath that tent they'd put up covering the hole. What would an innocent householder do in these circumstances? Go out, perhaps bearing cups of tea to revive them, and ask how they were getting on with digging out the corpse lain buried, unbeknownst, in her garden? Stay quiet, and go to work as normal? There seemed to be no middle course.

In spite of the good dinner Adam had provided the previous evening, Susan felt hungry. Her usual breakfast was a cup of coffee, toast and marmalade, but today she fancied a boiled egg, so she prepared one. The condemned

man's last supper, she thought, as she ate it with appreci-
ation. She cleared away and tidied up the kitchen.
Everything must be left meticulously neat. There was
washing of her own to be done and she went upstairs to
fetch it. The bin in Martin's bathroom contained some
soiled clothing, and that reminded her; he had had his
supper on a tray in his room on Thursday evening; he
hadn't brought it down and she'd forgotten all about it.

She went into his room. The tray was on the floor,
pushed into a corner; the bed was unmade; discarded
clothes were scattered about. She gathered them up, and
the tray, and took them downstairs. After she had put the
washing machine on and dealt with the dirty crockery,
she returned to Martin's room to change his sheets. They'd
make another load. Then she ran the vacuum sweeper
over the carpet. She did not dust. She would not move
any of his possessions.

His computer sat on its desk, a blank eye watching her
as she moved around. Perhaps there were hidden files
locked behind a password inside its mysterious intestines,
records of his life, his loves and hates. There were hates.
He hated her. She wondered if he hated his ex-wife, and
what about Paul, their son? Had he no feelings about the
boy, no curiosity? She had; she longed to see him or have
news of him. She never heard from his mother, or from
him, despite sending presents every Christmas and on his
birthday. Nowadays, ignorant of his likes and interests,
she sent him ten pounds inside a card.

She took the bedlinen downstairs to await its turn. Then, in the pale early light of day, she looked through the kitchen window to the end of the garden where the tent was standing. Shadowy figures could be seen outside it. She had heard some vehicle movement in the road; police cars must have been coming and going, even during the night, for the officers guarding the scene would have been on shifts that changed. All that would remain of Norman now would be his bones, and perhaps shreds of the clothing he had worn. As he had been washing the car before he died, he had not had his wallet on him. It was in the bedroom and she had emptied it of money. Then she had burned it and its other contents in the Rayburn. Gradually she had disposed of all his clothes, bundling them up, taking them to jumble sales and charity collections but not locally, driving miles to find distant outlets.

No one asked her what had happened to him. No one even asked if he had packed a bag before he left, for it was weeks before anybody mentioned that they had not seen him recently. People, in those days, had tact.

Seeing lights on in the house, Detective Sergeant Rodney Jones came and tapped at her door.

He was deferential.

'I see you're up and about, Mrs Trent,' he said. 'I just came to make sure everything's all right. I hope we haven't disturbed you too much.'

'Not at all,' said Susan brightly. 'I slept well. Not like you and your colleagues, in that tent.'

'No – well, the forensic team are getting going,' he informed her.

'How long will they take?' That was the sort of question she might be expected to ask.

'I can't say. It depends,' said Jones. 'Some hours, anyway.'

'I'm due at work,' said Susan. 'I suppose I can go, as usual?'

'I don't see why not,' said Jones. It would get her out of the way. The body could have been buried long before she came to live here. The post mortem would indicate an approximate date, and the victim's age. Experts would date the tree, and that would give a lead. 'Just tell me where you'll be, in case we need to get your permission about anything.'

'Is that likely?'

'Not at all. But we'd best know where you are.'

'Yes. And there's my son, of course,' she added. 'He may come home at any time. He spent last night with friends.'

'Do you know where?' The son might be needed, if later she should be distressed at the idea of a corpse being discovered on her property. So far, she seemed extremely calm, but then she knew nothing about it.

'I'm afraid I don't,' said Susan. 'He's forty-three. He leads his own life.'

She drove off to Rotherston some time later. In the office, Amy said that Linda, her flatmate, had seen that a tree in Susan's garden had been blown down.

'Yes,' said Susan. 'An old willow. It fell across Dan and

Fiona's garden. They're my new neighbours. It damaged the fence and some of their plants but luckily it missed the house.'

'Linda said Adam went over to see if you needed any help,' said Amy.

'Yes. It was so kind of him. He knows Linda, then?'

'He met Linda and Jo in the pub one night. You know Jo, don't you?'

Susan did. Her father and Martin were contemporaries, and before she retired, Susan had taught her.

'Yes,' she said.

'Will clearing up the tree be an awful job?'

'I'm not sure. I don't think so. There's an old chap, Fred, and his grandson, who sometimes help me out, and they came round at once to start sawing up the branches. They'll manage it, I expect.'

'The insurance should pay up,' said Amy.

'Yes,' agreed Susan. 'I hope they will.'

But she didn't care. It was not going to be her problem.

All day she expected either a telephone call to summon her back to the house, or the entry of several police officers with a warrant for her arrest, but nothing happened.

Jim arrived at Debbie's house at ten o'clock. The little girls were watching for him at the window, and as soon as they saw him they scrambled to get to the front door, but neither was tall enough to reach the latch.

After a few moments, Debbie opened the door. She stood back from him, warily. Part of her longed to fling herself into his arms but another part of her wanted to belabour him and pound him with her fists.

Jim made a small, hopeless gesture with his arms, as though he, too, wanted to be closer, but then he bent to the children and gave a hand to each.

'Say goodbye to Mummy,' he instructed, and, perfunctorily, they did, going off with him without a backward glance.

'Martin's upstairs,' said Lily, as he buckled her into her seat. 'He came in the middle of the night. He hasn't got up yet. Isn't he lazy?'

'Sounds like it,' said Jim. 'Does he have a job?' he asked, whilst despising himself for questioning her in this way.

'Not really, I don't think,' said Lily doubtfully.

Jim left it, trying to interest them in a tape he'd just bought. With both of them clamped into the back, conversation during travel was extremely difficult. Had he any right to criticise Debbie's choice of boyfriend, when it was he who had abandoned her for Kate? Martin might, in his view, be an unsuitable person to be in the company of his children, but that did not mean he had evil designs on them. Why couldn't she meet some nice man whose job did not demand travel, whose hours were predictable and who would be reliably with her, taking care of her?

He gave it up. They were going to Windsor for the

day; he hoped the girls would like seeing the castle and the Queen's doll's house. It would give him a hint of whether they would appreciate the domestic-sized one that he was making for them. Kate was working; he would have no help with the lavatory problems, but with two of them together, entering the ladies', surely, in Windsor, they would be quite safe? If they were a long time, he could ask a kindly-looking woman to see if they were needing any help.

Jim had come equipped with spare pants and tights. Best be prepared.

Chris had not returned, the night before. It boded well for his love life, Adam thought, making toast. He had slept badly, dreaming anxiously about his father as a troubled boy, wandering through a forest where the trees, lashed by strong winds, caught at his fleeing figure. The whole incident of Norman Trent's death must have clouded the rest of David's life. Young people, even now-adays, were often idealistic; he would have seen himself as a knight errant, riding to the rescue of his lady. If he was suffering from a weakened heart, digging a hole deep enough to bury a body, and making good the surrounding ground, would not have been the best activity for him to engage in; how much had that act of chivalry affected his health subsequently?

We all die of heart failure in the end, he thought, even

if we are initially felled by other diseases, but David had met his end too soon.

Roger came into the kitchen while he was entertaining these reflections.

'There's been a bit of excitement in the village,' he remarked.

'You mean the body found under a fallen tree?' said Adam, thus depriving Roger of the pleasure of breaking the news to him.

'So you know about it?'

'I should think it's all round the village by now,' said Adam. Of course, Roger would have heard of it officially. 'I was round at Linda's – Jo was there, too. There was some gale damage at Field House, but nothing much, and I saw the tree down in the next garden. I went across to see if Mrs Trent needed any help.'

'Did she? Was he there – Martin?'

'She was shocked,' said Adam. 'Who wouldn't be? And no, Martin wasn't. I don't think she knew where he was.'

'Not drunk in custody, anyway,' said Roger, cracking what was, for him, a joke. 'Maybe with some luckless woman.'

'This doesn't come under your jurisdiction, does it? This body?'

'No.' Roger was quite sorry; it would have been interesting to delve into something that must have happened a long time ago. 'It may take a while to identify the body,' he said. 'Ring dating on the tree will establish when it was planted, which will help, unless it's a really old body, going back several hundred years. It's more likely that someone planted the tree to cover up a grave.'

Testing of that kind would not be necessary, Adam thought. Forensic scientists would give an approximate date, and then it would be a short step to connecting it with Norman's sudden departure. Besides, hadn't that wily old man said the body was wearing a watch? If that proved no help in the identification, DNA testing might be all that was required; even from a corpse that had been long interred, it could be extracted, and a match made with Martin or his sister. His sister: should she be contacted?

It was not for him to say; that was Susan's business.

He wanted to ask how long the removal of the body would take, and how soon it would be identified, but he must not show too much curiosity. Even if the police suspected that Susan had killed her husband, it might be difficult to prove, after so long. There was no point in subjecting her to a lengthy and traumatic legal process, then sending her to prison, for what was probably an act of self-defence. Maybe she had stabbed him. She'd told him nothing about the actual killing, or the weapon used. Perhaps a knife would be found in the ground, with the body.

'The press will soon be round, I suppose,' he said.

'They've probably got on to it already. I expect the officer in charge will issue a statement, but as it's an old crime, it won't attract much notice. Not unless some juicy scandal surfaces,' said Roger. 'I wonder who lived there before the Trents.'

That was an interesting question, but pursuing it would not delay the police for long.

'Perhaps the person died naturally,' Adam hazarded, remembering not to give a gender to the victim.

'It's possible,' said Roger. 'Though unlikely.'

'How are you getting on with your robberies?'

While they were talking, Roger had fried three rashers of bacon and two eggs and had made some toast. He'd have another breakfast in the canteen, if time allowed.

'We've picked up a car they used. They'd left their masks in the boot,' he said. 'Silly buggers. If we get any suspects, there'll be traces to link them with the masks.'

'I hope you crack it soon, before anyone else gets hurt,' said Adam.

'So do I. These guys are good at finding small, fairly quiet shops and post offices where a raid can be carried out quickly. They've a good chance of clearing off with few witnesses. It's bad for the staff, though. Very scary. Upsets them for weeks.'

'I'm sure,' said Adam.

'What are you going to do today?' Roger asked, surprising Adam with his interest.

'I might go and see if I can help that old man and his grandson deal with the fallen tree,' said Adam. 'He's the old fellow who does the paper round. Maybe you've seen him in the mornings. He and his grandson help Mrs

Trent in the garden and they were there yesterday, clearing the neighbours' garden where the main branches crashed. The police were letting them go ahead. It was a big tree. The roots, where the body was, were a good distance from the upper branches.'

'Curious, are you?' Roger asked.

It was no good denying it. Roger was far too fly for that.

'I suppose so. And it might be no bad thing to be around if Martin comes home,' Adam said. 'You've seen what he's like. Mrs Trent's got some dreadful bruises on her face. The girls — Linda and her friend who works in Marsh's office with Mrs Trent — are quite anxious about her.'

'Well, whoever is under the tree, Martin can't have put him there — or her — since the tree's so old,' said Roger. 'I'm off now. Cheers.'

'Cheers,' said Adam, who, since arriving in England, had quickly learned to reciprocate this colloquial parting expression.

He walked up to get a paper after Roger left, but he did not meet the old man, Fred. Adam skimmed through *The Times*. There would be no Jo arriving at The Old Chapel today, as it was Saturday. Would those girls go on being nannies indefinitely? Or was it an occupation until they found the right man to marry? That might be difficult, since they spent their time with small children. At last he gave up on the paper and walked down to Cedar Cottage.

No one came to the door when he rang. Had Susan been arrested already? Surely not: identification of the body would take time – days, at least, he thought – unless she had crumpled and confessed. Then he heard the sound of a circular saw. Would that be Fred, already on the job? He decided not to approach by way of Dan and Fiona's house, realising that as it was the weekend, they would probably be at home. He would have to walk up Susan's garden to the police barrier and try his luck at finding out what was going on from there.

A uniformed officer soon barred his way, so Adam said that he had come to see if he could help remove the branches of the fallen tree from the neighbouring land. He displayed a strong pair of secateurs which he had borrowed from among Roger's tools in their garden shed. Roger need never know.

The constable, exasperated beyond bearing by the intermittent whining of Fred's saw, thought anything that accelerated the end of operations was worthwhile. He gave permission, adding that the use of secateurs was infinitely preferable to the saw. He couldn't think why Fred was being allowed to use it; the chief inspector, who had come to see how the scientists were getting on, had soon left the site; he didn't have to listen to it.

'Seen Mrs Trent today?' asked Adam nonchalantly.

'She's gone in to her office. Works in Rotherston,' said the bored constable. 'Might as well keep busy. Nasty for her, having this lot turn up in her garden.'

'Very nasty,' Adam agreed.

'Can't get too worked up about it,' said the constable. 'It's not as if it's recent, or a missing kiddie.'

'True,' said Adam, moving on. He felt as if the area was a minefield; at any moment, or more probably in several days, the whole thing would blow up, and then where would Susan be?

There was no point in thinking she should face up to what had happened; not after all this time. No one would connect David with this, for Susan would not mention him. His father's youthful, if misguided, chivalry had saved her; it was not up to Adam to undo his sacrifice.

He joined Fred, who was pleased to see him. Soon afterwards, the sound of the circular saw was heard no more. Owen had brought long-handled, very strong secateurs, the property of his father, and a pruning saw; with those, and the secateurs Adam produced, they dealt less noisily with the branches. Tackling the main trunk, in Susan's garden, must wait until the police had finished; then the saw could come into use again. Dan and Fiona's garden started to reappear from beneath the boughs. By midday, they had cleared as much as could be done for the present, pilling it up into manageable heaps. They'd make a bonfire of the twiggy bits, said Fred. It would have to be on Susan's land, where there was space, and on a still day when it would pose no threat or nuisance to neighbouring houses, some of which were thatched.

Fred and his grandson prepared to depart, Owen on

his bicycle, Fred on foot. As the boy pedalled off, Adam walked with Fred through Susan's garden to the road.

'The police wouldn't have let us even this near if that had been anything recent,' Fred remarked. 'Course, it's still a big garden, Mrs Trent's; she sold off the patch adjacent, where the young folk are, thirty years ago or more. Nice couple built the house; they were here for a long while, then moved. It's changed hands a few times since then.'

'I didn't know that,' Adam said. He'd noticed that Dan and Fiona's house was not in the vernacular style of the surrounding buildings, though it fitted in harmoniously. If he'd been an architect, like his father, he'd have seen it instantly.

'No – well, it was hard for Mrs Trent, with them children to raise,' Fred said. 'Brought her in a tidy sum of money at the time, as it seemed, but nothing like what it'd fetch today.'

'I suppose not,' said Adam.

'Now we know why she didn't sell off a bit more land,' said Fred.

'You think so?'

'Might have dug a swimming pool, mightn't they?' said Fred. 'Folk have more money than sense, these days.'

Adam laughed.

'What's your interest, then?' Fred asked.

'Mrs Trent's a nice person, and I don't like that son of hers. Martin,' Adam said.

'You're not the only one. Chip off the old block, he is,' said Fred. 'She should chuck him out.'

'I don't suppose it's easy. He is her son, after all.'

'About time that boy of his came down and took a bit of notice,' said Adam. 'Martin's boy, that is. Lives with his mother up Edinburgh way. Must be about Owen's age by now.'

'It'll get into the papers,' Adam said. 'Bound to. Maybe he'll get in touch then.'

'If his mother lets him.'

'Isn't he old enough to decide for himself?'

'Maybe,' said Fred. 'I expect she's sent him presents and that, all this time.' In fact, Fred knew she had, because his sister had run the village post office until eight years ago and she had told him so. Maybe the mother didn't let him have them.

If his grandmother were to be charged with murder, the boy was better out of it, thought Adam. They walked up the road together, parting at Chapel Row. Adam was keen to return Roger's secateurs before their owner missed them. But probably he'd be looking for his robbers over the weekend.

Fred, continuing homewards, met a journalist who stopped to ask him where the body had been found, and Fred took great pleasure in telling him he'd come to the wrong spot, sending him in the opposite direction towards the farm occupied by Jo's parents. If he got that far, they might mislead him further, once they knew the score.

Adam made himself a cheese sandwich. When he had eaten it, washing it down with a can of Heineken, he went back to Cedar Cottage. Somehow he felt compelled to keep a vigil, waiting there, perched on a low wall which ran beyond the terrace behind the house, away from the quiet, controlled scene at the end of the garden. He heard vehicles arriving in the road outside and the sound of voices. A plain black van reversed into the driveway, stopping near the garage. Then he watched the small procession as the body, covered on a stretcher, not in a body bag – that was to keep the bones together, he supposed – was loaded.

He did not watch it leave, turning his head away. He sat there, feeling numb, thinking about the young man who had buried it, his schoolboy father.

He needed company and it was Saturday. How could he find those nannies, or better still, Amy?

20

Debbie had begun to think about Christmas, which was only a month away. With the children out for the day, there was an opportunity to go shopping without them and she had planned to do that before Martin turned up.

Tentatively, after the girls had gone, she mentioned it, and to her surprised relief, Martin thought it an excellent idea. With her car available, it would be a chance for him to do the same, he said, with transport for his gifts. He fumed briefly about the injustice of having lost his licence, and Debbie kept quiet, for she had mixed feelings. She wanted to take his side and agree that it had not been fair, but she knew he drank too much, and if he had driven in the state she'd sometimes seen him, then he should be allowed nowhere near the controls of a car and it was as well that he had been arrested.

They decided to go to Reading, where there were large stores and a variety of smaller shops, very different from what Rotherston had to offer. For Debbie, it was quite a treat; she hadn't been there since she and Jim separated; and Martin was pleased to go where he wasn't known. He'd got his credit card; he could use that if he bought anything; he'd have to get something for Lily and Rose, he supposed. There was some money in his account, so he could draw out enough from a cash point to fund the day. He'd have to pay for their lunch and drinks, but he enjoyed making grand gestures when he could justify their cost. They had to buy petrol on the way. Martin sat in the car while she filled the tank, and as Debbie paid, she could not suppress the fleeting thought that it would have been nice if he'd offered to pay for it or given her money towards it, but she chided herself. The trip was her idea, to benefit her and the girls. He was sure to take her out to lunch somewhere nice; that was all she could expect.

At first, he set out to charm her. From his point of view, to be out with a young woman who adored him, no longer handicapped by the presence of her demanding children, was an agreeable way to spend the day. Shopping bored him, but he would indulge her. They went to toy departments and played with novelties, Martin at his best as Debbie drew his attention to this or that attraction. She found a number of small items to put in the girls' stockings, and wished she could afford a Wendy house as their main present; they would love one. Instead, she got them Barbie dolls, and some games.

'I suppose I should be saving up for a computer,' she said.

'They're much too young,' said Martin. 'It's good for them to play games with you and each other, not a machine.'

'I suppose you're right,' Debbie replied. 'But some of their friends have got them.'

'Resist the peer pressure,' Martin said. 'There's time enough.'

Debbie knew he was getting impatient. Men hated shopping.

'What about your mother? What will you get for her?' she asked.

Martin shrugged. He hadn't thought that far ahead.

'Some soap. Bath essence,' he said. 'She likes that sort of thing.'

'Shall we look for it?'

'It can wait,' said Martin.

Debbie thought he was lucky that he still had a mother to buy things for, but the old lady sounded quite a tyrant. She was fortunate that he chose to live with her.

They went to a pub for lunch, choosing steak and chips. Martin ordered a beer. Debbie was tempted to ask for wine, but she was driving, and though one glass would be acceptable, she would not risk it, asking instead for ginger ale.

The bar was busy; while they were eating, a burly man came past their table, which was in a corner near the window, and, as a customer left a seat not far from them, took his place.

Martin did not recognise Roger Morris, but the policeman remembered him. Devouring his steak and kidney pie, Roger watched him covertly. The woman he was with was a pretty little thing; she looked scared, giggling in a forced way at remarks Martin made, not saying much herself. She was picking at her food; what a waste. Martin took his empty glass to the bar for a refill, and briefly a desperate expression crossed her face.

Debbie was thinking, what am I doing here, in a stuffy, smoky pub with a man who – and she admitted it to herself, albeit fleetingly – frightens me?

When he returned, she gave him a bright smile and resumed toying with her steak. Martin gulped down several mouthfuls of his pint. Would he drive after this? Roger, not deterred from the pleasure of his own meal, glanced across from time to time at the pair. The woman made a remark and Martin replied, but they were not having an animated conversation; that, however, did not mean they were not content together. Who was the woman? He saw that she wore a wedding ring; Martin lived with his mother, so this was not his wife; was she two-timing a husband? Roger saw so much of the dark side of life that he often forgot that there could be another.

He saw Martin finish his pint and go to the bar for a refill, after sinking part of that he went off to the men's room. In his absence, the woman glanced at her watch and again seemed to sink into an apparent state of misery. Martin bullied his mother; did he also bully this woman? Some were born victims, and she looked like one. He lingered, planning to follow the couple when they left the pub; if Martin got behind the steering wheel of a car, Roger would intervene. He would use his warrant card to prevent Martin driving off, and he would summon a patrol car with a breathalyser to the scene. Now the woman was looking at her watch once more; she seemed to indicate that it was time for them to go. Martin still did not hurry; he finished his pint, and seemed about to fetch yet another but she spoke again, putting her hand on his arm, looking at him pleadingly. She was attractive, in a wan, defeated way; Roger hoped she knew what she was doing, with this man.

The pair got up and started putting on their coats. Martin's was an anorak, hers a black and white speckled tweed. She looked smart. Roger followed them from the pub and along the street. They were heading towards a car park. He walked behind them into it, and went with them in the lift to the level they were seeking. The woman did not know him, and Martin was revealing himself as an individual who saw nothing beyond his own nose; he never glanced at Roger. When the lift reached their level, he did not wait for the woman, nor stand back to let her leave first, stalking off down an aisle, the woman, who was wearing black leather ankle boots, almost trotting to keep pace with him.

They went up to a brown Nissan Micra, and the woman unlocked it. Roger saw her getting into the driver's seat while Martin Trent moved round to the passenger's side. In a way he was disappointed; he'd have liked to harass Martin. Roger made a mental note of the car's registration; he'd check out whose it was.

He wondered if Martin knew about the body unearthed in Bishop St Leon. Adam had said he wasn't there; doubtless he had been with this forlorn, pale woman. Even so, surely, when he discovered what had happened, he'd go back?

Debbie had been fretting about getting home.

'The girls aren't due back till this evening,' Martin said.

'I know, but sometimes Jim comes early,' she said. 'I hadn't warned him I'd be out.'

'You can't be at his beck and call,' said Martin.

'No, but I must be there for the girls,' said Debbie, managing to speak firmly. 'Besides, I want to get the parcels in and hidden.'

'And what about me? Don't I count for anything?'

'Of course, Martin. We've had a good day – don't let's spoil it with a quarrel,' Debbie said.

'Who's quarrelling? I'm not.' Martin's tone was truculent.

'Nor am I.' Debbie, concentrating on getting out of Reading, felt herself starting to tremble. She set her lips together, peering through the windscreen. It had begun to rain, and she turned the wipers on, while beside her, Martin sighed noisily. After a time he switched on the car radio and twiddled with the knobs, which distracted Debbie; she got flustered when she had an adult passenger, for it was so rare; she was used just to having the children in the rear and that was often difficult enough. Various bursts of music and talk alternated, and then Martin picked up a local news station. They both caught the tail end of an announcement that after the recent gales, a body, so far not identified, had been found beneath a tree that had been blown over in a village near Rotherston.

The report did not name the village.

Roger, back at his headquarters, asked a constable to trace the car whose number he had taken down. She soon came up with Debbie's name and address. After that, he got on to the officer in charge of the Bishop St Leon incident, and told them where they might find Martin Trent, if he was not at home and they wished to locate him in the light of any further developments. He learned that the body had been taken to the mortuary, but had not yet been identified. The pathologist had so far said very little; it was certainly not a recent burial. The body was male, and there was a wound to the skull which was probably the fatal injury; more than that could not be said at present.

*　　*　　*

Adam had rung Amy at Marsh's office; as she had been working the previous Saturday he wondered if she would be there today. He hoped Susan wouldn't answer; he would feel embarrassed at revealing a personal interest in Amy. However, a male voice answered, and soon he was speaking to Amy.

At first she hesitated, but then she agreed to go out to dinner with him. They arranged when he would pick her up at her flat, and he rang Chris in his workshop for advice on where to take her. Achieving this, he felt considerably cheered.

He had not mentioned the body; discussing its discovery could wait.

Roger spent a busy afternoon at headquarters catching up on paperwork. So much policing was bureaucratic; hours were spent collecting evidence and statements, preparing cases which, when they went to court, were shot down by clever barristers fighting wars with words. Roger had always preferred being out catching villains. Now, so many got away with it, and knew how to play the system; young louts, and girls too, mocked the law.

He was off duty that night, and had nothing planned. For want of a better idea, he'd go to the Crown, within walking distance of his bed, so that he could have a few drinks, listen to what was being said around him and find out what village gossip had to say about the body. The discovery would be the talk of Bishop St Leon by this time, and the media would be on to it, though as it could not relate to any recent missing persons inquiry, it was unlikely to attract much attention. Mrs Trent would be upset, however; it must have been shocking for her. He wondered how long she had lived in Cedar Cottage, and who had been the previous owner. Once the body had been dated, those would be the obvious questions the investigating team would ask. Lately, a number of un-solved murder cases had been reopened because scientific advances had made it possible for fresh evidence to emerge. Those who had got away with murder for twenty years or more, and were feeling safe, might now be called to account. Judging by the head wound, this was likely to be the body of a murdered man; perhaps it was an intruder who had been killed in self-defence by a terri-fied householder. Then, as now, the innocent householder would fear arrest, but years ago he would have been more likely to escape a charge than he would today.

At last it was time to go home, and no new major case had arrived for Roger to attend to; there were simply the normal thefts, road accidents and minor fights on his patch, and ongoing investigations were proceeding in their normal slow way. The post office robbers were no doubt counting their spoils; they wouldn't be out today, when their targets closed at midday. Monday would be the first time they would strike again, but there were always inter-vals between their raids. Money for drugs was probably what they wanted and they'd be quiet now until they needed fresh supplies.

When he got home, Adam was in. He was upstairs, showering, whistling to himself. Roger went to his own room and changed into a sweater and jeans. Then he ate a bag of crisps. He'd bought some at the pub at lunch-time. Strangely, they didn't taste as good as usual. Even so, he took another packet with him to the sitting room, where there was a larger television set than the one he had in his own room. He put it on; he might whip up some interest in the football results.

He was sitting there when Adam entered.

'Hi,' said Adam cheerfully.

'Hi,' Roger replied, sounding surly. Then he made an effort. 'Going out?' It was obvious; Adam was attired in dark trousers, a polo sweater and a cord jacket.

'Yes.'

'You got a date with one of those nannies?'

'Not a nanny, no, but I've got a date,' Adam admitted. Then he relented and added, 'She shares a flat with Linda.'

'Oh, does she?' Roger said.

For a mad moment Adam felt like suggesting they ring up to see if Linda could join them, and make a four with Roger; then he thought of Linda's probable reaction and held back.

'What are you going to do?' he asked, instead.

'I'll go to the Crown,' said Roger. 'I expect it will be buzzing with guesses about the body.'

'I expect it will,' said Adam, and his high spirits shrivelled. This was the lull before the storm. Susan's day of reckoning could not be long delayed.

Roger noticed the sudden collapse of his elation. Why?

'I saw Martin Trent today, in Reading,' he said. 'He didn't notice me. He was with a woman.'

'Oh.' Adam was not interested in any woman who might be involved with Martin. 'Well, if he's with someone, he won't be bullying his mother,' he said.

'True,' said Roger. 'I don't suppose he knows what's happened here.'

'He'll soon find out, I imagine,' said Adam.

'Yes,' said Roger.

'I expect it will take your lot some time to find out whose the body is,' Adam said.

'Probably,' said Roger. 'There's no hurry, in a case like this. Whoever stowed it away in the earth may be long dead themselves, and in any case, isn't likely to be a danger to the public.'

'That's so,' said Adam. 'Well, I'd best be off.' He turned to go, then, as a waft of vinegar reached his nostrils, he said, 'Roger, I don't want to offend you, but those crisps you eat smell terrible. It's like having a case of bad breath. Couldn't you try plain salted?' and he went away, leaving behind him a wake of aftershave, which Roger could not smell above the crisps.

*   *   *

Linda was in the flat when Adam arrived to collect Amy.

She knew about the body; she had seen the police arrive at Cedar Cottage the day before, but had not learned of the discovery until Jo telephoned with the news that morning. It was she who, when Amy returned from the office, had told her.

'When you phoned, I'd no idea,' Amy said to Adam. 'You didn't mention it, and nor did Susan. Not one word.'

'Fancy her even going to work,' said Linda.

'She probably thought it best to carry on as usual,' said Adam. 'After all, do you arrive all smiling and announce, "By the way, a body was found in my garden yesterday"? That's not Susan's style.'

'But all the same – to say nothing,' Linda said.

'It's dreadful.' Amy shivered. 'Poor Susan. As if she hadn't got enough on her plate, with Martin.'

'I wonder who it is? The body, I mean,' said Linda. 'It may have been there for a hundred years or more. Perhaps they'll find others. Perhaps it was an old burial ground.'

'Perhaps,' said Adam, feeling himself an utter hypocrite. Then he turned to Amy. 'Shall we go?' he said, and smiled, somewhat apologetically, at Linda.

She read his mind.

'I'm going out,' she said. 'Jo and I are going to the cinema with two guys she knows. Should be all right.'

'I hope it is,' said Amy.

'As long as one of them's not Roger,' Linda said.

'It isn't,' Adam answered, thankful that he hadn't given in to his wild impulse.

As they drove to the restaurant, Amy asked whether Adam knew if Roger was on the case of the body, and Adam explained that it was outside his area. They discussed it for a while, and then they talked about themselves. Adam asked Amy how long she had been in the district, and she told him about her army boyfriend. It was serious, she said, and felt better for the confession.

He told her, truthfully, that his father, who lived in New Zealand, had died recently, leaving him some money, and that he had decided to spend some of it on a sabbatical, in England.

They enjoyed their evening, and when he took her home, dropping her at her door, he kissed her lightly on the cheek, a kiss which she returned.

He felt bleak, leaving her.

21

Susan was in no hurry to leave the office. She wanted to postpone returning home, but not for the usual reason of avoiding Martin, if he had returned. Would he come back when he heard about the body? And when would that be? By now it would have been removed, she hoped. Would the police have packed up their tent and gone? She had little idea of what happened at such times; images of television news bulletins, following such discoveries, were all she knew. She was prepared to find a police officer standing at her door, ready to arrest her, but there was only one officer outside. There were several journalists, though, with microphones and cameras, which they thrust at her as the policeman beckoned her forward, asking the reporters to stand back and give her passage.

Susan drove through the gates. If she knocked someone down, that was their fault; she could not be in more trouble than she was already. Somehow, she negotiated the driveway; a police car was parked beside the garage but it did not block her passage as she put the car away. The police had already asked about the Honda in the second garage; she had told them it was her son's car and was not taxed or insured because he was so often abroad. If they were curious, let them find out the real reason for themselves.

The police officer closed the gate behind her, and a colleague appeared from the site of the discovery, where piled up willow branches in Dan and Fiona's garden prevented access from that side. The constables told the media to go away; Mrs Trent had nothing to say, and there would be a police press release later on that evening.

The police were kind. They shielded her as she went into the house, advising her to lock the doors and draw the curtains, only letting someone in if she knew who they were. Susan agreed, but she did not put the bolt across the door. Martin might return, and she could not stop him from entering.

At the office, neither Brian nor Nigel had commented on her drawn appearance – she knew she looked a wreck – and as they did not know about the body, they attributed it to the tense situation between her and Martin. Susan feared that she had only partially succeeded in deceiving her colleagues about the reason for her bruises; Martin and she had an uneasy relationship and that was an accepted fact. She still hoped that they would not believe that he attacked his own mother.

Later, she went into the garden, through the back door. The exterior light came on as she moved away from the house, towards the tree. Selling off some land for building had been prudent; the money had been very useful. The agent had tried to persuade her to let more land go, but Susan had to keep the willow and its secret within her boundary. Gardens big enough for children to play football in were increasingly scarce; new houses were packed densely into small plots with what were mere back yards behind them, but there were plenty of good-sized gardens in the older properties in Bishop St Leon. Both Susan and her neighbours had long gardens, and hers was wide, but so much of it was grass – some lawn and some rough orchard – that as long as it was mown, maintenance was minimal.

She went towards the site. The tent was still up, and two officers were guarding it. The opening was half towards her, away from the bole of the tree, and other figures were working within its shelter. There lay the hole into which David had tipped Norman's body on that fateful night. What else had gone down there with him? Had David dropped a vital clue which would have lasted all these years – a handkerchief marked with a name tape, as was customary then for schoolboys, or some other object? It was before the days of large plastic bags for rubbish; he must have used the wheelbarrow to wheel Norman there. The old galvanized one had long gone; its lighter replacement was made of green plastic. Or had he carried Norman slung across his shoulders, or dragged him by his heels? She had not asked, and she would never know now; that boy had borne his secret to his own grave. The action, however it was carried out, might have weakened his already damaged heart; that was something else to which she would never know the answer.

The police officers did not speak to her, nor she to them. She walked slowly back to the house, entering the way she had left, through the back door. Then she walked through to the sitting room. She lit the gas fire, but she did not turn the light on, sitting in the semi-dark, hunched into a corner of the sofa, remembering.

While Jim was driving back to Rotherston from Windsor, Kate rang him on his mobile.

She told him that a body had been discovered in a village near his destination.

'Might be interesting,' she said. 'It's been there ages. A tree blew over and there it was, a skeleton beneath the roots.'

'I'll stop and ring you back,' said Jim, who did not like using his phone while he was driving.

He was travelling along minor country roads; away from heavy, fast traffic, it was easier to communicate with the children, and in daylight there were things of interest to see, but it was dark now. He soon found a place to pull in off the road and ring Kate back.

She had heard about the body while at work herself.

'They found it yesterday,' she said. 'So far there's been no identification. There may be a story in it, even if it's been there several hundred years. It's in the grounds of a house in a village called Bishop St Leon.'

'I know where that is,' Jim said. 'Thanks, Kate. I'll get along there.'

If there was anything in the story, he'd pass it on to a colleague who might use him in the follow-up.

He didn't want to tell the girls about something so gruesome. Luckily, further along the road, he saw a fox running on ahead of them. He slowed down; the animal was held in his headlights and he pointed it out to the girls, who watched it as it turned and seemed to look at his vehicle, its eyes gleaming in the dark. Then it ran across in front of them and vanished.

That diverted them.

He had meant to have a talk with Debbie about her friend Martin. Now there wouldn't be time; others would already be at Bishop St Leon ahead of him.

Debbie came to the gate as he pulled up.

'Sorry – I can't stop,' he said, handing her the bags containing what they had acquired in Windsor. 'We've seen such a wonderful doll's house,' he added. 'Tell Mummy all about it,' he instructed as he started to unbuckle them. Windsor was a good place to go, he had decided, with a swimming pool and the safari park, as well as what was in the town, and it had a pantomime each year which sounded as if it was the real, old-fashioned sort, aimed at children. Why hadn't he discovered that sooner, when he and Debbie were together?

Because he hadn't given enough time and thought to it, just as now he was hurrying off after this tale of a body instead of tackling Debbie about her inappropriate choice of company.

'I've got to chase a story,' he told her, and she saw how his face had lit up with excitement at the prospect. 'Some old body's been dug up at a house in Bishop St Leon.'

'Old body?'

'Been there ages. Years and years,' he said.

'Martin lives in Bishop St Leon,' she said.

'Does he really? And is he there now, or inside, waiting to get his hands on my daughters?' Jim's tone was bitter.

'How dare you?' Debbie's furious response was instant. 'How dare you insult my friends? Why —' and she was about to say how generous towards the children Martin was, but he had never bought them anything.

'I've no time to argue,' Jim said. 'We'll discuss it some other time.'

By now the girls, being lifted from the vehicle, had picked up on their parents' acrimonious voices, and they had both begun to cry. Debbie, already laden with the parcels, clutched their hands, shepherding them inside. She banged the door.

Jim stood for a moment in the road, angry and frustrated. Then he got into the Daihatsu and drove away.

*　　　*　　　*

Martin had not wanted to be there when Jim returned, but he had nowhere else to go, except home or to one of the pubs. It was comfortable in Debbie's house, and once the children had related the tale of their day's activities, they would soon be off to bed, so that he could have a cosy domestic evening with their mother. He was prepared to be a father figure for the evening, even to the extent of reading to them when they went upstairs, but Debbie, who seemed upset after her encounter with Jim, said that she would see to them. She sounded firm. Martin was very willing, over this, to yield to her wishes, and he sank back with the paper, which he had bought in Reading. He might try the crossword; lately, he hadn't bothered.

Debbie, hearing about the great big church they'd been to, and the armour they had seen, and the lovely doll's house, listened and made comments while in her mind Jim's accusation echoed.

Martin would never – had never – no: she would not even think about it.

'You weren't getting on too well with hubby, were you?' Martin could not refrain from taunting her, when she came downstairs. 'I heard angry voices.'

'He's in a hurry. Some news story in Bishop St Leon. Some body that's been found,' she said.

'Body? In Bishop St Leon?'

'Yes. An old body. Prehistoric, maybe,' Debbie said. 'He's gone to chase the story.' She left him, going into the kitchen. They'd have some supper; then, eventually, bed-time would follow. She dreaded it. Jim's accusation had been slanderous but even so, having Martin in her bed when the girls were there did seem wrong, and since the night she and Jim had spent together, she had not wanted Martin to touch her. But without him, she was alone.

Prehistoric? That might be interesting. Martin decided to find out more. He picked up Debbie's phone and dialled the Crown.

When Des answered, Martin said, speaking formally, 'Good evening, Des. It's Martin Trent.'

'Oh, Martin. Well?' said Des. The telephone was not in the bar; he had to go behind to answer it. 'What is it?'

'Someone's just told me a body's been found in the village,' Martin said. 'A prehistoric discovery.' His mind was racing on, as he wrote up the significance of the find, salvaging his academic reputation and receiving plaudits for his scholarship.

'I don't know about prehistoric,' Des was saying. 'It was underneath that big willow in your garden. It blew down yesterday, and the body was beneath the roots. Been there a while, it's reckoned.'

Martin banged the telephone down. His heart was thumping and his head was spinning. Under the old willow, Des had said: that tree had been there for years, as long as he could remember, almost.

Almost: he could remember that it wasn't always big, but as he grew, so did it; its long branches, in the summer, made a tent, and his stupid sister played inside it with her dolls, calling it a palace.

When was it planted? Why couldn't he remember? And then, in fragments, wisps of memory returned. He heard loud voices and felt pain.

He must get over there. Something terrible had happened, but not now; it was long ago, and he was very small.

Martin flung his anorak on, grabbed Debbie's car keys from the bowl in the hall where she kept them and rushed out of her house. He scrambled into her car and drove away.

Jim had called at the Crown for directions and had been told only that there was nothing to see. The body, not identified, had been removed. There was nothing of interest to the media.

'This gentleman may be able to help you,' said the landlord, not eager to aid a journalist who would only add to poor Mrs Trent's troubles.

A large man with faded ginger hair had detached himself from a group around the bar.

'Detective Inspector Morris,' said Roger. 'There will be a press release later this evening,' he advised. 'The police press officer will have any information.'

Jim knew that this would be so.

'Where was it found?' he asked.

'Oh – where some tree blew down,' was all that anyone would say. 'Several did, around the area.'

They'd all clammed up, particularly Detective Inspector Morris. Jim recognised a dead end when he met one; nevertheless, he drove on down the road and knew he had found the site when he met the tapes and the constable on duty. Two tired, cold reporters, one from the local paper and one freelance, remained there, maintaining vigil, as a light rain began to fall. Jim strolled over and introduced himself. They had little to add to what he had already learned. The house owner, a Mrs Susan Trent, aged sixty-plus, had returned from work and was inside; there was a son, but he was not at home. The body was unlikely to be interesting, except that it had been interred a long time ago.

'Did anyone go missing, many years ago?' asked Jim.

Neither of his informants knew.

'Maybe we should see if we can find out,' Jim suggested.

But where to start? Not in the Crown; no one there was talking. There were two other pubs in the village.

The three of them decided to move on and try their luck in one or both of them.

They were long gone, and the policeman on the gate was chatting to his colleagues in the garden when Martin drew up outside in Debbie's car.

*　　*　　*

He had not driven for months, and her little car, without powered steering and so small, felt alien. He crashed the gears and even stalled the engine. Fortunately he knew the tank was almost full.

He stopped in the road, just past Cedar Cottage. A police patrol car was parked beside the garage, and the gates and fence were draped with tape to keep people out. Martin could not see a police officer, but those from the car might not be far away. Cautious now, he stepped under the tape by the front gate. He had his key.

Susan never heard him opening the door. He came quietly into the sitting room, where she was lying on the sofa.

'Well, Martin. You've heard the news, I suppose,' said Susan. He had turned the light on and the sudden glare made her blink. She must have drowsed off.

He was looking at her strangely, almost not focussing. When he spoke, his voice was slurred.

'Des said a body. Under the willow tree,' he said.

'That's right,' said Susan. 'It's your father, Martin. The police don't know that yet, but they'll find out, soon enough, so you may as well be told.'

'But he went away. He left us. You made him go,' said Martin, still speaking in that strange tone.

'I didn't, Martin. You did. You were so gallant. You were only a tiny boy, but he had been hitting you, and then he started hitting me. He slipped and fell, and you picked up a fire iron and hit him on the head. Probably you killed him, Martin, or it may have been because he hit his head when he fell, like those times I fell and hit my head. Remember?' She wouldn't mention David, even now.

He didn't remember, but then, perhaps he did. Strange echoes sounded in his ears. Martin stared down at her. She was smiling and relaxed, not scared at all. He didn't like that; he needed her to be afraid.

'You buried him. You planted trees,' he said.

'The willow tree grew well,' she said. 'He would have killed me, one day.' Susan spoke dreamily. 'Maybe he'd have killed you, too. Don't you remember how he used to hit you? You'd bumped into his car when he was washing it, that day, with your little tricycle.' She could see it now, so clearly, and Norman's enraged, purple face.

Martin did remember. He remembered fear and anger.

'It was your fault,' he said. 'He took it out on me because of you. It was always all your fault.'

She was still smiling as he picked up the table lamp with the heavy marble base that stood on a table near her, pulling its wire from its socket, and as he hit her with it, it was Norman's angry face she saw before she lost consciousness.

22

In the Crown, the talk was all about the body. Des was pleased at the way he and Roger had headed off a nosy journalist; and others during the day had been misdirected, not only by him but by those who wanted to protect Susan Trent from harassment. People were hazarding guesses as to who it was, buried there so long.

Roger asked who had lived in Cedar Cottage before Susan but no one in the pub could remember that far back, though some recalled several past owners of other houses.

'Field House was once the doctor's surgery,' Nicholas Waters, captain of cricket, recalled. His parents lived in the village, down-sized into a small modern house in a development where once there had been allotments, and Nicholas and his family had taken over their Georgian house in the square. 'I can remember going there,' he said. 'Then the new surgery was built behind the village hall, and they moved away.'

'They?' asked Roger.

'The doctor and his wife. Dr Fraser, that was. There was a son, too. He lived abroad.'

Fraser: that was the name on Adam's passport. Adam Wilson Fraser.

'Whereabouts, abroad?' he asked.

Nicholas did not know, but he thought the parents had retired to Spain or Portugal.

'My mother probably remembers,' he said.

Roger let it go for the moment. Why had Adam hidden his connection with the village? Why had he come to Bishop St Leon?

'Martin Trent rang earlier,' said Des. 'He asked about the body. He'd heard about it on the news, and wanted details. I told him it had been found under the fallen willow in his mother's garden and he rang off. I guess he'll be in here later.'

There were some groans at this.

'How long ago did he ring?' asked Roger.

'I'm not sure,' said Des. He glanced at the clock above the bar. 'Quite a while. An hour, maybe. Perhaps less.'

Roger thumped his glass, half full, down on the bar counter and headed out of the pub, off along the road. When last seen by him, Martin had been well tanked up and time had passed since then; he'd have had more by now. Roger ran clumsily, not cut out for speed. There'd still be officers at the site where the body had been found. They'd stop Martin and question him, but they could not deny him entrance to his home unless they were also barring Susan. This seemed unlikely, since whoever had lain buried there so long was not the victim of a recent crime.

As he ran, a car came rushing towards him, headlights full on, swerving wildly. Leaping out of its way almost into a hedge, Roger looked after it, dimly making out part of the registration. He had taken special note of a Nissan Micra earlier in the day; he was almost sure this small car, hurtling by, had the same number.

The house was locked and silent. No lights showed between the curtains. Roger knocked and rang, but there was no answer, and soon one of the officers on duty came round the corner of the house to challenge him.

Heads might roll later, but not now. Roger produced his warrant card and asked if anyone had seen Mrs Trent that evening. Yes, she had come home, and had walked up the garden later. She'd seemed quiet, and they'd let her be, because the poor woman deserved some peace. They'd managed to get rid of the press because their guvnor was going to make a statement later.

'Did you see a Nissan Micra? It nearly ran me down just now and I believe it was being driven by Mrs Trent's son,' said Roger.

They'd heard a car drive away from somewhere close

at hand, roaring off in low gear, but they hadn't seen it.

Roger told the constable off for not leaving someone on duty in the road, warning that he'd hear more about it later. Then he told the man to accompany him as they went round the house.

The back door was unlocked.

Roger went in, putting on the light. Slowly he walked through the house, the constable following. Susan Trent could be with a neighbour, Roger was thinking, and she might not have locked up, since police officers were allegedly on guard. He was like a panther, thought the following constable, alarmed already about his own future; such a big man but so quiet.

No one was in the kitchen or the dining room. Roger opened the sitting room door. There were no lights on, but the gas fire was flickering, a representation of glowing coals. Susan Trent was lying on the sofa, her sightless eyes staring upwards, and her face a pulp. Roger had seen too many dead bodies during his career not to recognise another instantly.

He stretched out a hand to stop the constable from entering.

'This is a murder scene,' he said. 'But I'll just check she's dead.'

There was no doubt. The weapon lay beside her on the floor, a heavy lamp, now spattered with blood.

'Get on to your guvnor,' Roger said. 'Martin Trent is

the person to be asked about what happened here. And put a call out for this car.' He pulled out his notebook, in which he had written down the registration.

This had been feared. Now it had happened. Why, at this particular moment?

He waited at the scene until the local CID officers arrived, and explained that since he had been living in the village, he had become aware of the uneasy relationship existing between Martin Trent and his mother, the dead woman. He said that by chance he had seen Martin Trent in Reading earlier that day, and, observing that he had had a lot to drink, followed him to make sure he would not attempt to drive, hence his knowledge of the car's number.

It should be picked up pretty quickly. Martin might try to flee the country, or he might dump the car and lie low. Driving recklessly, he might crash the car and cause an accident to someone else.

Roger left the scene as soon as he had passed on the information in his possession and walked back to Chapel Row, where it was still quiet; Adam and Chris were both out on their dates.

Good luck to them, thought Roger, and was about to reach out for a pack of crisps when he had a thought.

Five minutes later he got into his Mondeo and drove off.

*　　*　　*

Debbie knew Martin had left the house. The door slammed behind him and then, to her astonishment, she heard her car start up. She was sure it was her Micra, but to make certain she ran to the door and opened it. True enough, it had gone.

What had made him dash off without a word? More to the point, he had had too much to drink, and had lost his licence. Her car was insured third party only to save money, and though it wasn't worth a lot, it was a lifeline. How would she get the children to their playgroup, herself to work, even escape the confines of the house without it?

She'd upset him, somehow, but what had she done?

It must have been Jim. She thought back to their last exchange. Jim had been in a hurry to get off because of a story that had broken, a body found in Bishop St Leon, prehistoric, probably. She'd mentioned it to Martin and gone into the kitchen. Not ten minutes later, he had driven away.

His mother, the old witch, lived in that village, but that was mere coincidence. Perhaps he had wanted to make certain that it wasn't close to where he lived. Debbie dithered, frightened and uneasy. She was getting used to Martin's mood swings, but taking her car was something else; he called a taxi when he wanted to go home.

Maybe he'd tried to get one, but the lines were busy.

Now she wondered if she'd heard the telephone click when she went into the kitchen, but she'd closed the door to keep the smell of food inside. Martin had complained about it once or twice. Slowly she crossed to the instrument, lifted the receiver and pressed the redial button. She had to hold on for a long time before a male voice answered, 'Crown.'

Crown?

'Crown where?' she asked.

'Bishop St Leon,' said the voice, sounding impatient.

'Sorry. Wrong number,' Debbie said, and replaced the receiver. She felt rather sick, and her heart was pounding.

For some reason, Martin was in such a hurry to get to the Crown in Bishop St Leon that he didn't even try to get a taxi, though why he had telephoned the pub was a mystery. She went back to the kitchen and put away the meal she had been preparing. She wasn't hungry. Probably Martin would return the car eventually. If not, it would be at his house in Bishop St Leon, she supposed. Or at the Crown. She wouldn't need it tomorrow, as it was Sunday; she'd rather hoped they might take the children out for the day, but they'd just been to Windsor.

Debbie made herself a cup of coffee and went into the sitting room, where she turned on the television. There wouldn't be a news bulletin until much later, and the programmes that were showing were unappealing, but she let a comedy pass before her eyes while the day's events ran through her mind, ending with her angry spat with Jim.

It was always work with him. It came first every time. Why, when Rose was in the hospital, he hadn't cared. Sitting there, Debbie managed to work up a great fury against him.

He would know what had happened in Bishop St Leon. That was why he had left so suddenly; he'd phone some friend with the main story and hope to get a spin-off. She could ring him on his mobile and ask about it, but surely a prehistoric body wasn't all that exciting? People dug them up all the time, didn't they? It wasn't like a modern one, a recent crime. This one might be interesting, but scarcely urgent. She wouldn't demean herself by calling him; she wouldn't give him the satisfaction of finding out that Martin had taken her car to go over there.

Of course, Jim didn't know that Martin had no licence, but he wasn't going to pile up her car, so there was no need to worry about the insurance. If he didn't bring the Micra back either later, or tomorrow, she could telephone him at his mother's house and tell him she was coming to collect it. She had the spare key. It would mean taking a taxi to get over there. She couldn't possibly ask anyone to take her, as a favour; you didn't interrupt families on their Sundays. Nor did she want to advertise the difficulties she was having in her relationship with Martin. Maybe, once she'd got the car back, she should end it. It wasn't going anywhere, and it was causing trouble between her and Jim, not that he could talk, with that Kate person. But without Martin, she would be alone again, and he could be nice; he'd been nice today, until he'd got bored.

It was the drink, really. If he gave that up, everything would be fine, but would he? Could he, even?

Debbie was still sitting there, with the television on, when she thought she heard a car draw up outside. She snapped the sound off and started towards the window. There was the Nissan. It was working, anyway; even if he'd scraped a wing, he hadn't smashed it up. And he'd come back to her. A warm glow filled her; he needed her. Whatever had been so urgent mattered less than she did.

As Martin got out of the car, he seemed to be stumbling. She rushed to open the front door for him, and he almost fell through it. She drew him into the hall, closing the door behind him, and then she saw the blood. The front of his anorak, which was unfastened, was splashed with it, and so was his sweater. She touched it, and her hand came away all sticky.

He had had an accident, after all, but he was alive and he wasn't badly hurt or he couldn't have driven.

'Where does it hurt? What happened? Have you cut yourself?' Debbie asked. 'Come into the kitchen and let me see to you. Is it your head?' It must be; he was so dazed. Head wounds bled extensively. Maybe he'd pitched forward through the windscreen; she hadn't seen if it was shattered.

Martin allowed himself to be led into Debbie's kitchen. He let her ease his anorak off; she bundled it, lining outwards, into a corner. Then she made him sit down, pushing him on to a chair. He did not resist. She took a clean tea towel from a drawer and ran it under the tap, coming back to wipe his face.

'Where does it hurt, Martin? Tell me,' she said, and added, as if to one of the children, 'Let me make it better.'

Roger hadn't put it all together yet.

Adam, returning after an early end to his evening out, found a note on the table in his room.

In confidence: Susan Trent is dead. News not released yet so keep quiet and your head down. R.

Adam stared at it, horrified. Susan was dead! No great mystery about the killer, that would be for sure, unless it had all been too much for her and she had taken her own life. Why had Roger given him this news, and why the advice to keep his head down? Adam was baffled. Had Roger guessed his connection with the village?

Then he remembered his briefcase. He had left it, unlocked, in his room the day before. Had the nosy bastard poked about and found his passport? If so, what had made him curious?

Was it his interest in Susan Trent, which might have appeared extreme for someone who had met her only recently? Had it seemed strange? After all, Roger was a policeman. Adam tore the message into tiny fragments, took them downstairs and burned them in the sink, thinking he was behaving like someone in a gangster film.

He couldn't go to bed, after hearing this news. He put the television on and sat in front of it, like Debbie, taking very little in.

There was no way of knowing which direction Martin had taken, after leaving Bishop St Leon. Sometimes people committed suicide after such a crime – murdered their children so as to take them away from their ex-wives, and then killed themselves; shot their faithless wives so that no other man could have them and then shot themselves. Martin might do something similar, though as he had grabbed the table lamp and killed Susan with it, he must have done it on the spur of the moment, in a sudden rage. Maybe she had mocked him, jeered at him. But what was he doing driving that woman's car?

Roger knew that every patrol car in the area would be looking for it. He would go and ask the woman why Martin had taken it.

He drove slowly into the quiet, residential road where Mrs Deborah Grant lived. There, outside her house, was the Nissan, not neatly parked but halted at an angle. Roger parked his car on the other side of the road and took his big torch from it, then got out and locked the car. He walked over to the Nissan and shone the torch around it.

There was a big scratch along one wing; it looked fresh. He flashed the beam inside, and thought he saw drops of blood on the upholstery.

Martin Trent, having killed his mother, was most probably inside this house.

Debbie couldn't find a cut of any sort. Maybe Martin's wound was underneath his clothing.

He was still trembling and shaking, submitting to her dabbing at his face and sponging his hands.

'What happened, Martin?' she tried asking, but he didn't answer. 'Where does it hurt? Did another car run into you?' Even in this crisis moment, she turned her question round, not asking if he had hit someone else. Yet he must have been involved in an accident; why else would he be in such a state? Perhaps it was his fault – probably it was – hence his flight back here.

She turned away and poured him a glass of water. He had had too much to drink; water was a remedy. Then she put the kettle on, thinking, tea for shock.

Martin gulped at the water; some dribbled down his chin and she dabbed at it; his jaw was stubbly; Jim's, by evening, would rasp her face like sandpaper but she had never liked to mention it. The drink seemed to steady Martin a little. He took the glass from her, holding it with both hands, which shook. It was no good trying to question him while he was in such a state; besides, what did it matter? He did not seem to be seriously hurt, and her car was driveable, since he had got here in it. Perhaps he was concussed; that was why he wasn't registering.

'It doesn't matter about the car, Martin,' she reassured him. 'You're all right. That's what matters.'

Martin turned a blotched and haggard face towards her.

'He's dead,' he said. 'He was dead all this time. Not gone. Dead. And she says I did it.' He spoke jerkily, the sentences coming out like pistol shots.

He'd killed someone. He'd been in an accident and someone had been killed. A witness had declared that Martin was responsible, and the chances were that this was true. It had been a hit-and-run. Well, that part was over now; as there was a witness, ambulances would be at the scene so she had no responsibility as far as that was concerned.

'You didn't mean to,' she consoled.

Suddenly, he turned on her. Pushing down on the table with his hands, he stood up and glared at her.

'You silly, stupid bitch,' he yelled. 'How do you know what I meant to do? You're another one, a useless cow, a balls-eater, no good to anyone.' He looked wildly round the kitchen and saw a rack of knives, high on the wall, intended to be out of reach of childish hands. He grabbed one from it, and as Debbie, unbelieving, terrified, took a step away from him, he advanced towards her.

'Martin, no, stop! I'm your friend,' Debbie quavered.

He'd gone mad. Whatever accident he'd been in had made him flip. She had to calm him down, and if he went on making such a noise, the girls would wake. 'We love you, Martin, the girls and I. Please sit down and let me give you a cup of tea.'

'Tea,' he snarled. 'Tea. That's all you want, tea and cakes, shopping, nice and tidy. Where's your brain? No wonder that husband of yours walked out on you. No wonder my father—' and then he stopped suddenly, took a deep breath and another step towards her.

Debbie had moved so that the table was between them. She edged round a little more, until Martin's back was now towards the sink and hers towards the door. She must try to calm him down. If she made a run for it and shut him in, he'd easily get out, but it was what she'd have to try and do.

Martin's mind was whirling. Images, long suppressed, of the last time he had seen his father, were blurring in his memory. Terror, blood, the savage face of the angry man he knew as Daddy, bending over, beating him and hitting at his mother: then, nothing.

She'd killed him, all those years ago. She'd provoked his father with her stupid ways, and he'd struck out, but she, intent on vengeance, had rounded on him, killing him, and now she was accusing him, a tiny child, of murder. Well, he'd punished her, that evil bitch, his mother. Only here was another one, another selfish, brain-less cow who was clucking at him, wanting him to be a good, quiet boy and then nobody would hurt him. This one was talking about a cup of tea.

Martin lashed out with the knife, stretching across the table, but he couldn't reach Debbie. He was edging round the table so that now it was she, retreating, who had her back to the sink and he had the freedom of the house behind him. She had missed what chance she had to run for it. Then, to her horror, she saw, standing in the doorway, Rose and Lily, holding hands, white-faced and, so far, silent. She put her hand to her lips and edged round again; she must get him back to the other side.

'Sh,' she said loudly, as she saw Lily open her mouth. 'It's a game,' she cried, and as Martin, his attention briefly faltering, turned to glance behind him, she put her hands under the table, lifted it up, and pushed it over, into him.

He didn't fall, but he stumbled and he dropped the knife. Debbie was round him in a flash and out of the door, taking time to bang it shut behind her. Then she grabbed the girls, just as the front door bell pealed. She opened the door and practically fell into the arms of a uniformed policeman.

23

Adam was waiting up when, at three o'clock in the morning, Roger arrived back in Bishop St Leon. He was in the sitting room, the lights on, the fire burning, a bottle of whisky, water, two glasses, two packs of plain salted crisps, and a plate of sandwiches, covered in foil, on the table. The door was ajar, and Roger went straight into the room.

'Seems you've had quite a night,' said Adam. 'Have a drink.' He poured out two stiff tots, and pushed one glass over to Roger, who pulled off his leather jacket and sank down on the sofa, facing Adam. 'Get him, did you? Martin? I assume he is the guilty party.'

'Yes, we got him,' Roger said, with satisfaction, and he took a swallow of his whisky.

'Bit too late,' said Adam. 'Everyone was worried about her, but none of us stopped it.'

'He lost it,' said Roger. 'I don't know if he'll be found fit to stand trial.'

He slit open a pack of crisps and began absent-mindedly stuffing them into his mouth.

'I made some sandwiches,' said Adam. 'In case you'd had no supper.'

'No, I had no supper,' Roger agreed. He'd been the arresting officer, and he had discovered Susan's body, so on two counts he had had to go to the local police station to make statements and see Martin charged with assaulting Deborah Grant; the count of murder, over Susan's death, could wait. Bail would be opposed, when he came before the magistrates on Monday.

'Here you are,' said Adam, lifting the foil from the sandwiches.

At half-past one, he had realised that Roger might be gone for hours, but he could not go to bed himself, not without some answers, and the man was sure to be hungry; he always was, even when he'd just finished eating. Adam had made preparations for alternatives and supplements.

'You'll make someone a lovely wife, Adam Fraser,' Roger said, taking a sandwich.

'How did you find that out?' Adam, who already looked tired and somewhat haggard, now turned pale at hearing Roger use his proper surname.

Roger tapped his nose.

'Never mind,' he said. 'But maybe you can identify the body found beneath the tree. Before we do it, that is, taking blood samples – all that.'

'Who do you think it is?' Adam now gulped his whisky.

'I think it might be Norman Trent, a nasty man from all acounts,' said Roger. 'And I think it may turn out that Susan murdered him, a long time ago, forty years or so, and buried him in the garden, planting a tree above the body.'

'It is Norman. She told me so,' said Adam. It did not matter now; Susan no longer needed protecting. Then he realised, with a shock, that though she had accepted knowledge of the crime, she had not actually said that she had been the killer. Was it possible that someone else – his father – attempting to save her, had been responsible? Surely not? 'I had a chat with her last night – Friday night, that is,' he added. For it was Sunday morning now.

'Probably manslaughter. Self-protection,' Roger said, robustly. He bit into a second ham sandwich.

'Will it all come out now?'

'May do. There'll be an inquest on him, as well as Susan,' said Roger, chewing.

'What about identifying him? Norman, I mean?'

'There may be something on the body. There'll be the teeth, of course, but it's a long time ago to look for records.' There was facial reconstruction, too, but in this case that would be unnecessary. A blood test, matching the body's and Martin's DNA, was all that would be required. Susan was unlikely to have been unfaithful, though nothing would surprise Roger.

'There was a watch. The body had a watch on,' Adam said.

'That might be traceable,' Roger agreed.

'What happened to Susan?' Adam asked at last.

Roger poured himself another strong tot and ate a third sandwich. 'Martin heard about the body being found,' he said. Deborah Grant, calming down eventually, had explained about her estranged husband's return with the children, and his mentioning it because he intended to follow up the story. Martin had taken off in her car, returning later covered in blood and in a state of shock. 'We traced the car he was in,' said Roger, not revealing the part he had played in this, except to say that it had nearly run him down. 'It seems he was having an affair with this woman.'

There was no need to tell Adam that Martin had been threatening her with a knife. Roger had been prudent, at the house in Rotherston. First, he had called for support; then he had gone round to the back of the house and had witnessed something of what was happening in the kitchen as shadows moved behind the blind drawn across the window. He had decided to force an entry without waiting for reinforcements, and at the same moment Debbie had tipped the table up against her assailant, escaping from the house just as support arrived.

'Poor choice of boyfriend,' Adam said.

'Single mother. Two small girls. Vulnerable.'

Deborah Grant's husband had turned up soon after Martin had been taken away, while a policewoman was making tea and Deborah and the children were in the sitting room. Icy calm now, Deborah had quietened the children and told them Martin wasn't well. He was going into hospital.

'But there's no ambulance,' said Lily.

'The policeman's taking him,' said Debbie. Martin had been led away, handcuffed, by two uniformed officers but by then the large man with red hair had bundled her and the children into the sitting room and closed the door.

Martin had just been driven away when a mudstained Daihatsu drew up outside and a frantic man was prevented by police outside from entering. He was the children's father, a television sound operator who was pursuing the story of the body found in Bishop St Leon. After talking to various people on the outskirts of the village, each of whom sent him off in a different direction, Jim had parted from the other two reporters and was returning to the Crown to demand proper information when a police car, blue light flashing, passed him. Jim went after it, and it led him back to the house in whose garden the body had been found. Talking to a couple who emerged from a house opposite Cedar Cottage, he learned that its owner had been battered to death. The couple were extremely upset and kept saying, 'If only we'd done something.' They said that Martin Trent, the woman's son, was on bad terms with her and only a few days ago had injured her.

'Was the son here tonight?' he asked.

They didn't know; they'd been indoors with the curtains

drawn. They didn't know if he'd been back since the body had been found in the garden.

'Where would he be?' Jim pressed them.

'He's got a girlfriend in Rotherston,' Mary told him. 'Debbie something, I think Susan said.'

'Martin. Martin Trent.' Jim stared at the couple for a blank, shocked moment. He hadn't known the surname of Debbie's unattractive lover, but Debbie had said he lived in Bishop St Leon. He couldn't be the same man.

Yes, he could. The best way to find out was to go straight back to where she was living with their daughters. Jim sprang into his vehicle and was gone.

After a time, the police let Jim into the house, having asked Debbie if she would like to see him.

The girls answered for her. Jim was welcome. He took the children upstairs and read to them while Debbie gave her statement.

'What happened? Why did he take my car? Did he have an accident?' she kept asking, while the interviewing officer tried to get her to give an account of his attack on her.

The big man with the red hair, who had been sitting silent in the corner, intervened.

'Mrs Grant – Deborah—' he said. 'Did you know a long-buried body has been found in Bishop St Leon?'

'Oh, yes,' said Debbie. 'Jim told me. He brought the

girls back and then rushed off to find out more about it. A prehistoric body, wasn't it?'

'Probably not as old as that,' said Roger gravely. 'Did Jim tell Martin this?'

'No. But I did,' Debbie said. She gazed at him, bewildered. 'I don't understand,' she said. Then she gave a little gasp.

'You've remembered something,' Roger said.

'He rang up the Crown Inn. He used the phone, then rushed out and drove off in my car,' said Debbie. She wouldn't tell about his having lost his licence. He was in enough trouble already. 'I redialled to see who he'd rung up,' she added, sheepishly.

'You had a right to do that,' said Roger.

'It's in Bishop St Leon. The Crown. His mother lives there,' Debbie said. 'I said it was a wrong number and hung up. Please, tell me what happened. Did he hit another car? Was someone hurt? I don't mind about my car,' she added, wildly.

'He didn't hit another car,' said Roger. 'There was another sort of accident, and his mother's dead.'

'Oh – the witch!' gasped Debbie. 'But that's awful. Poor Martin. He wasn't very nice about her but I expect he loved her, really.'

'Who knows?' said Roger, adding, 'She was no witch. A much respected lady, by all accounts.' He had never met her, while she was alive.

He nodded to the other officer, who went on with the

interview. Debbie explained how she thought Martin had been injured because there was a lot of blood, and she'd washed it from his face and hands, but couldn't see where it was coming from. She'd left his stained anorak in a bundle on the kitchen floor.

'We'll be taking that away,' said the officer.

'But whose blood—' Debbie looked from one man to the other. 'Not his mother's. He didn't hurt his mother.'

Roger said, 'We don't yet know quite what happened, Deborah.'

'It must have been an accident,' said Debbie.

It was certainly not premeditated murder. Few murders were, in Roger's experience. Often they were the result of blind panic when a robbery went wrong, or a quarrel between partners or spouses got out of hand.

'We'll find out,' said Roger.

There was not much more that she could tell them. Her statement would be typed up and she would read it through and sign it, but that could wait. It was arranged that a policewoman would stay at the house overnight. Debbie didn't seem to have a friend whom she could ask to come, and no one liked to enquire if Jim would be remaining. Roger thought he would be off to file his story; he'd almost had a ringside seat. There might be other reporters clustering around when news of Susan Trent's murder was announced but there was a good chance that they would not connect Deborah Grant with the suspect. Not yet. Roger knew that she wouldn't be able to put him out of her mind for a long time; there'd be the trial, which would not be for months even if Martin admitted what he had done. It would be a corker of a story, if it came out – as it must – that Susan had killed her husband Norman forty years ago.

'A lot of what happened has to be kept under wraps for now,' Roger told Adam. 'The girlfriend mentioned that Martin has a sister. She's being traced – a neighbour knew where she lives, in California.'

'This will all be a dreadful shock for her,' said Adam.

'Yes,' said Roger. 'Are you going to tell me what your interest is in all this?' he asked. 'Was Dr Fraser your father?'

'You've heard about him, have you?' Roger was no mean sleuth. 'No – he was my grandfather. My father died recently in New Zealand, and he left some papers indicating that he knew the Trents. I'd never heard of them. I was curious.' He hesitated. Everyone concerned was dead now. 'My father may have known that Norman was dead,' he allowed Roger to learn. 'He was just a schoolboy at the time.'

'He helped Susan bury the body.'

'Who knows?' said Adam. 'Possibly. I think he supplied the willow. There's one at Field House, older than the one that blew down. It's more sheltered there. It's still standing. You grow new ones from slips pushed into the ground. It's very easy. Maybe you know that, Roger, you're such a good gardener.'

'You can grow a lot of things like that. Rosemary, for instance.'

'Rosemary – for remembrance,' Adam said, and earned a puzzled look from Roger. 'I wonder if my coming here set off some fatal process.'

'You didn't make the tree blow down, and we both know the people around here were worried about the situation. What could they do about it, though? It was for Susan to get her act together and turn him out.'

'But she had such a secret in her past,' said Adam. 'Maybe she felt guilty about depriving Martin of his father.'

'So she should,' said Roger. 'Not that he seems to have been one worth having.'

'No,' agreed Adam. 'If you want to know about him, ask old Fred, the chap who helped Susan in the garden. He and his grandson were cutting up the branches of that willow.'

'What'll you do now?' Roger had finished up the sandwiches and opened the second crisp packet. 'Will you stay around?'

'I don't think so,' Adam said. 'I won't be needed as a witness. I've found out what I wanted to know. There's an old brass plate of my grandfather's at Field House; it's among a lot of junk they haven't yet got rid of. I might see if they will let me have it.'

'Are you going to tell them you're his grandson?'

'I don't see any need for that,' said Adam. 'I've been

here such a short time. I'll be forgotten, long before all this blows over.'

'The girls will be sorry,' Roger said. 'The nannies.'

Adam smiled.

'They're great. Why don't you try your luck with one of them?'

'Not me,' said Roger. 'They wouldn't give me half a glance.'

'You're all right,' said Adam, wondering whether to mention Roger's image. Better not. 'My father left me a house in New Zealand,' he said, instead. 'I've been working in the States, but I think I might give that up and move there.' He could set up his own business.

'Good idea,' said Roger. He was thinking of Deborah Grant. Poor girl – she was little more than a girl – deserted by that newshound husband, who had left the house as soon as the girls were safely asleep, telling Roger as he went that he had never liked that man getting near his daughters.

Roger wanted to ask why he had abandoned them, but heard himself saying, 'I had a daughter once.'

'What happened?' Jim paused long enough to ask.

'She died in a road accident,' Roger said.

'I'm sorry,' Jim had replied, then left, punching a number into his mobile phone as he did so.

Roger decided not to reveal this piece of his own history to Adam.

'We'll have a drink together before you go,' he said.

Adam felt a twinge of guilt about his tenancy, and it was likely that Chris might not be far behind him. Still, that wasn't his problem.

Roger was thinking about Deborah Grant. It was going to be tough for her now, and she'd feel stupid and ashamed. He might go round to see her some time, suggest taking her and the children somewhere, Whipsnade perhaps; it wasn't far.

'We must get some sleep,' he said, rising to his feet, picking up the empty plate and crisp packets. Adam, following with the glasses and the whisky, hid a smile; Roger was becoming house-trained. 'Martin Trent said an extraordinary thing, as I arrested him,' Roger added, going into the kitchen. He threw the packets in the bin and took the plate over to the sink.

'What was that?' asked Adam.

'He hasn't yet been charged with killing his mother,' Roger said. 'I was arresting him for assaulting Deborah Grant. The fight had gone out of him. He was quite meek, sitting there in the police station. He said, "She smiled at me." He didn't mean Deborah Grant. He meant his mother smiled at him as he bludgeoned her to death.'